THUNDERSTRUCK

Project Livewire, Book One

ELIOT SUMMERS

JaCol Publishing Inc.
Copyright 2020 © by JaCol Publishing Inc.
Illustrations Copyright © 2020 by JaCol Publishing Inc.
SECOND PRINTING
September 2020
All rights reserved
JaCol Publishing Inc.
195 Murica Aisle
Irvine, CA 92614
818-510-2898
Editor-in-Chief: Randall Andrews
www.jacolpublishing.com

ISBN: 978-1-946675-47-7

Cover design by Sarah Kil Creative Studio

I want to thank all those who helped me along the way with this novel. For my boys: Bub, Tater and Turkey, who have shown me the strength of boys with big hearts. For my husband, who shares his wife with her imaginary friends. For my mom, who let me stay up late reading under my covers.

And for my friends, who helped me find myself.

I also want to thank my editor, Randall Andrews, who challenged me every day to be a better writer.

I'm so grateful to all of you and to any I may have missed. None of this would have been possible without you.

Contents

Chapter 1

The noise had always been in the back of my mind. It whined just loud enough for me to hear it in the background until something triggered it—the simplest and strangest things—and the volume cranked up. Heat would fill my skull, and the high-pitched sound filled my ears. That afternoon in the cafeteria, it was the protein substrate on my plate. It smelled like meat, it looked like meat, but I knew the taste would never live up to the real thing. The noise changed from its normal low whine into an overwhelming squeal.

I shouldn't have known anything about meat. Wards of the state raised inside the Tower, like me, couldn't afford it; it was reserved for those who could pay. The more I tried to figure out how I knew, the louder the noise wailed. The cafeteria melted away, and delicate hands put a roast on a worn wooden table. Her kind but tired blue eyes smiled through a curtain of black curls like mine. I belonged to her. I reached for her, but she disappeared. Darkness, thick and clawing like tar, sucked me in. The noise grew unbearable; the heat followed.

As suddenly as the strange feelings and sights took over, they disappeared. I gasped for a full breath, on my feet, though I didn't remember standing.

"Glitch alert!" A piece of bread flew from down the table and hit me in the face.

Rat stood. "Leave Arlo alone." Our table fell quiet. "Mind your business." He was the only reason that Glitch was the worst thing I got called...at least to my face...at least to his.

I was different from them, always alone. Always on the outside watching. My ward-mates didn't have noise in their heads, and they felt the difference as much as I did.

The smell of the fake meat turned my stomach. Rat caught up to me as my tray clattered into the dish return. His sharp fingers dug into my arm. "You aren't a glitch, but you are a wet blanket! You're just gonna let them mess with you?"

I shrugged. What else could I do?

He let go and turned back to the table and silenced the sniggers and jeers that followed me across the long room. "Where are you off to in such a hurry?"

I walked the tips of my fingers across the counter.

He always looked a little like he took a swig of lemon juice—all edges and angles. The thought that I could glitch out again and someone might take me away to the mental ward underground with the rest of the freaks and glitches like me pulled his lips and eyebrows into a deep pucker. I was scared, too—always scared—but I'd made it a decade without getting locked up. I either did a good job of hiding my moments, or the Wardens just didn't give a crap. He sighed and stepped aside. "Fine, take yourself for a walk and get that bird's nest off your face because I got you a pass for this rally thing tonight."

The thought of leaving the Tower put an uneasy, sick feeling in my stomach. I let my hair hide me.

He batted it aside and forced me to meet his eyes. "Come on, I'll Ro Sham Bo you for it. If I win, you come with me. If you win, I stop asking you to come and let you be a hermit."

I drew an X over my heart and raised my eyebrows. The nickname fit. He misspelled his given name, Stuart, as S-T-U-R-A-T sometime in primary school. Stu-Rat eventually shortened to Rat, and it stuck.

Rat rolled his eyes. "Yeah, I promise. Let's get this over with. Come on, one play wins it all." He held one fist over the other open palm.

I could read his face like a book, and he knew it. He had an angle, but I wouldn't know what it was unless I gave in. A burst of air vibrated through my lips and raised my hands to mimic Rat's.

"Rock, paper, scissors..."

Rat's lip twitched. He'd play Rock.

Paper covers Rock.

"Shoot!"

I held my hand out flat, palm down. Paper.

Rat played Rock, but instead of letting me slap his knuckles to announce my win, he faked a punch at my groin. "Paper might cover Rock, but Rock crushes nuts. You're going. I'll go get Beryl. Wait for Marta here."

The sun sat heavy on the horizon and threatened to dip below the edge of the Frontier. Outside the floor-to-ceiling windows, the dense city surrounded Central Services Tower. Four roads spoked out of each of the six sides of the Tower and concentric circles of streets, like ripples in the pond in the Public Garden, intersected the spokes. I rested my hand against the cold surface and let the light white out my vision.

"Can it be true?" Marta's voice startled me; my head knocked into the glass with a hollow thunk. "My Rebel is going down to the mean streets?" Hers was the first face I saw when I stepped off the tubes at seven years old and the only Warden who took the time to talk to me even when I wouldn't answer her back. One hand rested on my back, and the other pushed my hair away and smoothed over the smarting spot. "Sorry. I didn't mean to spook you." She tugged at her blue Warden's uniform and smiled wide. "Is this pass I just approved for real? You're going with Rat and Beryl?"

I wished I could answer, but all I could offer her was a shrug.

"Do you want to go?"

I tucked my chin to my chest. She always seemed to know what I was thinking.

"Oh, so Rat threatened you, and now you think you have to?"

I shook my head but couldn't meet eyes with her. She made a face like something smelled bad. The approaching clap of boots on polished cement saved me from Marta's questions. Her face turned white; sweat beaded on her brow.

I pressed my back against the wall and let the wild bramble of my hair fall over my face. A patrol of green uniforms approached. Commander Escher eyed me with cool disinterest and turned his glare on Marta. "Wofsy."

His cold voice sliced the still air. Marta flinched, and all her warmth withered. "Commander Escher."

The harsh corridor lights flashed off the silver at his temples. Escher pushed my hair aside with a pen; his light eyes bored into me. "This is our mute?"

I forced myself to stay still, but anger washed off of Marta like static electricity. "Yes, sir. Arlo is Non-Verbal." Eidolon recognized Non-Verbal Linguistics as a language and culture with its own embassy. The rules were different inside the Tower.

"Non-Verbal suggests language, Wofsy." Escher pushed my hair aside with a pen. "He has no speech, no documented use of any hand signs. He's just mute."

I kept my eyes on the perfect polish on the Commander's boots, wishing I could sink into the cement floor and never come back up.

Marta bit her lip and looked away from him. "I tried to get him sent to the NVL Embassy for lessons when he first came to me, but you denied it, sir. Any lack of language is our fault. Not his."

Escher's forearm snapped over her throat and held her against the wall. The green-clad soldiers who followed him around drew their batons and charged the electric prongs at the ends. Escher watched with cruel fascination as her face turned pink, then red, and her hazel eyes began to bulge. "Watch that lip, Wofsy." He dropped her and walked away, entourage in tow.

"Yes, sir." She coughed, gasped, and caught her breath. I reached down to pull her up, but she wouldn't let me touch her. She fought for me over and over, and I watched her take flack for me, too cowardly to even move.

Rat and Beryl's voices bounced down the quiet halls ahead of them.

Marta scrambled to her feet and wiped the tears from her cheeks.

Rat's eyes paused on her swollen neck and red eyes, but he said nothing and slapped my back. "Time to see the city without three inches of glass in the way."

Marta brushed off our standard-issue clothing and fussed at every flaw. "You two blabbermouths keep an eye on Arlo. If you get into trouble and Patrol shows—"

"I know, I know!" Rat pocketed the passes, despite Beryl's objection. "They got their little things that scan our fingerprints, but ours got smudged." No swirls, no grooves etched my fingertips, but I'd never noticed. "We gotta say our name and our ward into the reader, and it IDs us."

She tsked her tongue at Rat. "They need to carry their own passes; that's the law. You have to have it on you at all times when you're outside the Tower." She waited for him to hand them back and tugged my collar, demanded my attention. "Yours is set so that anyone can say it, but you can't expect the officers down there to understand. Stay close to Rat, you got me?"

My throat ratcheted down tighter and tighter with each staccato heartbeat. I nodded.

She grinned and shoved me to the open Tube. "Go have fun and be careful. Your passes expire at midnight. Don't be late." The doors closed, and she was gone.

Chapter 2

The compartment dropped so fast my guts rose up in my throat, and my ears popped. I gripped an overhead handle and forced my feet onto the floor. An advertisement blinked onto the screens in the walls.

"Persaud BioMed, making our city stronger one Citizen and Resident at a time. See your Central Services Resident Health Center to apply for clinical trial opportunities. Earn extra allotment funds and help your fellow Residents."

Rat snorted at the screen. "You wouldn't catch me down in the Resident Death Center unless I was too far gone to say, 'hell no, let me die in peace!'"

I shuddered at the thought of the underground hospital that serviced the one hundred fifty-six floors of Residents. But the Underground wasn't just a hospital. It was a hospital, a prison, and an asylum for anyone who couldn't care for themself. Bad things happened down there. Below ground was a death sentence, but I didn't know how I knew that.

The doors slid open with a smooth hiss, and we stepped into the Terminal at Central Processing. Outside the Tube, the inner walls of the tower atrium climbed over a quarter of a mile—sixteen hundred feet of steel, glass, and concrete with a tiny circle of blue sky like a jewel at the top. Green spaces and nutritional greenhouses flew above, spiraling toward the sky at ten-floor intervals. The Public Garden filled the ground floor of the atrium. It surrounded the Justice Center. Glass walls kept the Justice Center's shining dome in view at all times.

Wardens in glass cubicles inspected our passes and reminded us of the rules. "Your passes are for six hours. If you are caught causing any trouble, you will be remanded to Central Processing and taken to Juvenile Detention for a minimum of six weeks for Behavioral Therapy. There you will be rehabilitated and reminded of the standards we demand of our Citizens and Residents. If you do not return within ten minutes of your pass's expiration, you will be remanded to your floor warden and given extra duties. Any other passes will be revoked for a minimum of six weeks. If you are more than one hour late, you will be remanded to Juvenile Detention. Do you understand the conditions of your passes? If so, state your first and last name, ward, and floor and place your fingers on the scanner." The elderly warden held out a finger scanner.

Rat stepped up first, placed his finger on the tiny screen. "Stuart TowerWard. D ward, floor 47."

"Beryl TowerWard. D ward, floor 47."

The white-haired man's bushy eyebrows knitted together into a solid line of straggly white fur, but he still held the scanner out to me.

I hesitated, but Rat shoved me. "Put your hand on."

I gave my smooth fingertips one last look and placed them on the scanner screen.

Rat leaned into the microphone. "Arlo TowerWard. D ward, floor 47."

The flummoxed warden shook his head. "I guess that's fine. Behave yourselves, boys; be back by midnight."

My first breath of Tower City air felt thick and strange. It hadn't been through the Tower's filters and cleaners. I yawned, my ears popped, but all the new sounds and colors left my head feeling close to capacity People brushed against me from every angle, all in such a hurry. The starch in their bright, stiff clothes scratched me. My skin hurt from the stiff scrapes. TowerCloth felt soft and thin, nothing like the sharp lines and bright colors.

Patrol officers roamed among the Citizens; their neon safety vests stuck out in the crowd that already looked like a moving garden. They didn't pay us any attention, but I couldn't look away or shake the feeling that I needed to get back to the 47th.

Rat punched my arm. "What are you staring at?"

I pointed up at the Tower; my feet took charge and moved back to Central Processing.

He yanked my arm. "Nope. You're coming with me. Don't worry about them." The tram slowed to a stop, and he handed Beryl and me each a small card. "You gotta pay to ride. It isn't like the Tubes. They pay for everything down here." We swiped our cards and stepped onto the long open-air trolley. A few Citizens watched us find seats together, but most didn't look up from the tiny screens in their hands. Rat pointed to a screen like in the ones in the tube walls hanging from the tram's roof. "They got the Simulcast right in their hands."

The tram lurched forward, and I gripped the seat. "Relax!" Beryl quipped from across the center aisle. "The Tube goes quicker than this thing."

Maybe so, but the Tube didn't feel like it might buck me out at any moment.

"You look like it's your first time out, Glitch." Beryl draped his arms across the back of his seat, despite the uncomfortable shuffling of people on either side. "Wait, is it your first time?"

"Shut up." Rat's bulldog style protection didn't go unappreciated.

"Well, why?" Beryl didn't bother to glance my way for the answer. "It's not like we have to stay in the Tower all the time. What about all of the trips they took us on when we were kids? We went to the Frontier center and the Outer Rim parks, where was he?"

I glanced sidelong at Rat.

Rat smirked and crossed his arms over his chest. "He's right here, you know, and he doesn't like it when you do that."

"What's he going to do about it?"

I glared at my feet. Nothing. Everyone knew I wouldn't do anything.

"Here?" Rat inspected his fingernails. "He won't do anything while we're here, because you aren't worth getting sent down. But you better watch yourself when we get back."

Beryl shuffled in his seat and looked away. The discussion of why I'd avoided the city for a decade, thankfully, over.

We stepped off the tram, and the bright vests of the Patrol caught my eye again. Rat nudged me. "Don't worry about the Patrol. They're just security guards. If anything goes down, they call the Wardens out, and we know what to do with them, right?"

I nodded. Stand still, back to the wall, eyes down, hands out. Pose no threat and hope like hell that they go away quickly.

Beryl stretched his arms over his head. "Yeah, and when the shit really hits the fan, they call Retainment, the goons in green. They're the ones you want to worry about."

Rat spat on the pavement, earning him shocked squeals from passersby. "They won't call the goon squad for a bunch of kids. Those brainwashed apes are all out at the borders making sure no one talks too much."

My Adam's apple felt too big for my throat. I turned around to get one last look at the Tower. I wanted to be back inside the chain-link and razor wire. Maybe I was a glitch, but everyone knew it and left me alone.

Beryl turned too but looked away. "Looks like a prison with all of the spikes and lights and fences."

Rat grinned and rubbed his hands together. "That shit's just for the sad sacks below ground, the criminals and crazies on lockdown. Not us." He slapped me on the back. "Let's go see this rally, maybe I can make someone pee their pants and run home to Mama."

Chapter 3

On the 47th, Rat's list of friends took up one line, four letters: A-R-L-O. He had followers who were afraid of him, but he didn't think of them as friends. The moment we stepped into the hall, a girl with a purple jacket and a painted face squealed, "Stu," and ran to him like she and he were very well acquainted.

I cocked an eyebrow. Rat never let anyone but the Commander call him anything but Rat.

Rat scowled. "Not a word, Arlo." He turned on a megawatt smile, and she rushed into his arms. Out of the side of his mouth, he said, "Don't agree to anything. Don't believe anything they say, but smile like you're thinking about it."

The girl jumped on Rat and cooed a high-pitched greeting. Another followed in her wake and shoved paper leaflets at Beryl and me.

Beryl tossed his over his shoulder. I marveled at mine until Rat pulled the girl off his body and settled her at his side. "Don't read that bull, Arlo. It's crazy talk."

I held my hand out, palm parallel to the floor just like when we played Rock, Paper, Scissors.

THE SYSTEM IS BROKEN. SEPARATE IS NOT EQUAL!

WE DEMAND A RESET! ATROCITIES IN CENTRAL
SERVI—

Rat ripped it away and squashed it in his hand. "I know, real
paper. It must be nice to have credit to spare on something you
throw away."

The girl swatted his chest. "Play nice, Stu!"

Rat rolled his eyes, grinned at me, and ignored her. "See, it's just
a game to them." He turned to the girl, looking like a predator. "I
don't play nice. That's what you like about me, right, Beautiful?"

She blushed and giggled. "You want to introduce me to your
friends?"

"Not really."

"If I don't know their names, I can't find them someone to keep
them company while you talk."

Beryl pushed to the front. "I'm talking, too! I'm Beryl."

She grinned. "Eager beaver, huh? What about this one?" She
turned to me. "You got a name?" She dragged her fingertips up my
arm. "Cat got your tongue?"

Simulcasts and school said that Citizens and Residents were the
same, but these people were not the same as us.

Rat pulled her away, back into his side. To her, it must have felt
like he was acting possessive of her. She giggled and blushed some
more, but I knew that I was the one he was protecting. "That's Arlo.
He doesn't like new people; I'll set him up."

Her simpering smile could have stripped paint off a wall.
"Awwww, shy guy. Beaver?" She glanced at Beryl. "Come with me."
She took Beryl by the hand and led him away.

Rat found a place where we could keep our backs to the wall but
had a clear path to the well-lit stage and podium. Someone called
his name. "Wait here, but keep your eyes on them the whole time
and don't believe a word they say. They'll do anything to get ahead
of one another, whether they have to buy it, snort it, screw it or
inject it into their eyelids. They are compulsive social climbers or
die-hard quacks who believe those papers they throw away."

He pushed his way through the crowd.

My heart thumped in my ears. I wanted to go back.

The boy speaking wasn't any older than me, but his passion flowed into the audience like nerve gas. It ramped them up and made even the smuggest look interested. "My brother didn't ask to be different, and we loved the person he showed us hid inside that withering body he was born with. By the time he was sixteen, we were desperate. We needed help caring for him."

They were desperate. They needed help.

The noise squealed and wailed. My breath caught in my throat while those words echoed against the sound. I gasped, and the room came back into focus.

A pair in bright yellow uniform sweaters sauntered in sync, arms linked, and communicated with flicks of eyebrows and mouths that I didn't have to understand to dislike. The girl's palm slid across my neck like a snake, and her perfume filled my nose. "Teá said you're shy, but you don't have to talk to us."

I ignored them and kept my eyes on the stage.

"My parents were going broke, and Jaron was too heavy for my mom to lift on her own. She applied for assistance, and Jaron was accepted into Resident Care. For a while, things seemed good. But no one tells you that accepting their help means that you sign away any right to making decisions on your loved one's life and care."

Something, somewhere deep in my brain, shifted...twitched. Light flashed behind my eyes, but when I went to look at the source, all I got was a sharp jab of feedback. I grunted and rubbed my ear, accidentally baring my neck to my two companions. They descended on me like a pair of vampires while I tried not to react.

"Jaron got sick. The doctors said there was no hope; they wouldn't even try to save him. We appealed to everyone we could, but everyone said we were cruel and selfish to keep him in suffering. He never suffered until they got involved."

A hard nip at my skin hurt too much. I jumped away, but the boy's arm wound around my waist. The girl batted her mascara caked lashes. Whatever made her voice purr and her words slur, blew her pupils out until they swallowed the green of her irises. Her vacant smile unnerved me. She latched her mouth to mine—her tongue dove down my throat. My mind screamed to push her off, make her stop, but I froze and waited for it to be over.

And then it was. Beryl and Rat dragged them off and tossed them aside.

The girl snarled at him. "Don't they teach you Tower Trash any manners? I could deal with your big friend here, not saying a word to me, but you don't touch me."

Rat moved, her nose inches from his chest. "Or what? You'll call Patrol? You're not supposed to be here either."

Rat followed her escape step for step, and she whimpered. "Please. Don't hurt me."

She wasn't worth us getting hauled to Juvenile Detention. I grabbed Rat's elbow.

He shook me off and shoved his hair back from his eyes. "What did I tell you, 'Lo? You can't get messed up with these Eidolon girls; they're all nuts. They only want one thing."

I only wanted one thing. I held up four fingers and then seven.

"47? You can't go home now! We got hours left! Beryl and I still have to talk to these weirdos!"

My chin dropped to my chest, and I repeated the number with the primitive gestures.

47.

Rat scrubbed his face with his hands. "Marta will kill me if you get lost on the way back, and I have to speak for these idiots, or they won't pay up." He stared at the stage, and a grin spread across his face. "Come on." He led me up some stairs, through a curtain to a dark area backstage, and opened a door. I struggled to adjust to the sudden brightness of the well-lit room. "Found this place, looking for somewhere private to take that blonde on one of my last trips and knew I had to show you. I remembered how much you liked this stuff when we were little."

I blinked, and a room full of musical instruments came into focus. I forgot the rally, the pair in yellow, and the Patrol officers, and moved among the instruments. Each of them felt like an old friend. I plucked strings and ran my fingers along well-worn keys. The Eidolon Symphony sent volunteers to the Tower to offer a little culture to the less-fortunate children when we were kids. The others quickly lost interest, but I fell in love. The instruments spoke the only language I could speak.

The light bounced off the oiled mahogany of a violin in an open case. It was my favorite of the symphony's instruments. My fingers whispered across the strings; the reluctant little hum of each one greeted me, and a smile stretched my face.

I put it to my shoulder, placed my fingers carefully on the neck, and drew the bow across the strings. My hands knew what to do, and a sad lullaby sang out. My mind went somewhere else. Even the noise in my head went away. The music led me into a contented haze.

I could have played for hours, but a scream and a male voice over a loudspeaker interrupted my private sanctuary. "This is Eidolon Retainment. Proceed in an orderly fashion to be itemized and sorted. Cooperation is imperative. Any resisters will be processed."

The violin hit the floor with a hollow clunk.

▭

RETAINMENT OFFICERS with clubs and crowd shields blocked the doors. I should have hidden. I should have gone back to the room with the instruments, locked the door, and snuck back to the Tower once everything got quiet, but my feet wouldn't move.

The kids who looked so happy in their bright clothes lined up in a sad rainbow with downcast eyes and contrite faces. Patrol Officers sent nervous glances to the green-clad soldiers among them as they walked down the lines scanning fingerprints and sorting people into different groups. Every door was guarded; there was no way out. I wouldn't know how to get back if I tried. I didn't even know if that card thing had fare for another tram ride or if the Tram ran at night.

"You, on the stage. Freeze." His hand rested his holstered club. "Pass, floor, and name." My hand itched to get into my pocket for my pass. "Pass, floor, and name. Now." He waited, but there was nothing I could do. Rat was supposed to stay close so he could say it. "Cooperate, or you risk incarceration."

His eyes focused on someone or something behind me. I turned; he nodded, and the electrical sting of a stun gun hit me in the neck. It burned from my chest to my scalp, scorched down to my toes, and took away my control over my body. Convulsions rocked my limbs, my skull flamed, and pain drilled from my right ear down my shoulder. I was dying, and if I wasn't, I wanted to.

A harsh scream filled my head. The searing heat relented; I realized the sound wasn't in my head. The cry was my own voice. The hoarse, grating sound scraped up my throat like shrapnel, added to the war waging inside my skull. My hands clawed at my head, tore at my hair, trying to let the flame out. My body rolled and writhed without my permission.

"Shit." The officer grabbed my wrist; his eyes locked on my palm. "Kid, I know you don't understand, but you will soon. This is for your own good." He held fast to my wrist, turned his head, and put his own stun baton to my neck.

Lightning, white, and purple, and hot, filled my vision and silenced all thought, the room, maybe the whole city. Bile gathered in my throat. My fingers tingled and went numb.

Blue eyes with delicate laugh lines around them smiled at me. The warm sun on her back kept me from seeing much, but I knew her. I knew that I belonged with her. Cool, earthy soil squished between my toes. Other children played around the blue-eyed woman and me; their laughter wafted in with the fresh breeze.

Words formed in my head, and my mouth moved to try to make them. "Who are you?" They sounded right in my head, but the syllables fell apart and rearranged themselves somewhere between my brain and my mouth.

Her smile fell, tears glossed her eyes, and she turned away from me.

I tried to reach for her, but my arms wouldn't move. "Come back!" The same thing happened: a garbled jumble of syllables replaced the words I wanted.

The backlit figure stopped and turned back, but it wasn't the woman I knew. This person had dark eyes and thick black eyelashes but wore a respirator over her face. Her voice was muffled, but she talked about me, not to me. I fought her and asked where the other woman went, but she ignored the stream of noise.

A flash of heat on my cheek and a spark of pain pulled me from my stupor. My chest ached, and for a moment, I fought the Retainment officer sitting on it. He slapped my cheek. "Breathe!"

As if they were waiting for the order, my lungs opened up. I gasped and gulped air.

"That's it. You back with me now?"

My head felt too heavy, it lolled on my neck when I tried nodding, and my eyes threatened to snap shut. He slapped me again when I gave in and let them.

"No, you can't sleep right now. You'll wake up deep underground if you let yourself sleep. Stay with me until I get you headed somewhere safe. What's your name?" He waited, his eyes endlessly scanning the room. "You don't have all night, Kid. This is no time to be shy! You were screaming your head off a minute ago, so you can't play mute with me now."

I'd never screamed before. That would have gotten me dragged below ground for sure. Foggy and confused, my mouth opened, but what came out was the disjointed babble I made in my dream.

His eyes widened; his Adam's apple bobbed. "Shit." He looked around the room, face white. "Riley will know what to do with you. Come on."

The change in altitude as he hoisted me up made my head spin. My legs stumbled—knees rubbery and unstable.

His end of the day stubble brushed my ear. "Don't go back to the 47th, whatever you do. Resident Health won't let you out; Escher will find other uses for you." My supposed savior kept his eyes trained on the Patrol Officer at the head of the sorting lines and hushed his voice. "Don't let them take you to Central Processing. You'll be underground, strapped to a gurney for the rest of your life before you can say 'boo.'"

My teeth chattered, but sweat poured down my face. The man's words washed over me as if they were in another language. Underground was bad. I remembered that: restraints and bad people who hurt me.

A new pain shot behind my ear and down my neck. My legs went out from under me, and my eyes rolled back.

"Whoa!" We dropped together. "Stay with me a little longer. I gotta get you in the right van before you give up on me."

I slumped against him; my cheek pressed against the deep green uniform. Wardens wore their last name on their chest, Patrol too. The badge on my officer's chest only said, "Retainment." I tapped the badge.

He looked and seemed to understand. "You can call me Guinn." He stood, dragging my sagging body with him. "Keep your head down." I did as I was told and drooped, let Guinn drag me along. "Chasney, I have one going to NVL. He's a fighter; you might want to dose him before we even try to load him up."

Chasney glances up from her screen, and a smug smirk tilted her mouth. "Either our definitions of a fighter are very different, or you're losing your edge, Guinn."

He shrugged. "I stung him twice. He's not exactly a lightweight. If you want to chance him waking up and going ape shit on the way there, that's on you." He lied without a bead of sweat or an extra flush on his cheeks. His heartbeat, slow and steady, pressed against my side.

She stepped closer and flicked a piece of hair out of her way. "Why are you sending a Resident to the NVL?"

Guinn scoffed. "These Resistance nuts are crazy. They dress up like Residents for these dumb talks. Didn't your superiors brief you?"

"We didn't have time for more than a call for all available officers and being handed identity tablets!" She held her tablet out. "Just let me log this mess of a kid in, and we'll be on our way."

His heart rate soared. "I checked his papers. He's starting to come to! Give him a tranquilizer syrette, and let's get him loaded up."

The female Patrol Officer stood so close that her perfume irritated my nose. "I have to check him, and you know it. I don't want your brute squad coming for me."

He dropped his voice low. "Chas, just do it. Send the heat to me if you get flagged. You didn't see anything; you followed orders from a higher-ranking officer and put this kid on the truck to the NVL."

A needle pierced my neck, and the hot flush of tranquilizer bloomed under my skin. My legs gave, but I didn't care. My head spun, my eyes drooped, and I fell away from the chaos.

Chapter 4

Lingering electricity raced up my spine; my muscles twitched and spasmed at random, but I couldn't move them on my own. It was dark; I couldn't have seen my hand in front of my face if I could have lifted it. The floor of the patrol van had ridges that dug into my back more with every pothole and rut in the street surface. Still, the tranquilizer Chasney and Guinn injected did its job and, combined with the engine vibrations, lulled me into a strange state of half conscience. I didn't know how long I'd been out, or if I was asleep before the truck stopped. The garish beam of a streetlamp sliced the darkness and the frame of the cloth stretcher they strapped me to shuffled into the night.

The dense city lights blocked out the stars, but I remembered them. Not in the Tower, but before. I'd always had those little flashes of memory that scared me, but this was new. I remembered the patterns and how bright they were. I remembered the stories of ancient deities that...someone told me but was too tired to dig through my mush-for-brains for whom.

Too soon, the stars were replaced with overhead lights. I closed my eyes. The rambling sway of the stretcher stopped, and someone pressed my hand to a scanner. A monotone, computerized voice punched the quiet night. "He's not ours." I tried to move away.

The male Patrol officer flinched too, rocking the stretcher. I wondered what would happen if he dropped me. Maybe I'd wake up back in my room in the Tower, and all of this would be a bad dream. "My orders were to bring him to the NVL and tell you to let someone named Riley know he's here. He's your problem now; call Retainment if he's in the wrong place. They'll pick him up when they're done cleaning up the Academic district."

Doors closed, feet shuffled, and cool hands touched my face. The quiet sunk in, and the lights dimmed. A man and woman peered down at me. His hair hung down his back in thick ropes as big around as my fingers. The woman's movement caught my attention. Her sandy brown hair fell over her shoulder in a long tail. The part above her left ear had been shaved smooth, fitted with a metallic receiver, bejeweled with blinking lights. The glittering tech in her head was the least interesting thing about her. Her hands danced, her face contorted, and her body moved in a beautiful ballet. I followed every motion, every expression, and my mind wailed for more when she stopped. My body wouldn't respond to my attempts to roll or sit up or even wiggle my toes, but the fog cleared. I wanted to know what her dance meant. I could have kept watching for hours, but a knock stopped her.

The door opened, and a tiny man with a white coat that brushed his knees with every shuffling step entered, and his coat was all I could focus on. Trapped in a body that felt full of sand, I panicked. My heart pounded like a bass drum in my ears, and I lost sense of where I was—in the dark, quiet room where the woman said things I didn't understand with her dance or strapped down to a hospital bed somewhere else. Bright lights shone in my eyes, and syringes in gloved hands surged toward me.

The woman's cold hand on my brow brought me back, but I toggled from dream to reality. She patted my cheek gently and then with more force when I couldn't make myself respond. "Dr. Zachili, help me. He's burning up."

A deep, graveled sound ground in my ears. It brought me out of the dream and away from the masked faces and gloved hands to another needle coming toward me. My body gave a pitiful twitch when I told it to run, and the tiny doctor stuck me with no problem. Dr. Zachili held his fingers to my neck and ran his tablet over me. "I administered a light sedative to help him remain calm. I've only seen a fever this high with dissociations when an implant malfunctions."

"That's not possible; he can't be more than seventeen. Certainly not old enough to have completed conscription and gone through the implantation approval process." The woman smiled. She seemed nice, but she wasn't mine.

"Don't kid yourself, Laurel. You of all people should know not to believe the propaganda. I'll stay with him until I can get the fever down. What do we do after that? Call Retainment to take him back?"

"We'll figure that out once he's stable. He's not going anywhere in this condition. Let him sleep. Send me a message when you've finished with him, and I'll come back and let you get some sleep." As if her statement was a command for me, my eyes shut, and sleep took me.

Soft linens filled my nose with gentle soap, not the sterile fumes of sanitized laundry from the Tower. My arms and legs weighed too much, but they at least dragged across the sheets when I tested them. A soft voice kept up a constant stream of chatter, and I forced my head to the side to find the source.

"You're stuck with me because I'm the Embassy nuisance. They figured I could watch you and get someone when you woke up without causing too much trouble." She sighed and tucked into the seat of a chair with her legs underneath her. "They're wrong, of course. I'm not one of mother's lab assistants, after all. We tried that. 'Imma, stop your prattling and give the subjects some peace. Imma, follow procedure, this is no time for what ifs!'" She mocked her mother in a high-pitched, snotty voice. "I fit in there as well as I do here or in Father's office. I don't really fit anywhere. Not that Mother cares."

She started into another tirade of high-pitched mocking. A

sound rumbled out of my mouth with all the suave gentility of a leaf blower. I slapped my hand over my mouth but, it leaked through my fingers. My shoulders shook. My eyes strayed to her, worried she would run in horror.

But she stayed. "Don't laugh! I can't do anything right."

It had been so long since I laughed. Maybe I never had.

"Hello." Her voice trembled with nerves, and her tailored black, white, and red uniform hung off her small frame. "Can you hear me?" Her thin frame and wide eyes reminded me of a bird—a strange creature with a delicate beauty all her own. "I didn't see an implant or even a scar." Her head cocked to the side. "My name is Imma. Do you understand me?"

I nodded.

Her smile grew wider. "So you can hear me?"

I nodded again.

"What's your name?"

I had nothing to write with. In the Tower, I would fog up a window or scratch in the dirt in the gardens, but the window was across the room. I traced the letters in the bedsheets. A-R-L-O, and she repeated them aloud.

"It's nice to meet you, Arlo. I'll be right back. They'll want to know you are awake."

IMMA CAME BACK, holding hands with the woman with the gestures and the partially-shaved head. Imma broke away. "Arlo, this is my sister, Laurel Pressman. She's the head of the Embassy School." Her hands moved as she spoke, the same gestured dance.

Laurel nodded her head, and her hands danced.

I didn't know what she was saying, but I wanted to. I needed it. The hunger for more was like nothing I'd ever felt before, but my slack-jawed awe made Laurel frown. She flipped her long ponytail behind her. She switched to speaking. "You don't sign, and you have nothing to identify you besides an expired leave pass from Central

Processing." Her words came out muddled and imperfect. She raised a brow. "Can't you speak, or won't you?"

The noises that came out of me after a lifetime of silence haunted me. I shook my head.

She scrutinized my face and pulled a small black box, no bigger than her palm and thinner than her small fingers from the pocket of her black trousers, and held it out to me. "Why didn't you have your TalkBox when they arrested you? It might have saved you from being taken in at all." The box dropped on my leg. "Tell me the truth."

I turned the device over in my hand. It had a screen covered in words, but I didn't know what to do with it. I handed it back and shook my head. Imma bolted forward, pushed the black box back at me. "I know it's not yours, but isn't it better than nothing?"

My fingers slipped and touched the screen. The synthetic monotone voice rattled off random words.

Laurel sat in the chair. "You should have had a TalkBox as soon as you were old enough to be classed as Non-Verbal."

I scrolled through pages of words until I found the right ones. "Can't," the voice stated. "Speak."

"Since when?"

I shrugged. "Always."

Imma's eyes sparkled like I was a puzzle she wanted to solve. "You don't know?"

The anger came out of nowhere, enveloped me in a wave. It didn't matter. My head was killing me. Everything hurt. I didn't have answers. I dug my hand into my throbbing temple, but the pressure wouldn't release. "Where. Here."

Laurel's small hand cooled my forehead. "The dormitories at the Non-Verbal Linguistics Embassy School. Patrol brought you to us. You're burning up but safe here."

Imma perched on the bed, her thigh pressed against mine. "Arlo." A dreamy smile fell over her. "Are you a fortress? Arlo means a fortress on a hill."

Laurel groaned. "Go get Dr. Zachili, it's too early for your nonsense." She stared me down long after Imma disappeared. "You might have my sweet, silly little sister fooled, but I'm who you have to convince." She sat back, waited, but I didn't understand what for. "How did you get here?"

I shrugged. "Patrol." The newfound defiant streak burned inside me, and I couldn't back down.

"Don't mistake deaf for stupid. I know more about the Tower than most." Her face tightened, and she sat up. The imperious expression changed everything about her. "Pressman. Laurel Pressman." She looked enough like Secretary of Corrections Dell Pressman from the tube video. She studied my fingertips. "Identity erasure like that is only supposed to be enacted on criminals who have no chance of ever coming above ground. It hasn't been done to anyone in over twenty years." Her face twisted and contorted like she had to fight to get words out. "I also know that nothing inside that building is as it seems. Please, tell me the truth. I can deal with anything but you being an escaped murderer."

I searched the long lists for the right words. "Not kill. No run."

"That's a start, but I can 't help without all the facts."

"Green. Police. Man. Said can't go Tower. For my good."

"A Retainment officer told you not to go back to the Tower? I give up. I was willing to help you, but you're just another delinquent looking for kicks....drop the act and tell me your name and Warden so I can return you."

The rage, quick as lightning and just as hot, filled me, and I shot forward and grabbed her arm. Her skin bulged between my fingers. Sound poured out my mouth, harsh and painful to my ears. I let go of her and clapped my hand over my mouth, heart racing. If anyone at the Tower heard that, they'd send me straight to Resident Health's Psych ward.

I reached for the TalkBox with a shaking hand. "Please. I stay. Guinn say talk Seb Riley."

She stared at me in awe and swallowed as she pulled a small tablet, similar to the TalkBox, out of her pocket and began to type rapidly, then settled back into the chair, arms crossed. "How have you gotten this far without...anything?"

What choice did I have? No one ever offered any other way.

Reading and writing came easy because I wanted it so bad, and I had a few friends willing to work through it with me. I scrolled through pages upon pages of words and grunted in frustration.

Her finger hovered over the screen. "If you know the words you want, you can go to the ABC tab and type it out. The pages of words are for 'quick' answers, but sometimes it's just quicker to say what you mean."

I typed what I wanted to say with my thumbs. "Watch. Listen. Use face. Write words."

"Write words on what? Like I said, you should have had a TalkBox long ago."

"Glass. Dirt. Hand."

She let out a soft laugh and sat forward. "I grew up in a house where no one signed. Here, at school, everyone spoke my language, but at home, they told me they fixed me, and I needed to use the gift they gave me. They didn't understand that the gift they gave me was sending me here to be with others like me." She pointed at the receiver. "Not this."

The TalkBox weighed heavy in my rubbery arm, weak with sedative, but I managed to find and tap the words I wanted. "Want words." My eyelids felt heavy.

Her eyes glowed, full of pride. "And I'm going to make sure you get them."

Chapter 5

Time lost its meaning. I don't know how much passed before Imma came back. She slid a tray onto the table and rearranged the two soup bowls, dishes of bright vegetables, and sweet fruit. Her eyes pinged from my face to the tray. She smiled, but her lip trembled. "They all stare at me in the dining room. I'm just an outsider to them, but I'll eat in the hall if you'd rather be alone."

We were both outsiders. We had to stick together. I offered her the chair the only way I knew how: a gesture.

Her smile was almost as debilitating as Guinn's stinger. "Thank you." She placed the tray on my lap and pulled the desk chair closer. "Eat up. I took a little of everything since I didn't know what you liked."

I reached for the small bowl of soup. It seemed like a safe place to start. Heat seeped into my skin and crawled up my arm. Instead of hot, salted water, silky, fragrant broth coated my tongue. Herbs that I knew the perfumes of but never tasted filled my nose.

Imma pulled her legs up underneath her and held a steaming mug close to her body. "Laurel used the pass she found in your clothes to track down someone from your ward."

I almost dropped my soup in my lap. Imma relieved me of it, and I typed in the TalkBox frantically. "Who?"

She waited for me to hold my hands out to ask for the bowl back. "She didn't say, just that they were coming later today. They should be here soon." She sipped at her own bowl and smiled into it. "My nanny used to make me soup anytime I hurt myself when I was a child. So, when the dining room had soup, I thought I should bring some to you."

I didn't know what a nanny was but would have had to put the soup down to pick the TalkBox up and ask, and the warm broth tasted too good to do that.

"I was always falling out of trees or tripping over my own feet. Nanny was ready with a warm washcloth, a bowl of soup, and a cup of chocolate milk."

I decided it had to be her word for mother. Marta never fixed a scraped knee with food, but washcloths to a scraped knee and a sour cherry out of the packet in her uniform trousers were her versions of the same thing. Maybe some things were the same in the city as they were in the Tower.

Imma put a blueberry in her mouth, but her eyes strayed to the single slice of cake. "The blueberries are fresh and ripe from the bushes out back." I pushed the dessert toward her. Her eyes grew bigger than before. "You don't like cake?"

I bit into a slice of peach and started tapping. "Never had it."

"You've never had cake?"

"No."

She nudged me a fork, and the first sweet bite melted on my tongue. Two times overlapped again. Imma receded. Other faces smiled, and the cake had a large number five drawn on it with strawberry chunks.

"Happy Birthday, my darling," a voice whispered inside my ear.

I couldn't think through the slow burn sizzling in my skull. I gripped my hair and yanked, clawing to release the heat. I thought the sheets would burst into flames.

Cold hands pushed mine away. "Arlo?" Marta's voice broke through the heat. She sat next to me, and I wasn't sure whether she was real or another whisper from a dream. Her hand brushed my scalp but pulled away with a hiss. Laurel handed her a few chemical cold compresses, and Marts pressed them to the sides of my head. Instead of thanking her, Marta glared at Laurel. "How long has he been like this? Why didn't you contact me sooner?

Laurel huffed. "Imma, your mother is waiting in my office. It's only a matter of time before she busts out and comes to storm the citadel. Go before she takes down the whole Embassy."

Marta fidgeted. She looked pale, like when Escher confronted her.

"Imelda, now." Laurel pulled Imma out the door and shut it behind them.

Smudges welled under Marta's eyes with none of her usual spark of teasing humor, making her appearance match the harsh sound of her voice. She closed her eyes; her skin turned a shallow green like she might be sick. "I know you didn't know anything, so you couldn't know to keep away from them. That woman, Doctor Persaud, she's the reason you were with me, and she has more power under her pinky fingernail than you or I will ever have. It's only a matter of time before she brings a shit storm down on top of us both!" Her words hung in the air between us. They floated like a feather and wafted in the discomfort between us. Her hazel eyes clouded, and her cheeks blanched. I wanted to reach out, but every-thing about her pushed me back. "Are you going to tell me what's going on here? Or are we going to keep pretending we're back on the 47th, and nothing is wrong?"

Typing out the events of the rally seemed endless, but having to watch Marta's face go through an entire spectrum of emotions while we listened to the playback was worse. Her eyes bulged out of a blanched face. Her freckles stood out against her pale skin.

"Speak."

She looked up from picking at her uniform slacks. Laughter rolled out her mouth, but her eyes held none of their normal sparkle. "Imagine that: you telling me to speak. What a strange day. You're sure it was Guinn?"

I drew an X over my heart with my finger.

"Damn him. He should have brought you back to me so that I could follow proper...."

The door snapped shut. Marta jumped to her feet. "Arlo should have been here from the start." Laurel closed the door behind her. "If his family needed help communicating, they should have come to us instead of surrendering him. He was five; we could have done so much for him!"

I held up seven fingers, my heart ached. I was seven when I walked out of the tube and onto Marta's ward. Marta shoved in next to me on the mattress and wrapped me up in her long willowy arms. "You people," she spat, "Too high and mighty to even consider his feelings before you just drag his life around like it's Simulcast headlines."

"Arlo, I'm sorry..." Laurel hung her head. "I just assumed you remembered."

Marta's eyes narrowed. "Resident files are confidential."

"I have my ways past that." Laurel turned on the same look she gave me when she told me she understood the Tower better than most, a mix of pride and contempt.

Marta snorted. "It's very cute that you think a daddy card will work on me, Miss Pressman." She smirked and slouched. "You look like him."

"It's almost as cute as you think it has anything to do with you. Patrol showed up at the Embassy in the middle of the night with a kid whose brains turned to soup because he was stung to the point of scrambling. He had no prints, no way to speak, and nothing to identify him besides a note in his pocket saying to deliver him to our lead technical supervisor. None of it made sense. I called in a favor, so I didn't welcome an escaped psychopath into my school."

"He's not a psychopath just because he lives in the Tower."

"Of course not," Laurel soothed, "but I have other people's children here. Their safety is my first priority, and now he is included in that. You obviously care about him. Help me do what is right for him. If you sign a transfer, we can give him what he deserved from the beginning!"

"I can't," Marta whispered. "He's red-listed, non-transferable.

I've been petitioning to get him to you from the first day, but it has to go through Commander Escher himself, and I can promise you, nothing will come of it."

MARTA DREW INTO HERSELF, looking like she did when Escher terrorized her. "Guinn is an idiot. He always was."

Laurel jumped in and said the words before I could start to type. "Wait, you know the officer who did this?"

Marta smiled at something I couldn't see. "Guinn and I grew up together. He was always trouble. Seems like maybe Retainment training doesn't brainwash them as much as the Resistance wants us to believe."

Laurel stiffened in her chair.

"He and I were inseparable. I didn't know where I ended, and he began. When he aged out, he tested for Retainment. I tested out conscripted and came back as a warden." Her palms rubbed against her slacks, puckering the fabric. "I didn't know anything but inside. Service was the only way to have some of the freedoms of Citizenship but still be... home."

"Why would he do this? Make Arlo absent without a pass, though?"

Marta sighed. "Because that's what he does, makes messes, and hopes someone else can clean them up." She buried her face in her hands.

Laurel and I waited while she stewed and argued with herself. She bolted up, red-faced with a deep ravine between her eyebrows and turned to Laurel, eyes fierce. "You really want to help him? Even if it might mean the ruin of your whole family—sister and stepmother included? Before this goes any further, I need to know that you're willing to do that."

Laurel took her time, her expression fixed in a serene mask. "My loyalty lies with my students, not my parents. My stepmother is a snake who needs her head chopped off with a shovel, and I haven't seen my father in person in six years. Eidolon and the Secretarial have always come before family for him."

Marta nodded and stood. She checked the hall and locked the door. "You both have to understand that Arlo and the others on the 47th aren't just unwanted or battered children living as wards. They were chosen, one by one and surrendered to the state as part of a biomedical experiment called Project Livewire. They are the next generation of Retainment, groomed from childhood."

Me? A part of the goon squad? No. No way. The glitch of D Ward couldn't become a mindless brute; then again, Guinn didn't seem so mindless. Bile filled my throat, but she kept going.

"They were implanted as children, to repress their memories and emotions. When every other kid goes to test into conscription and find their career aptitude, the kids from the 47th go to your stepmother. Their implant–or in Arlo's case, implants–is deactivated, and they go through a rigorous training protocol. What comes out is a soldier, fit for the border."

"But implanting children... the law says—"

Marta interrupted, "Senator Pressman has her ways around rules because I have two hundred fifty kids with microscopic impulse technology in their heads. What Guinn did was not just forcing Arlo to go AWOL. He used a stinger and deactivated Arlo's implant, and then told him it was for his own good. There is no going back to D ward, Arlo. You have two choices, kiddo, and neither of them is great. You can't hide the changes in you. They will notice and send you down to the underground Mental Health Hospital. They need you silenced."

I swallowed; my tongue felt too big for my mouth. "Other option?"

"You stay here. I clear your missed return on a pass as a computing error since Rat and Beryl both made it back in time."

Rat and Beryl both made it back by curfew? They left without me? They knew that I would need them if we got caught, and they left me. It was too hot, but the blankets felt like they weighed too much to move. A cold pack hit my ear, and I gasped. The sharp contrast between it and my skin dizzied me, and I closed my eyes.

Marta hovered inches from me. "I know. He was supposed to stick close. I'm pissed, too. It's okay to be mad. Don't try to fight it. Let yourself feel it even though it's new but, don't let it take control." I didn't like the feeling, but knowing I wasn't alone softened it.

Laurel interjected, "The Tower has cameras everywhere, logging Resident faces. When his face isn't captured, his normal number of times, it will alert them. I have people who can erase video footage, but I can't superimpose his face in real-time."

Marta's eyes widened. "You can hack through Tower security protocols?"

Laurel flushed. "Not me, but I know someone who can."

"Good to know. I'll need more time to work out getting Arlo in and out to get his face seen. Luckily, he spends most of his time hiding in grow houses where there are fewer cameras with his hair in his face. His quota is low."

"Thank goodness for small favors." Laurel rubbed her hand across her forehead and scrunched her nose. "There's so much we're still missing."

"Can your friend make passes, credentials, and hack the database?"

"Yes."

"Good. I'll need your contact information. We'll make it work." Marta turned to me. "No matter how airtight we manage to get our plan, we can't gloss over the stakes. If they catch you, Arlo, all three of us will be processed, tried, and likely imprisoned. If you go back now, you'll be locked away but treated well. Maybe they'd approve you for lessons from Miss Pressman. If you try to make it out here until you age out and get caught, you won't go to Mental Health. You will be incarcerated, and I probably will be too. Miss Pressman's family will be destroyed."

They shouldn't have risked so much for me, but my heart hurt and my mind wandered back to Laurel's signs.

"I can't tell you what to choose, Arlo," Marta said, "You have to make this choice, but know that I wouldn't have given you the option if I didn't think you being here was worth the risk. It's only a few months." She cupped my cheek. "I've watched you, surrounded by people, but so lonely. This is your chance to be part of it."

Laurel cleared her throat. "What about the reactions he's been experiencing? The sudden fevers and hallucinations?"

Marta paled. "I will go over the post deactivation first aid protocols with you before I leave, but the worst should be over. If he continues to spark, contact me. We're all in this together, and his hallucinating in public is attention we don't need." The sad smile on her face soured, and it scared me. I wasn't ready for good-bye.

She clasped my face tightly between her palms. "If it goes wrong and Escher's thugs come for you, you go quietly. Don't fight back. Don't give them any reason to use force." She sniffled and hugged me till it hurt. "Keep your head up and your eyes open. You've got friends now; it's okay to ask them to help you. You know the right people, and knowing the right people is everything when you're just starting out. I know you can do this." She turned on her heels to Laurel, "Miss Pressman, a word in private?"

Laurel nodded, tight-lipped. "Of course. Follow me."

They left me, all alone in this new world, with an unfamiliar brain.

Chapter 6

A sound in the room startled me, and I jolted awake. I searched the room for Rat and only made sense of his absence when I realized I didn't know where I was. The door clicked, and my lungs pulled out of their shocked stall. Everything from the rally on came back—Guinn, the NVL, Laurel and Marta, and our plan to keep me safe. It was the start of the new life that they chose for me.

A knock came at the door, and Imma peeked around the slab. She dragged the desk chair closer to me. "You can tell me to go away if you want. Everyone else does." She waited behind the chair for my answer.

I patted the seat, and my lip hitched up on its own when she grinned.

She curled up like a cat, taking up as little room as possible on the already small chair, and pulled a TalkBox from her pocket. "It's almost time for the Simulcast; I thought you might feel more, I don't know, normal if you could watch it. It always helped me get my bearings when I first started my internship."

I nodded and tapped my heart.

"Is that your gesture for 'thank you?' "

Another nod.

She made a gesture, touched her chin. "This is ours."

She watched me mimic the motion a few times, giddy excitement wafted off her like perfume. "You're a natural. We'll have you caught up in no time!" Her head cocked to the side and her face grew sad. "I can see all the questions... it looks like they're going to start dripping out of your ears if they don't get answered soon. Think of the rest of us, washed away in a tidal wave of unspoken thoughts and dreams." She let out a dreamy sigh and smiled. The chiming introduction jingle for the Simulcast sounded.

On the 47th, meals were scheduled to start after the Simulcast, and we had to report to the dining hall before it started. The others would go in playing and joking, but the commander stepped in, and two hundred fifty voices died at once. Every sound, every movement stilled. Every person stood at attention.

After a cursory once over, he said, "Recite the Pillars." The twenty-five glass cafeteria tables hummed to life at his command. The surfaces lit and produced a three-dimensional image of Central Services Tower. My ward mates voices dropped an octave, boys and girls alike, to chant in homogeneous cadence.

Each of the six sides of the Tower glowed as it's corresponding value rolled across nearly three hundred tongues in unison. The lights of the Tower image pulsed, the heartbeat of a million citizens and residents beating as one. The image faded with each pulse, and a polite fanfare led in the daily Simulcast.

I swung my legs over the side of the bed, ready to stand at attention even if I couldn't recite the pillars.

"Where are you going?" Imma said. "I don't think they want you up and moving around yet. Sit down. Watch with me."

The news started, and I sat. Everything was supposed to be the same whether you were in the Tower or the city, but from what I had seen, nothing was. No standing at attention, no reciting the pillars, she didn't even look at the screen. Her face relaxed, her eyes glazed; she went somewhere else. She stayed dazed until the chimes sounded again and Silvagni said:

"As one, we stand apart."

The sound cut, and before I could breathe, she started talking. "Did you know that when lightning strikes soft enough organic material, it leaves scars?" From the dreamy look on her face, she didn't hear a word of the Simulcast. She leaned in closer, tapped the screen a few times and showed me picture after picture of people with skin marred by crackled red lines. "They're called Lichtenburg figures, and they look like the lightning. Wood, soft rock, even human flesh can get them, and the scar will always be there, like a tattoo. Even if you live through being struck, it never lets you forget it. You'll always have the mark of someone who was thunderstruck."

I blinked. How did a person exist with things like that in their head?

Before I could even pick up the TalkBox, let alone think of a response, her face lost the dreamy haze, and her attention snapped to me. "Why did you stand up? I've only ever met one Resident, and he hates my guts because of who my parents are. I never got to ask him any questions. Would you mind?"

I shrugged and picked the TalkBox up off the side table. "Slow."

Her short hair kicked out in whisps and feathers that wobbled when her head cocked to the side. "I need to go slow? Or your answers might be slow?"

"Yes."

Her giggle danced between us. "We both need to go slow. Got it. I'll do my best. Why did you stand up when the Simulcast started?"

I started typing but snuck a look up at her every few words.

She smiled. "I don't have anywhere to be, I promise. Take your time." I went back to the TalkBox. "It's kind of stupid that all of the adaptive tech puts the burden back on you. You already have a disadvantage. Why should you have to sit there and type out your answers? I wonder why no one makes it easier for you."

The poisonous thought bloomed without warning and brought back what Laurel said about my parents. They surrendered me. I'd survived on the belief that my life in the Tower was better, that I'd been saved by a Services intervention. Services didn't save me from my family; they saved my family from me. Adaptations weren't made to make life easier for people like me. Adaptations made living with me and my problems easier on them. My family adapted by not having to look at me anymore. Services locked all of us problems away in the Tower.

I hit the button that made the awful voice speak. "We have to stand. The others all speak as one; I pretend I am one of them. The sound hurts. It feels like getting hit. Trust." I mimed being punched in the cheek. "Autonomy." A punch to the jaw. "Frugality." An elbow to the gut. She turned away. A lone tear trailed down her cheek. "Reciprocity, Transparency, and Justice." The same heat that gripped my chest when Marta told me that Rat and Beryl got back to the Tower took hold.

She sniffed and wiped her cheek on her shoulder. "I thought only conscripts had to do that. We certainly don't. They make it so we have no choice but to have it on, but we have no ceremony beforehand."

I felt terrible for making her uncomfortable. She was the only person trying to make things easier for me. I pointed between the TalkBox and Imma's handheld. "Why do you have a TalkBox?"

She shook her head. "You've never had an HHD?"

I'd seen them in the hands of people on the tram when Rat, Beryl, and I rode to the hall for the rally. I'd never seen one before that. "Seen. Never had. Not allowed."

She looked down at the device in her hand. "Jack has an HHD; he's a Resident." Her eyebrows knitted together, and she twisted her fingers against one another. "Maybe you couldn't have one because you're a ward? I guess Services can't be expected to pay for one for each of you when they could just put big screens up on the walls." That sounded as plausible as anything else. "A TalkBox is different. HandHeld Devices connect to the Services system. TalkBoxes are just for speech generation and dictation. The only people who have personal TalkBoxes are the Services liaisons who choose not to have implants and need the box to translate the speakers around them." She knew about things I didn't know existed. "I wish they made something like that for people like me. Something that would make other people make more sense."

We had that in common. I'd watched my ward mates for years, wondering what made me different from them. It couldn't just be speech. I typed the words and handed her the TalkBox. "What kind of people are you?"

She scoffed and shook her head. The box dropped onto the mattress, and her hands went into her hair. She twisted the short strands until they stood out from her head. "I'm supposed to appeal to everyone, but the more appealing I try to be, the more people find me annoying. My sister convinced my father to let me spend my internship here with her to help grow my confidence. Everyone loves Laurel, they always have. I'm pretty sure my own mother doesn't like me."

"Mine gave me away. Parental Surrender." Ten years—well, twelve, but I wasn't ready to face that yet— later, the pang of loss in my chest was still fresh.

She shrugged. "I wish my mother would surrender me. I'm going to be eighteen in eight months, and you'd think I still played with dolls and needed help tying my shoelaces the way she fusses. 'Don't eat so much. Don't wear that you'll look trashy. You cut your hair short again? I told you we were growing it out. A woman wears her power in the way she presents herself. No one will ever listen to you if you don't look as smart as you are.'" She sounded like she did when I first woke, and a low chuckle slipped out again. I held my breath to keep in any other random sounds that attempted to escape.

Laurel cleared her throat from the doorway. She stood with her arms crossed over her chest. "You could start by getting to your classes when you're supposed to instead of sneaking around the boys' dormitory."

Elder sister caught younger by the elbow as she passed and held Imma's face between her palms. "Her opinion doesn't count. You wear your power however you want." Laurel pulled Imma's forehead to meet her own and smiled when their noses rubbed.

LAUREL WAITED for Imma to get down the hall. "You look better —half-alive instead of half-dead. We have a lot to talk about." The man with hair like ropes came in behind her and closed the door. He had part of his head shaved, but no blinking receiver lights.

She set a stack of red and charcoal gray clothes on the desk and rested her charcoal clad hip against it. A red geranium decorated her lapel. "When you start venturing out, you need to put a uniform on; we don't need you drawing any more attention than any new student would."

The man put his hand over hers, and she smiled—the hidden kind of smile that I'd seen countless girls use on Rat. He'd tied the thick locks of dark hair back this time, allowing me to see the kind eyes and wide smile I was too affected to see before. Laurel squeezed his hand. "This is Seb Riley, my lead technological staffer. Seb, this is our resident fugitive, Arlo."

Seb extended a long, sinewy arm encrusted with tattoos barely a shade darker than his skin. I shook it.

Laurel kept going, "He and Marta have been in contact and have set up a plan to keep all of us as safe as we can hope to be."

I had so many questions swarming my brain. I couldn't make sense of the noise, but they cleared as soon as Laurel said Marta's name. "Marta? O-K?"

Seb's lips never moved. He held up an HHD twice the size of Imma's, and his fingers flew over the screen. The voice that answered fit him, warm and deep. "Marta is quick as a whip and twice as snappy. She checked in regularly while you slept off the worst of the scrambles."

I pointed, so shocked at the human voice coming from the machine that I forgot I had words at my disposal until Laurel tapped my hand holding my TalkBox. "Doesn't sound bad. Why?"

He reached for my TalkBox, concern mixed with excitement in his eyes, and went to work tinkering with setup screens and other workings. Laurel rolled her eyes like she and I were in on the same inside joke. "He can't hear it, so he thinks you mean broken when you say bad."

She put her hand on the device, and they had another conversation I couldn't understand. They shared a laugh over the miscommunication. He typed on his monster machine to answer me in the detached human voice. "If you get on my good side, we can talk about recording and synthesizing your voice."

Laurel's hands moved while she spoke. "Seb is the authority on dictative and text-to-speech technology. He can use recordings of speech sounds to synthesize a more personalized voice for hearing Non-Verbals to interact more easily with a TalkBox outside the community."

"Imma said TalkBoxes just to borrow."

They shared a look of amusement. "Imma is still very new here, and an outsider. There is a lot she still doesn't understand. There are things she never will understand.

"Most of us choose not to use TalkBoxes unless it's necessary. They are cumbersome, impersonal, and off-putting to those you want to communicate with. For people who have to live outside the community or have little hand dexterity to sign with, a TalkBox is a lifeline. Most of our matriculating students choose not to be implanted for the same reason. Our language isn't an impediment to us. It is the heart of our culture and our community." She stood and came closer, sat on the edge of the mattress. "It can be yours now, too."

I wanted that. I'd always stood on the edges and watched while my ward mates made friends, started romances that always ended badly, and talked about what they would do someday. I never wanted anything. I never dreamed of anything. Somehow, the implant took that away from me, and now that I had it back, I wouldn't run from the things I wanted.

A wide grin spread across her face. "That's the kind of hunger I like to see in my students. You'll start classes as soon as you feel up to it. We'll start with you in the beginner's class. We don't have an adult class starting for another two weeks, and I don't want to risk wasting a moment for you to learn. So, in the morning, you're going to work your way through the different classrooms. It will help with immersion and giving you words at the right vocabulary level. In the afternoon, when all the interns leave class to work in the Embassy, you will work with Seb."

Seb sobered and nodded. He folded his body into the small metal chair and hit play on his HHD. "So far as Marta or I have been able to tell, the only tabs they keep on you are that your schoolwork is completed and that they catch your face on their security footage a consistent number of times in a given period. I hacked you a back door into their system to do your schoolwork. You can do that in my office so that no one accidentally walks into the computer lab or Laurel's office and sees your screen. When you're done with that, you can help me.

"When Marta sends me word that everything is in place, I will get you some documents that will get you into the Tower and through Processing. She told those you've lived with that you were approved for an educational release, and none of them know that they're red-listed. They won't know it's not supposed to happen. After three messages back and forth with that woman, I'm going to take her word that she has everything well in hand."

Marta could handle herself against anyone. Everyone except Escher, the person who would be after all of us if this went wrong.

I held up my hands and shoved my smooth printless fingertips under Seb's nose.

He pushed my hand away but grinned. "We have ways around that."

"We?"

Laurel glared at her partner. "We'll talk about that more once Marta gets us word that she has everything in hand in your ward. For now, we need to set the ground rules to keep the three of us safe and out of scrutiny from the students here."

Her hands trembled in the air, and she blew out a shaky breath. "The students here will think the same as your mates from the Tower. You are on an educational release. They will likely think nothing of it, but you need to be very careful what you tell them. We need to be as secretive as we can without seeming like it." Laurel narrowed her eyes. "Imma sees something in you. She normally shies away from people. I hate to discourage that, but she needs to be kept out of this. Her mother and my father would shit bricks if they knew I let her anywhere near you and would make me eat the brick if they knew I got her mixed up in what we're doing. I know you don't need any more pressure on you, but this is important to me. Please, be her friend, but keep her out of this."

Chapter 7

I wanted to keep my promise to Laurel, but when Imma turned up that night after I had a shower, I forgot all about it. She pulled her chair up until it touched my bed. "You've cleaned up. I can see your face." Her smile spread across her face. "You don't even need words; your face says everything you're thinking."

I let my hair fall forward, the wet strands hid my face.

Her cheeks and ears flushed. "Great, Imma. You made it weird." She raked at her short hair. "You do look much better."

"What was I thinking?" I handed her the TalkBox.

Her eyes flew over the question, and the blush on her cheeks grew darker. "You...you looked hopeful? Happy to see me? It was nice." She handed the box back without looking up. "I told you earlier, no one is happy to see me. They told me to take care of you so that I was out of everyone else's way." Maybe she was right. Maybe my face said things without me knowing. Maybe that was how I got along without words for so long. I had a few people willing to interpret what they saw. "Why don't you let the box say the words. You don't have to hand it to me."

I typed and hit the picture of a mouth. "Don't like the voice."

She chuckled and looked down at her hands. "It's not yours. I guess I wouldn't want to speak with someone else's voice either, but it's better than nothing, isn't it?"

I picked up the machine and found the words I wanted. "You sign because of Laurel?"

The light came back into her eyes, and when she spoke, her hands talked, too. "She was eleven when I was born and lived with her mother. After her mother died, she lived with us when she wasn't at school. I signed before I could talk."

So many movements, each at a specific place on her body. She calculated every facial expression and head tilt. It was all part of the language I wanted. I tried to mimic, tried to follow, but she moved so fast and fluid.

"I'm going too fast." She spread her skirt across her legs and kept quiet. She put her pinky finger next to her temple and moved it away from her face in a loopty-loop pattern. "This sign is mine. Laurel gave it to me when I was little."

I'd never had anything to call myself. My hand flew to my chest and patted. I wanted that.

She smiled but shook her head. "I can't give you a name sign; the others have to do it. I told you, I'm an outsider here. It has to come from them, but I can show you the letters that make your name." She made four little movements and waited for me to mimic them.

The hand that patted my chest and asked for my name tapped at the mattress, full of energy that I couldn't release. I needed more.

She made another. "Bathroom is always a good one to know." Her hands switched, and mine followed. "And this is 'eat.'" She met my eyes and covered a giggle with her hand. "You look like you're going to burst. More? More seems like one you will need."

I made the same motion and kept making it. No more yes or no answers to everything. No more pointing and hoping someone understood what I wanted. I needed names for everything and pushed off the bed. I pointed—bed, chair, door, shirt, blanket—and Imma gave me names for things I never had words for. I knew what everyone else called them, but those words she taught me were mine for the first time.

It started low, so low that I didn't notice it over my excitement.

"This is 'all done' or 'finished' and so am I." She shook her hands. She yawned and stretched her arms over her head, but her eyes held their brightness when she recovered. "You are full of surprises, Arlo–" She stared at me, a funny little half-smile frozen on her lips "–I don't know your last name. Your pass said Arlo Towerward and a bunch of numbers."

"No." My hands moved, but my shoulder hitched up to relieve the whine fizzing behind my ear. Sweat ran down my temple. "Name Arlo."

"Arlo is your only name? What if there is another Arlo?"

The squeal turned loud; my knees wobbled and dropped me. I dug my fingers into the carpet. A child screamed, and it melded with the militant noise. Another voice joined it. "Just tell me what you want! This? This? Use your words, Ar–"

"Arlo!" Imma crouched on the floor, her hands over mine. Heat blistered inside my skull. "I need to get Laurel. But I can't leave you. Think Imma, think!"

The fire fizzled out as quickly as it flared and left me panting with my forehead resting on the floor. "All done. Bed."

She yelped and jumped to her feet." What happened? Are you all right?"

I dragged myself up to all fours and crawled onto the bed. I didn't have the words I needed, and my hands shook as I typed. "Baby screaming."

"No one was screaming. You kind of…groaned, but no one screamed."

"Kid screaming. Woman. Questions." The TalkBox dropped from my hand.

She backed toward the door. "I think I should get Laurel."

I wanted to call her off, but the exhaustion that followed the heat and pain of the implant flaring consumed me. I couldn't lift a finger and was asleep before the door shut.

She brought Laurel back. I heard them even though I couldn't wake up all the way. The door opened, and light from the hallway spilled in. "He's sleeping now, Imma. I'm sure everything is fine. He took a hit to the head with a stinger. It's common to get dizzy spells with that kind of head injury."

Imma had none of her sister's calm. "It looked like he was having some kind of fit! His face turned red, and all of his veins stuck out. It was not just a dizzy spell!"

"Hush!"

I understood why Laurel wanted to keep Imma safe. Imma couldn't let go once she saw all of the inconsistencies in our story. "And he heard a child screaming and a woman asking questions. But there was no woman or child. I couldn't hear them."

Laurel responded with dry wit. "I'll take your word for it."

"He doesn't have a last name. It wasn't a typo like you said. He told me he doesn't have a last name. Just Arlo. What is going on, Laurel?"

"Things are different in the Tower than they are in Tower City. You know that. We all do even if we say otherwise. Arlo somehow fell through the cracks in the system. It happens, but he's with us now, and we're going to keep him safe. I need you to help me keep things normal for him and for the others. He has enough challenges without everyone seeing what you saw. He's gone his whole life with an untreated speech delay, who knows what other issues have gone undocumented. Keep tabs on him and let me know if he has another fit. We need to keep Dr. Zachili apprised if he needs to see a specialist. Can you do that?"

"Yes. Of course. He deserves to have someone on his side."

"He does. Now go to bed." The door shut, but I could still hear them in the hall. "And Imma, maybe we shouldn't tell your mother about Arlo until we have him a little better settled."

"Good idea. Good night, Laurel."

"Good night Arlo," Laurel said through the door. She knew I might be listening. She wanted me to hear what she told Imma so that I could do my part to keep her out of the mess I'd made of all of our lives.

Chapter 8

My new uniform crackled, stiff against my skin when I moved. I didn't recognize the person in the washroom mirror. I'd only ever seen myself in gray TowerCloth. The red sweater vest and stark white shirt made my eyes look bluer, and my hair darker. I pushed the wet strings back from my face—no more hiding. I had to face this new world.

"Arlo? Are you in there?" I opened the door, and my stomach flipped. Imma waited outside the bathroom. "You have a message, Laurel sent it to my HHD so you could watch it in private."

She held out her tablet. My hand shook when I took it.

She smiled. "It's queued up, ready to play. Take it to your room. I'll wait out here, and we'll go to breakfast when you're ready." The moisture in my mouth turned to paste. Cheeks flushed, eyelashes fanned on her cheeks, big brown eyes raised below them: she could fell armies with that look.

I reached out, hands shaking, and made the sign, "Together."

She lit up." Yes. Together. Very good."

"Wait?"

If her smile got any wider, I wouldn't be able to breathe. "I'll wait."

I closed my door and settled on the bed. Marta's face stared back, a smile on her lips but not in her amber-colored eyes. "Hey, kid. I hope you're hanging in there. I know you don't like new people, new situations, and this is a doozy you've got yourself wrapped up in, but it's the best thing that could have happened in the worst way. Take it and run with it."

She checked the closed door behind her. "Be careful, and listen to that guy...Riley. He knows his stuff. I'll send word to him when you can come for a visit. Be good. Show them that you are the same as them, maybe better. If you get sparky again, go straight to Miss Pressman. Do not let them take you to anyone but her or that doctor who patched you up. Have a good first day."

The screen went black. I wanted Marta back or, better yet, a good hiding place.

The hinges creaked on the door, and Imma plunked on the bed next to me. "Sparky? Is that a nickname or something? Like your friend is Rat?"

She wasn't supposed to know. Laurel asked me to keep her out of it, and Laurel had risked everything for me. I shook my head.

She frowned; a 'tsk' of disappointment escaped her lips before she could stop.

I left the HHD on the neatly made bed and walked to the window overlooking the school play yard.

Her soft hand wrapped around mine as two birds took off out of a small pine tree, flying together in a strange aerial dance. "Sometimes they move together, hundreds of them."

"What?"

"Swallows. The birds. It's called a murmuration when they dance together. I'm not sure if it's still called that for only two, but it should be. Look at them. Off by themselves; nothing to fear." She tugged me to the door, scooped up, and pocketed her HHD as she passed the bed. "Come on, we'll be late. You can sit with me. We can each pretend that the other kids are staring at the other."

I pulled in a deep breath and blew it out through my lips in frustration, nodded and, squeezed her hand in return.

The kids ate off real china plates, filled with eggs, pastries, and bacon. Fruit I'd only seen in books glistened on the white glazed plate. "Do you want more?"

Her plate held a small piece of melon, the smallest pastry she could find and a dainty portion of eggs. I didn't want to take more than they allowed, and my plate looked loaded down in comparison, so I shook my head. She led me to a table where five other kids, all in their late teens, and all wearing the same gray red and white uniforms, sat. I tugged at my vest.

Imma sat in a hurry and kept her eyes on her food. "This is Arlo. He's new, and I said he could sit with us."

A girl with rich brown skin and tight coils of hair around her face scooted her chair closer to Imma's and shoved some of her eggs onto her friend's plate. "You have to eat more than that."

I liked her.

Imma gripped a mug close to her chest. "Don't peck at me. I get enough of that from my mother."

"Blah blah blah." The girl shoved Imma a fork. "You weigh nothing, you don't eat enough, you're cute as a button. Shut up and eat before you disappear for the day." Imma hid behind the mug and hugged it like it could shield her. The other girl looked over to me and smiled. "I'm Rae." She held her hand out. "And you're Arlo."

I nodded.

"Welcome to the Embassy. That's Charlie, Tora, Lewis..." She let out a disgruntled hiss of air. "And Jack."

The kid across the table slumped in his seat. I recognized him but couldn't place where I could know him from.

We finished what we could before the lights flashed. "That's the signal for the end of the meal," Imma said. Everyone stood to clear their tables, except one little boy who glared at the movement around him, threw his plate, and let out a howl. The little boy gave a guttural roar as he took off into the kitchen where he climbed the counters and grabbed wooden spoons, mixing bowls, anything he could throw to fend off the teachers.

The crashes turned into breaking china. A pounding built in my head, pulses like lightning grew behind my eyes until they rolled back in my head, and I dropped to my knees. It felt like being in two places at once, but as quickly as it began, it ended.

Imma knelt at my side. "You must have stood up too fast."

I took the hand she offered and rocked on my feet. She hooked a nearby chair with her foot, slid it behind me. I signed, "thank you," like she taught me.

"I should be thanking you. You distracted everyone long enough for Laurel to get him somewhere more private. Poor Gage. He doesn't understand that we just want to help. He's a ward on a Special Education pass, just like you."

Laurel rushed back and straight to where I sat, cradling my head. She checked my temperature and sat me up in the chair. "Quite a way to start your first day. Let's get you checked out, and then I'll walk you to your class."

I shook my head and pushed her hands away. "Fine. School time."

She sat back on her heels, and a proud smile spread her normally serious face. "Marta warned me that you would soak it up like a sponge! Very well done."

I pointed to Imma. "Good teacher."

"She is a good teacher." She dismissed her sister, pulled me to my feet, and waited while I shuffled through the school halls. The door she stopped outside had been decorated with colorful letters and numbers. Eight small faces looked up at me, but the panic I would have felt if they were kids my own age didn't come.

Laurel signed to the little ones and spoke for me. "This is Arlo, and he needs to learn his signs. I expect all of you to be my helpers!" The teacher waved me over and patted a piece of open carpet beside her. The moment my backside settled, the others crowded around me.

▭

MY SMALL CLASSMATES picked everything up so quickly and were already months ahead of me in vocabulary. Exhausted and dragging my bruised ego behind me, I sat down for lunch and buried my face in the crook of my arm.

Jack planted himself across the table, and the other interns filled the seats around him. "Have fun finger painting?" He sneered and ripped off a hunk of bread with his teeth, contemplating me as he chewed. "Is that what you had in mind all along? Find yourself a nice cushy place out of the Tower to wait out a few months until Conscription and then book it for the Frontier? They can only make you a soldier if they can find you. You're going to bring heaps of trouble down on our heads."

Rae bounced a grape off Jack's cheekbone. "Just because you'd do it doesn't mean everyone would. Not everyone has your penchant for melodrama and crippling paranoia." She turned to me. "He likes to think he's special and you being here threatens that. No one is allowed to be more special than Jack. Eat up, lunch is short."

I searched over the heads of the eating students.

A grape hit me between the eyes. Rae popped one in her mouth and winked. "So. You're the mystery boy Imma can't shut up about."

"Where?" I struggled through fingerspelling her name.

Her smile at my rudimentary signs didn't last long. "Her mother showed up and took her out for the day. The senator is another special one. Just because her name is on all the Simulcast ads doesn't mean her kid doesn't need to go to school or have friends."

Jack snorted. "Boo-hoo. She had to cry to Mommy and Daddy to let her come and play with the other kids. You and me, Rae, we're the only ones here who actually fought for our places." He moved his food around the dish, a look of disgust on his face.

The others made themselves very interested in their plates and offered no objections to the insult.

I pushed the decadent food around until the lights flicked, and everyone set about their clean up tasks.

A hand squeezed my shoulder. Laurel smiled. "Come with me." She led me across the playground, through a gate and into the backdoor of the Embassy building. My heart rate jumped faster with every adult we passed. The door was marked "Adaptive Technology, Sebastian Riley." Laurel pushed a blue button and pushed in. Seb sat behind a desk, watching nonplussed as Jack signed.

The loud snap of the door latch stopped Jack's hands in midair. Laurel raised an eyebrow. "Jack, you're supposed to be in the offices, aren't you?"

Jack grumbled under his breath and made to leave but grabbed my arm as he passed. He kept his tone low and moved his mouth as little as he could to keep Laurel and Seb from understanding. "Everyone knows you've got a little crush on Imelda. Don't expect it to go anywhere. She is what is wrong with this world. And you? I know there's something not right about you. You're some sort of spy for Central Services. We've never had patrol show up at a gathering before. Suddenly the place is a riot, and half the supporters get dragged into Services Satellites, and you end up here the next day! I don't know if you called them yourself or if they did it for you. But you're part of it."

"Jack," Laurel barked, "go. You're already on thin ice; don't make me revoke your internship. You'd make a terrible soldier."

He skulked out, and Laurel locked the door behind him. "Some days, that kid is more trouble than he's worth."

Seb laughed and signed something to her that she answered with a withering glare. "Get your schoolwork done, Arlo. Seb will walk you back over for supper."

Seb beckoned me over to a small table in the corner, and Laurel left. "I hacked a back door into Central Services Educational Curriculum so that you can sign in just like you do when you're there and complete your daily work. No one monitoring your progress will know the difference."

"Tech Monitor?"

Seb smirked. "Please. You think I didn't think of that? It's not like it's the first time I've hacked their systems."

I sat with a huff. I couldn't do this. I couldn't keep this huge secret and endanger all those people.

"What do you need?"

No one had ever asked me that. I pulled out my TalkBox. "Sign.

Babies understand. Not me." Laurel and Imma both said I learned so fast and soaked it up like a sponge, but I didn't feel very absorbent. "I need it fast."

"You have time. It takes babies years to talk or sign anything more than one word at a time. One word at a time, that's all anyone can ask of you. "

"Can't we just put my voice in this dumb thing? It's not like I have anyone I can sign to outside this place!"

Seb tapped on the shell of his HHD. "If you didn't have hands, I might say yes, but this is a tool for you. It has its place. You're not going to be a ward forever. If you don't learn Sign, you won't have a way to speak for yourself, and all of this will have been for nothing. You'll be an outsider here the same way you've been on your floor in the Tower."

I couldn't go back to that. I tucked the TalkBox back into my pocket. "School now."

"Good." Seb signed slowly. "We can practice when you finish."

Chapter 9

The little boy, Gage, who somehow activated my failing implant at breakfast my first day, screamed in the next room from my morning class every day for the next week. The signs I learned the best from sheer repetition became, "watch me." I couldn't take it anymore. They couldn't leave the kid to scream forever. My classmates sat down at a tiny table for a morning snack, but I asked to use the restroom and slipped down the hall.

Gage was so engrossed in his tantrum that he didn't notice me sit on the floor. When I made myself noticed, he threw all of that anger and frustration at me, and I let him. I welcomed it and felt strangely homesick for it. My calm acceptance calmed the boy, and he sat down, knee to knee, and stared back with wary curiosity. When I signed my name, Gage glared at my hand, but his eyes lit up when I pulled a marker from my pocket and pointed at the writing board on the wall. His blonde hair flopped over his eyes as he gestured wildly that he wanted it. As soon as he had it, he drew and didn't stop until the board was covered with a female stick figure. He grunted and whimpered, and the duplicitous feeling I felt suck me in the first day of school made me feel like I was two places at once again.

They took me. They took me to a strange place, and I want to go home. I want my mother. I didn't mean to hurt anyone! I won't do it again if she'd let me come home. The lady in this new place is nice enough, but she's not mine.

As suddenly as it was there, it was gone again. Laurel crouched in front of me and called my name. I locked eyes with Gage, sucked a breath into my aching deflated lungs, and looked between her and the boy.

"Arlo." Laurel touched my hand.

I pointed at the board, at the stick figure Gage drew. My hand shook, and my brain reeled too quickly to find the signs I wanted. "M-A-M-A." My brain got some traction to start functioning again. "Want…mother." I spelled out all of the feelings I felt in that strange moment, "scared, mad, not understand."

Laurel sat back on her backside in shock. "He told you that?"

Gage smiled at me.

Is that what he did? If I said that to Laurel, she'd ship me back to processing with a first-class pass to Psyche evaluation. It sounded crazy to me, and I'm the one who felt it.

"You are something special, Arlo."

I didn't want special. I wanted normal—somewhere between the spaz of the 47th and Laurel's 'something special.'

She sat at a desk. I sat on the floor with Gage, and she watched me give him names for all the things around him. "I'm ashamed to say that I didn't know how to help him. He's so angry. Most children like him jump at the chance to communicate"

"He's like me." I knew it was true but had no way to explain what it meant. "I was angry…."

Pain ripped through my head, and a screech filled my ears, but instead of the images I'd seen the other times, my vision went white, searing my eyes like the heat and noise sizzled in my brain.

"Arlo!" Laurel's voice sounded strange like it traveled from above water that I'd become submerged in.

My heartbeat thudded through my whole body but throbbed in my head, each beat a hammering blow.

"Arlo stop!" Her voice grew clearer, my body rose closer to the surface of whatever ocean had dragged it under.

I could feel my knees digging into my chest and the telltale tingles of pins and needles in my feet. Laurel's hand carded through my hair. The thudding muffled, but the ache remained.

"Please stop."

I opened my eyes but wished I hadn't. The room rocked, and my stomach rolled. A pitiful sounding groan rumbled from my chest, and her hand pressed down. The room didn't rock, and the percussion wasn't my heart. Her hand padded my forehead from pounding against the hard floor.

"That's it. Don't hurt yourself."

My legs felt leaden, too heavy to move, but my knees digging into my abdomen added to my nausea. I forced them out behind me and rolled to my side.

Laurel turned my face. She 'tsked' and smoothed her thumb over my forehead. "That's going to leave a bruise. What happened?"

I rolled my eyes around; Gage cowered under a desk. He didn't do it, but he was the key to me unlocking what my brain wasn't ready to let go of.

"Don't know." I pulled away and rested on the floor, the cold tiles soothed my scorched skin.

"I'm calling Dr. Zachili and Marta."

I jolted upright, bellowed a protest, and cradled my spinning head.

"Fine."

"You're not fine. Aside from that episode, you could have given yourself a concussion banging your head like you were!"

Marta would worry. She would try to save the day if she knew, and her leaving unnecessarily would put her in danger. Her in danger meant I was in danger. "Doctor. Not Marta."

"I promised I would let her know if this kept happening, but they monitor unusual contact. I'll let her know the next time we talk. You rest while we wait for the doctor. I'm going to find someone to watch Gage."

I nodded off but came back to reality when Gage screamed. He wouldn't let Laurel move him, pointed frantically at me. I waved him over and fell asleep with his hand in mine, content that he felt connected to me as I did to him.

Dr. Zachili came with ice packs. He scanned over me with his tablet and checked the bruise forming on my forehead. "There isn't much more I can do, Laurel. I can take him with me and give him a proper concussion scan, but his temperature is dropping already." He caught me watching him and smiled. "He seems to be coming around now."

Laurel put her hand on my face. "I think it's best if you go back to your room and lie down, Arlo. The other students are going to ask questions if this keeps happening. We can try it again in a few days."

I sat up. "No. School."

"Give him another chance, Laurel," Dr. Zachili said. "Nothing is going to change if you keep him locked away in his dorm room. You'd be as bad as they are."

Her face soured. "Fine, but if it happens again today, we're calling it quits until tomorrow."

I nodded, and had to spell, "Deal."

<hr>

GAGE WOULDN'T LET me out of his sight. He trailed me into the dining room, gathering food onto his own plate and ate the same thing I did, bite for bite. Imma came up and smiled nervously.

Gage jumped to his feet and made one of the few signs he'd picked up in between fits of rage. "No."

I tapped his hand. "My friend. Tell her your name." That was all it took to convince Gage. He happily finished his lunch and went outside to play on the playground.

"You're just amazing with him."

I shrugged. "Marta give me; I give him."

"Gave you what?"

"A chance, a voice, a friend."

She seemed to see through my limited signs to my meaning. "He's lucky to have you. We all are." No one had ever said that to me before. I rubbed anxiously at the back of my neck as nerves ran over my skin like spider legs.

Rae's amber-brown eyes studied me as a smirk tugged at her lips.

I dragged my eyes up to meet hers and stared back for a moment before allowing a tentative smile. "What?"

"You're a mess."

I checked my shirt and wiped my mouth with a napkin. "Good?"

She laughed. "No. What's the story with your hair?"

"I like it. Not cutting it."

"Maybe if it didn't look like a beaver dam, people would stop trying to chop it off without your permission." She and Imma shared a look and a grin that made my stomach flip-flop. "Come with me. I'm good at taming beasts like that."

Imma shooed me away, and I followed Rae out of the dining room. She walked like she owned the world, hips swaying, arms swinging curls bouncing, head high, and people moved out of her way.

The hall that housed the girls' rooms looked identical to the boys'. I expected them to be somehow different, but Rae's room was small with light walls. The bed, desk, and dressers were in the same place as in my room, but hers were vibrant and full of life. Posters for things I'd never heard of and art I'd never seen papered her walls and a colorful quilt from home covered her bed instead of a plain charcoal and red blanket like mine.

"Sit here." She pulled out a chair at her desk and propped a mirror up in front of it. She carefully picked through the snarls and tangles and rubbed something fruity and rich into it.

"You know, I went through a phase when I was little where I refused to let anyone brush my hair. Everything felt so wrong, and I had no say in anything, but I could control who touched my hair and when. You know?"

I knew, but she didn't need to know that.

She picked and combed and sprayed girly smelling stuff on me, never looking up to the mirror to meet my eyes. "That was when my sister was still with us. Everything was chaotic at home then."

She looked up long enough for me to sneak a question in. "Why?"

Her curls shivered, whipping back and forth with her head. "She had...problems. My parents are academics. They each have a department at the university, and they thought they could handle her, but they couldn't. No one knew what to do, and my health was being called into question, so they gave in. They asked for help. For awhile services sent help to us, but then Kyla was just gone.

"My parents petitioned and protested and nearly got themselves locked up underground trying to get her back, or even just see her. They are blacklisted. Unless they are directly summoned, they are not allowed on Tower premises. I had to get special permission to be granted my internship. I worked so hard, and I almost didn't get it because Services stole my sister. I get to stay and really make a difference for kids like Kyla so long as I behave."

I didn't know what to say. "I'm sorry" seemed insulting.

She moved around to face me, hitched her hip up on the desk, crossed her arms, and stared at me. I wanted to melt, hide: anything to get away from the weight of her blank stare. "You are a puzzle, and Imma loves puzzles. She will go to ridiculous lengths to solve you, lengths that could make trouble. I can't have trouble. If word gets back that I was even in the same Embassy with that, I lose my internship, and the only way I can help anyone is by jumping on Jack's bandwagon!"

"What do I do?"

"Just try not to be so interesting to her." She laughed and let her hair fall in her face. "Never mind. She'd probably search for more every time you tried to distract her. She likes you. It took me a long time to get her to believe that I wanted to be her friend."

"What is she searching for? There's nothing to find."

She tilted her head and watched me. Sadness and pity filled her dark eyes. She hid it with a smile, and hopped down from her perch, returned to her detangling. It felt different, gentler, and she worked in silence. "You really turned that kid around earlier," she broke the silence. "Did you help with the other kids...you know, before?"

"Not a secret that I live in the Tower. No little kids in my ward. Little kids had their own place."

"No one is that good with kids unless they've been around them! They're like their own species! I do okay because I've got three little brothers, but even I was ready to dropkick that kid. Throwing things around and acting a fool like that. I get that he's homesick and all, but sheesh, he was like a wild animal. Feral."

"Doesn't have words. Didn't know where he was or why. No one explained to him. They took him from his home to the Tower and then left him here to figure it out by himself at six years old."

She stared at my reflection in the mirror. "I guess anyone would cry and throw a fit. Poor guy. That's why you said you're the same. You were the same age when you got taken to the Tower?"

"Imma tell you that?" Imma wasn't supposed to know much about why I was there or how precarious my situation was. She knew enough to make girlish gossip dangerous. "What else did she tell you?"

She smirked, but not maliciously, and went back to combing out mats and tangles. "Sorry, 'Lo. My loyalty lies with her, not you. Oh, and if you break her heart, I'll tear you up. Like I said. I've got three brothers."

Chapter 10

With time, both Gage and I became more comfortable at school. With Seb's help, I made good progress with signing. I passed that help on to Gage, but he still had his issues.

Passing through the halls on my way from Seb's lab and back to the school, the sound of a scuffle caught my attention. Tucked away in a little corner of the schoolyard, a crowd of little boys surrounded Gage. He crouched on the floor but refused to scream or kick back —until he saw me. His eyes lit up, and he launched himself at his tormentors. A guttural battle cry rang out, and he let loose a slew of misguided slaps.

The telltale ringing and vertigo of an implant repressed memory freeing itself filled my head. Heat blistered inside, and I lowered myself to the floor before I fell.

My bruise covered arms hugged my scraped and bleeding knees to my chest. A wall of bigger kids surrounded me. Some of them sported bruises and scrapes I gave them, but it wasn't enough. They were bigger, and there were so many of them. Jonah called my name; Jonah would make them leave me alone. The wall of legs wouldn't let me out or Jonah in. They squeezed tightly together, holding me captive, shoving me back, kicking and laughing.

"Come on, High Rise! If you get out, we won't call them to come get you and take you to the Tower where you belong!"

Jonah fought until an elbow jabbed back into his face. Everything they said was true, but they couldn't hurt Jonah. I launched off the ground, leaping on top of the much bigger kid—

Something cold and sloppy-wet spread over my neck; the kids, both in my head and around Gage, were gone. The twang of anti-septic cleaner vapor prickled in my nose. Upon limp-armed investigation, the wetness on my neck turned up a wad of wet toilet tissue. I pulled it off and tossed the soggy lump aside. "Where did that come from?"

"Bathroom."

I sniffed my hand; my eyes watered from the antiseptic fumes. "Bathroom? Or toilet?"

He shrugged. "It was clean." He scooted closer to me, big wide eyes pleading from a grayed face. "Why does that happen? Does it hurt you when I'm bad?"

I pulled my knees in and rested my head on them. I couldn't tell him yes. It would be cruel and wrong, however true. The real truth, or a slightly simplified version of it, felt right. I'd been lied to most of my life. I wouldn't do that to him. "There is something in my brain that shouldn't be there. When you scream, I remember things that the thing in my head made me forget." The room spun, and my stomach lurched in answer. A deep breath did little to steady either of them. "What happened with those kids?"

Anger sent blood rushing to his cheeks. He shoved me, throwing his weight into me. I careened back; my skull hit the floor with a dull crack. The clouds swirled above me, trails of light streaked my vision, and his little footfalls clipped away. Half cocked and upset like he was, Gage could take down half the primary school. I stumbled after him; my rubbery legs were still twice the length of his. I grabbed him and ducked into an empty classroom.

I leaned against the door, but he tore around the room, threw his body into everything he could. So long as he didn't take his maelstrom out to the other kids, I let him and took the moment to recover.

A deep, resonant hum of vibrating strings brought me to my feet and stopped Gage. It was covered with a blanket. He hit it and let his hand sit on the side, the reverberation sunk into him. The fight drained out. He turned to me, head cocked to the side like a curious puppy, and did it again. "You feel that?"

I nodded, moved closer. The quilted moving blanket hit the ground with a whoosh of air. The piano was old. Its varnish was cracked and peeling; its wood was dry and gray. The ebony and ivory on the keys chipped when I touched them. "Sit down. Back against it."

He did what I asked. My hands skipped across the worn keys, banging out chords that made him smile. Once he calmed, I moved around to sit next to him on the floor. "I was mad too. I think I got taken away because I was so mad."

"Me too. How do I make the others leave me alone?"

"I don't know. But you can't hurt people."

His stomach gave a loud growl. "Hungry. Dinner time?"

At my nod, he scampered off, but I stayed, sat down at the threadbare piano bench, and played the melody that haunted my dreams and played in the background of all my thoughts.

The door latched.

I slammed the keys closed.

Imma stood at the door with a dreamy smile on her face. "That was beautiful. I didn't know you could play like that?"

I scratched the back of my neck. "You never asked, and I didn't look for a piano in a place where no one can hear."

She pursed her lips, but a smile peeked through her attempt to look sour. "Rude. You're not the only hearing Non-Verbal person in Eidolon." She sighed and rested her elbows on top of the upright piano. "That song, it's heartbreaking and wonderful all at once. What is it?"

I'd always known that song. It comforted me when I was scared as a child. I hummed it when the other kids on my floor made fun of me or when the noise in my head got too loud. "Don't know."

"Did you write it?"

"No. I just know it." The people from the Symphony had asked me about it, too.

"How did you learn? Did you have piano lessons?"

"The Symphony came for a few months and taught us." I hadn't been able to play as well, then. It still didn't feel right. Something was missing.

She giggled. "I took lessons for years and sound nowhere near that good."

No one else from D ward or even the 47th did either. I had it in my mind that it was because they weren't interested, but maybe it was because of me. I shrugged. "It just made sense to me. Instruments. I could talk to them."

Her eyes lit up. She had that look like I'd given her another puzzle to solve. "I wonder... Will you play again? I want to see if we can't find a name for it."

"How?"

"Just play. I'll show you."

My fingers knew the melody by heart. I played, and she held out her HHD but frowned when I stopped. Her fingers tapped and swiped, but each movement deepened the crease between her eyebrows.

"Come with me?"

I nodded, tucked the piano back under its heavy padded blanket, and followed her out of the room, back into the main Embassy.

She led me into a room full of computer terminals, but no people. "These are Research Terminals. You need a passcode from Seb to access them, but they have access to more than the citywide system that the HHD's use." She sat down and typed in a passcode. "HHD's access current events, weather, messaging, and entertainment, these can access anything. You can learn about the other groups of survivors and the governments they've used, wars they've waged. It has access to every document that goes through the senate, department of services, and the Frontier department. Surely, it can tell us where this song comes from and what it's called."

I stared at the screen, a whine humming in my ear. The implant didn't want me to ask, "Can it tell me where I came from?"

She froze mid keystroke. "It might?"

"Is that a question?"

She rolled her lower lip in between her teeth. "For now, yes."

———

TEN DAYS PASSED. I got to the Adaptive Tech Lab to do my Central Services Education System Schoolwork and found Laurel in my usual spot. Her hands flew; angry slashes and shoves. Her cheeks flushed, but lips drained from the force she pressed them together with. She spoke too fast for me to keep up. "Can't believe....behind...back....my sister." She pointed her finger in Seb's face and stared him down. "No! Not bring.... in ..mess."

The hunger for more words, more signs gnawed at me and pressed me to keep eavesdropping even though I knew I shouldn't.

Seb scrubbed at his face and looked up. He smiled weakly at me. "Good, you're here."

"School first.'" I went to sign-in on the terminal Seb isolated the back door to Tower Education, but Laurel didn't move. I looked back to Seb. "Practice first? We always do school first. Did I do something wrong?" I turned to Laurel. "Don't make him stop teaching me! I need it! I'm getting better! I'm trying!"

"Arlo, stop." Exhaustion weighed on her and dug deep bruises under her eyes. "You're doing wonderfully, of course, he can keep working with you. That's not what we're talking about. What did you see?"

I fought the urge to put my hands out for inspection like I did back at the Tower and lost the battle to look her in the eye. She liked when I looked her in the eyes, but it was hard to fight a lifetime of looking down. "Nothing. Sorry."

She stood and closed the distance between us. Her finger moved up to tap my chin. "No. Don't do that. You're not in trouble. Tell me what you saw so I know what to fill in. This is about you, and I promised you that I wouldn't keep secrets from you."

I checked with Seb; I didn't want him or Imma in trouble because of me. Seb smiled.

"Imma is in Seb's mess."

She laughed harshly. "True, but that's not the real problem. Marta got us a message yesterday. She has everything in order; it's time for you to go back to the Tower. Seb has your credentials ready, we were just...discussing who should be your chaperone."

Seb leaned forward, drew Laurel's eye back to him with a wave. "Imma is connected to that place in every way she can be; no one will question her presence there. I already checked in with the Senator's campaign managers. They loved the idea of her going and spending time with wards her own age. She will be on her best behavior because it's a campaign stunt, and she won't even know she's involved."

Laurel stomped her foot like an angry child. "I will know! Miriam doesn't need any more reasons to pick Imma to death! Every time she turns around, Miriam tells her that every instinct of her own is wrong. I'm not going to manipulate her like they do! Not to mention, if word gets back to Miriam that she was there, I will no longer be alive! She will make me disappear. We cannot use her daughter in this. What about Jack?"

Seb shrugged. "He won't do it. He was my first choice, but he's still convinced that Arlo is a spy planted here to watch him."

Laurel rolled her eyes. "He's entirely too smart to be as dumb as he is sometimes."

I waved to get their attention. "I don't want Imma in trouble. I can go myself. Tell me what to do."

Laurel shook her head. "You have to have a chaperone. It's one of Marta's requirements. We are in breach of our part of the agreement if you show up alone." I could leave on a pass unaccompanied, but I couldn't go back without a babysitter. "You have to be accounted for. If you get lost, we all do, too."

"Why would they care about losing me? One less ward to feed."

The look Seb gave me made me want to cower. "You're not an ordinary ward. An ordinary ward wouldn't need to be smuggled in. Their warden would just sign an educational release that signed over guardianship to the Embassy, like Gage. You need this."

I picked up the card Seb shoved my way. My own face stared

back at me, but something was wrong, beyond the few bits of information about my residence and residency status. The face that stared back with blue eyes, just like mine, was more sculpted and angular than mine and the black curls were short and tamed:

Jonah Cooper

Eyes: Blue

Hair: Black

Residency Status: Citizen

Place of Residence: Outer Rim, Sector 16

Conscription: passed.

The faint sting and vibration filled the back of my skull, and sweat gathered at my temples. "Who is he?"

Seb's eyebrows raised in a question answered by Laurel's stony glare and pursed mouth. I'd never seen Seb so frustrated. He and Laurel never fought. "Someone I found with a database search. He looks like you. He's close enough to your age to be believable, and he won't know you borrowed his credentials."

I nodded and tried to talk myself into calming down, but the face on the card nagged my conscience. I couldn't be him. I wasn't him. I wished I was. I always wanted to be him. Always.

Grief flooded me, filled my every nook and cranny. Hot tears joined cold sweat in a slow waterfall down my face. I turned, ready to run, but Seb held me in place with an arm slung across my shoulders.

Hands shaking, the sign stuttered. "Can't."

Laurel kept her voice low and soothing. "You can't what?"

The melancholy was too big, sitting on me like a boulder. I couldn't go. I wasn't Jonah.

The mechanically calm voice of Seb's HHD interrupted my panic. "Imma will be with you."

Laurel made a sound of distaste like she sucked a lemon through the spaces in her teeth. Her body rocked with force. "No, she won't! I won't let you pull her into this!"

Seb ignored her protest, kicked me a chair, and beckoned me closer. "Hold your hand out, Arlo." He coated my fingers with adhesive and rolled cellular medium over each one. "When the adhesive dries, no one will be able to tell the difference between your skin and the skin I made you."

The small air bubbles disappeared, and the swirls and grooves of normal fingertips melted in. Seb held out a reader like the ones the Patrol carried at the rally and pressed my capped finger to it. On his screen, a text box with Jonah's face and his information popped up first. A second square approved Jonah for a day-pass in the Tower to visit Marta Wofsy in the 47th floor common area.

Seb beamed. "As good as the real thing."

Nothing but the real thing is as good as the real thing. I shrugged. "If you say so."

"You go through the visitor's entrance in Central Processing, hand the warden your credentials and scan your fingerprints. Once you get through, Marta has someone ready to meet you in the Public Garden. That contact will have clothes for you to change into and a place to change. After that, you take your normal Tube to your floor, make sure you look up a lot so that the cameras see and identify your face."

A bad feeling, sick and slimy, sat in the pit of my stomach.

Laurel squeezed my shoulder. "It will be okay, Arlo. You'll be back here later in the afternoon. Just keep calm."

"You said I can't go without a chaperone." I held on to hope that she would stand her ground, and I wouldn't have to go.

She huffed and glared at Seb. "Fine. Imma can go, but just this once. If Miriam gets wind of this, we might all wish that Arlo went alone and got lost along the way."

Seb wore his pride and his hesitance and his resolve to keep going all on his face at once. "Imma will come and get you tomorrow morning after classes. You need to act surprised. Laurel is going to tell her that you have some administrative tasks to take care of to finalize your transfer, so she won't expect you to be by her side the whole time." He took a deep breath and shook his hands out. He couldn't be nervous. If Seb was nervous, then how was I supposed to keep myself together? "Marta has a uniform waiting for you in the garden and a place to change. She'll meet you in the

Public Garden and escort you through the Tower and hit as many cameras as possible."

The fear I used to feel every day on the 47th wasn't real fear. The squirming in my guts, heart-racing, can't get a full breath in feeling, overwhelming every other thought and emotion as I sat there in Seb's lab was. "What if—"

Seb cut me off, put his hands over mine, and pushed them down. "We won't know if we've done enough until the reports go through. We can't worry about 'what if" we just need to push through. Can you do that?"

I would have to. I didn't have a choice. It wasn't just my freedom that hung in the balance.

____

Chapter 11

____

Imma loitered outside the classroom that morning. I'd moved up out of the kindergarten class. All of my eight and nine-year-old classmates ran out of the room and towards the dining room. "Arlo?"

I didn't want to look up. I could feel her hesitance from across the room, and if I looked, she would see mine on my face.

"Laurel sent me to get you. I guess we both have things that need to be taken care of at the Tower. She wants us to walk together." I followed her out. She seemed as content to keep our eyes off of each other as I was. "We can stop at the dining room for lunch if you want. I don't think I can eat right now."

The thought of food turned my stomach. "No, thanks. Not hungry," the TalkBox said.

"Good. I don't think I could even sit with you; I'm so nervous."

I jogged up so I could walk beside her. "Why nervous?"

She pulled the sides of her cardigan tightly around her. "My mother has never trusted me to be in front of anyone unless she is by my side to pinch me when I'm not smiling just right or standing straight enough. But today, she set up some public relations stunt where I have to go and speak in front of a bunch of kids our age at the Tower. I hate talking in front of people." She cleared her throat, and a shiver ran down her spine. "Laurel said you have to finalize some forms or something to get your educational release approved."

I shrugged. Anything more felt too committed. Too dangerous.

She stepped in front of me and stopped. "Are you okay? We have time; I could go with you first, and then we could go together, and you could be my emotional support while I do my speech." She blossomed before my eyes. "Neither of us would have to be alone."

I wished I lived in her world, where protocols could be side-stepped, and everything turned out in the end. But I didn't. And I'd jumped over too many protocols already. "Can't. Only Marta can come with me. Security."

She wilted. "Right. Well, we'd better get on with it then. There's no sense in putting off the inevitable."

The NVL embassy building wasn't on the inner-most ring around the Tower like all the other embassies. We took a trolley the three blocks inward and didn't say a word to one another. My feet hit the pavement. The Tower loomed over me; her arched doorways open wide to swallow me whole.

Imma leaned back, her nose crinkled, eyes locked on the faraway top of the Tower. "They really didn't do a good job making it look welcoming, did they? Are they trying to keep people in or out?"

Rat said the barbed wire and chain-link I'd noticed on our way to the rally were there to keep the people Underground in. The longer I stayed out and the more I understood about my past, the more I realized that it was just as much to keep Citizens out. Services put out warnings so that they would forget those who went into the Tower. "Both." I stepped forward. Together, we stepped through the high archway, into Central Processing. Stanchions herded us into lines to be assessed by wardens in glass booths. Imma scanned her fingers, handed her credentials through the gap in the glass, and passed through easily. My breath grated in and out like hiccups as I stepped up for my turn.

"Identification," the woman in a warden's uniform said. I handed over the card. "It says you have an adaptive device. I'll need to check it to make sure it can't broadcast while it's in the Tower, then you'll be on your way." She held out her hand.

My palms were so sweaty and slick that I was afraid the fingertips would slide right off. The TalkBox slipped in my grip, but I got it into her hand. "Nothing to worry about, Honey," she soothed with a kind smile.

I gulped; my throat too dry to swallow, but I placed my thumb and forefinger on the scanner.

"All set, Jonah. Have a nice visit."

Being called that made every hair on my scalp stand on end, but I put the TalkBox into my pocket and joined Imma on the other side of the booths.

"Why did she call you Jonah?"

I shrugged but smiled when she giggled at my response. "Old lady. Confused."

We passed through the turnstiles and gates, bypassed the familiar tube bank that I took with Marta my last day in the Tower and into the Public Garden.

"I'm sorry Laurel roped you into this." Imma wrapped her sweater around herself and drew her lips into a weak smile. "It's bad enough that Mother's constantly forcing me into her publicity stunts, but to use you is just disgusting!"

"Use me? How?"

"I don't know what her angle is, but she's never asked me to help with campaign stuff before, so there's an angle."

The head gardener, Gerald, stood on a ladder, tinkering with the misters for the tropical plants. The walls cut the garden off from the rain, so Gerald and his staff had to make their own. I tugged the leg of his TowerCloth trousers down to cover the cigar he kept tucked in his sock. He never smoked them, just carried the contraband around, and held them in his teeth when no one was looking.

"Hey, Kid. What are you doing down so far? You aren't in trouble, are you?" He didn't wait for an answer. "Of course not; you're a good egg." He clamored down the ladder and frowned. "You need a haircut, though. You look like birds have made a nest in there."

I shook my head until my face hid in the bramble of unkempt

hair. He and I met in one of the growhouses I tended to haunt when I didn't want to be found. His staff set up chairs in one of the clearings. My heart sunk. Gerald was my contact. Why would he risk himself for me?

Gerald looked up and smiled, but the worry dug deep into his forehead. "Who is this?"

My face got hot, and my breath caught in my throat for a moment. I couldn't tell the difference yet between a normal embarrassed flush and an implant flare. But nothing happened, so I pulled my TalkBox out of my pocket. "This is Imma. My friend."

The older man smiled. "Well, ain't that a neat trick—a voice box and a friend. What can I do for you two?"

Imma held her hand out. Her smile sat on her face, empty and meaningless, nothing like her normal smile. "My name is Imelda Pressman-Persaud. I'm supposed to be speaking this afternoon."

Gerald smiled. "We're all set for you, Miss Pressman-Persaud. The media censors took the press aside for a security briefing, so you should have a few minutes." He stretched and groaned, arms above his head. "This old body isn't going to hold up forever. Arlo, be a pal and go to the supply closet in the southeast corner and grab the garlic oil spray. Damn mealybugs are in the Paper Plants again. A trip to the rose garden will do me some good, especially with a young lady." He smiled at Imma, and she blushed. Over her head, Gerald shot me a hard look. A "you know what to do" kind of a look.

In the supply closet, on a slatted potting bench, a set of TowerCloth coveralls sat, ready for me. I slid them over my clothes; only my black shoes showed, and I hoped they would go unnoticed. Too much work went into me getting in and out to be ruined by a pair of shoes. The camera's facial recognition counts the average number of times per week it sees each face. I always had hair in my face, so my expected number of hits in the system was low. Seb said to make sure it saw me. Better safe than sorry.

I bent over, twisted the mass of snarls on top of my head, and secured it with one of the polymer straps Gerald used to tame young vines onto trellises and left the shed's safety. Reporters gathered around the podium, and Imma smiled as she greeted them.

A familiar, female voice rang across the foliage. "Gerald, have you seen my Rebel?"

Gerald chuckled at the nickname he didn't think fit me. "Haven't seen any rebels about, Sergeant Wofsy. I do have Arlo, here, though."

"Gerald, I'm twenty years younger than you; you shouldn't have to call me Ma'am. Please, call me Marta." She tucked an errant curl the color of the spire on the justice center behind us back into her chignon.

The skin around Gerald's eyes folded in on itself, all traces of worry disappeared.

"First names would be fine if we were in the city, Ma'am. So long as we're in here and you wear blue, I'll stick with Sergeant."

She sighed and turned her calming smile on me. "Arlo, I need you back upstairs. Have a good day, Gerald."

"You too, Sergeant Wofsy."

Marta bumped her hip against mine and chuckled when I stumbled. Reporters gathered around the podium, and Imma smiled as she greeted them. We made it to the Tube without incident, and Laurel and Imma's father welcomed visitors on the ad screen.

▭

THE 45TH FLOOR was quiet when the doors opened. Marta kept our pace brisk on our way to the suspended greenhouse at the center. I filled my lungs with hot loamy air. Each soil and compost laced breath sharpened by the green twang of chlorophyll was like a narcotic to my uneasy mind. It made me feel at home, but the Tower wasn't home. I belonged at the embassy, but it didn't feel like home. Where did I belong?

Marta grinned, though it didn't make it to her shadowed eyes. "Now, we can talk.

Did anyone see you? Did the girl suspect anything? I see Gerald got you some clothes to wear; he wouldn't let anyone else get involved once he noticed that he hadn't seen you. He was on the 47th banging down my door looking for you, and the only way to shut him up was to let him in on the secret."

My head spun with the speed of her words and the persistent whine at the back of my mind. One of her hands steadied me, and the other cupped my cheek. She stared, questions and worries carving little frowns and wrinkles into her face. "Are you with me? You left me for a minute."

I nodded and stepped out of the warmth of her touch. I couldn't fuel her apprehension any more than my latest episode already had.

"How often is that happening? The fevers and losing time?"

All the time. It was only getting worse. The fits happened more and more often and lasted longer. "Fine," I signed without thinking.

She covered the fleeting look of disbelief with a wide smile. "Such a sponge, but I have no clue what you said. I'm going to take Laurel's classes on the city educational resource system when I can. I've been a little busy covering tracks lately."

I pulled the TalkBox out. "I'm fine. I promise. I thought I was going to sneeze." I hated lying to her. "That all stopped."

Her nose wrinkled. "I never did understand why you liked it in here. It's hot, and it stinks. Makes me feel like I'm going to sneeze too, but it's the safest place for us to talk. There's less surveillance coverage on these greenhouses. Recreational spaces have more, but no one, well, no one but you and the gardeners really goes in the nutritional growhouses—"

"I like it. Smells like—" Home. It smelled like home. "—life."

She grinned. "I hoped that someday you'd open up and just start talking to me, tell me what was churning around under that mess." She reached out to ruffle my hair, but I blocked her and smoothed back the strands into the knot. "And here you are, having a conversation and letting me see your face at the same time." Her voice grew rough, and her smile wobbled despite her teasing words. "Riley couldn't find anyone else to walk with you? I'd rather we kept a lower profile, and that's pretty well impossible with Senator Persaud's kid acting as your chaperone."

I typed my answer and tried to swallow down the sour taste her disdain for Imma left in my mouth. "Imma doesn't know about me. She thinks I'm finalizing my education release."

Her grin grew, but tears filled her eyes. "Oh. It's like that, is it?" She chuckled. "I knew it when I saw you two together at the embassy."

My face gave me away again. "My friend."

She shook her head, and her hair shook free of its regulation knot. I'd never noticed because it was always tied back, but her curls were as wild as mine. "I warned you to be careful. The first time is the worst." There were no benches in the greenhouse; it wasn't meant for leisure. I liked the smell and the solitude and never minded sitting on the crushed brick pathways. Marta paced a few steps in either direction and sank to the floor. "Your first changes the shape of your heart, and it hurts so bad that you think you're going to die. You don't, but it feels like it sometimes. They build you up, and you can never go back to the way you were before you met them."

I sat beside her. "First what?"

She put her hand on my knee. "That voice is not what I expected you to sound like, but it's so nice to talk to you, finally." She let out a long sigh. "I didn't really expect this talk to be our first chat. You sure do know how to pick them, don't you? Of course, you fell for the first person you saw when you came to, and you don't even know the difference between that and the real thing. You're just happy that someone wants to be around you, and I don't blame you for that."

I searched the menu for one word that would break her out of her musing and into making some sense. "Explain."

She chuckled. "They didn't want to deal with any of the 'fraternization' they dealt with during earlier trials." Her face flushed, and she hid her face behind her hair. "It doesn't really matter if it's real. It will hurt the same either way, and I won't be there to pick up the pieces. This is such a mess, and I can't fix it for you!"

She hadn't explained anything, and my patience was wearing thin. "Never stopped you from telling me what to do before."

She sniffled and showed me her grin." Smartass. I always knew you would be a smartass under there."

Two words out of her ramble stuck out. I couldn't get them out of my head. "What is not real?"

Her eyes doubled in size. "Oh, Arlo, I…ignore me. I was just thinking out loud. Your friend seems very nice and cute as a button. I need you to keep your mind on what you're there for and on keeping yourself safe. I know you never really connected with anyone here like some of the other kids have, and I'm pleased that you have now."

"You want me to leave Imma be."

"Yes. Yes, I do. Between you not needing distractions and her mother being who she is, it's just safer if you two keep your distance."

Something twisted and knotted in my stomach, and I dug my fingers into the sharp gravel underneath me. She wanted to take away my friend. Imma made all of the changes, and all of the newness at the embassy bearable. She washed away the loneliness that clung to me for as long as I could remember.

"Hey, don't look like that. There are tons of other kids there. It will be okay."

I forgot the TalkBox and signed, "Imma and I are the same."

She mimicked the last motion. "Tell me what it means, Arlo."

"Same," the monotone voice said.

"You and Imma?" She balked and laughed. "How are you the same as Senator Persaud and Secretary Pressman's daughter? You couldn't be more different. She has grown up with everything handed to her, and you grew up here with me. You know how you got here now, Arlo."

"Forget it," I signed and stood up. It didn't matter. She didn't need to understand. I walked my fingers through the air like I did before I had other ways to tell her what I wanted.

She stood. "I feel like you just gave me the brush off, but I'm going to let it go. Just promise me you'll be careful."

I made an X over my heart with my finger and stuffed the TalkBox in my pocket. We left the greenhouse and rode up the extra two floors to the 47th.

She twisted her thick mass of auburn hair back into its tight coil and pinned it in place. "Everyone is downstairs at Imma's little talk. It would be just like you to be off hiding somewhere instead of being at something like that, so roam around and let the cameras get their fill of your face. I'm going to go check something at the warden station. We can go back down together in a few minutes, okay?"

I nodded but waited for her to turn into the warden station before I moved. I didn't know how to be there as my new self. My words and my feelings didn't belong there.

The room I shared with Rat was barely bigger than a broom cupboard, enough room for two beds and a locker for our clothes and a few personal items. Rat covered the walls around his bed with posters and leaflets he'd picked up at different rallies he'd spoken at. The walls around my bed were blank like no one ever lived there. I guessed no one ever had. The implant took away who I was before. It was up to me to find out who I wanted to be now that it was gone.

Chapter 12

Flashbulbs strobed all around Imma. The smile on her face sat like a mask, soulless, empty, and perfect. It stayed put while she shook hands and made small talk. She didn't look like the person I knew.

Marta watched her too. "See? How can you, who can get away with not being here because you don't let the cameras see your face be the same as her?" I didn't have an answer for her, but it didn't change how I felt. She saw that I had no intention of answering and let out an exasperated sigh. "Go get changed so you can get out of here without a hitch. I'll see you next time. You can teach me some more of your signs." She smiled, and I could see all the hope she was pinning on that. She wanted me to trust her and see her the same as I had before, but I still had so many questions. "Go get changed. Stay there until I get everyone herded back to the Tubes."

Rat put himself between me and the shed. "I heard she was from the same place they were keeping you. I thought maybe she'd tell me that you're okay and maybe get you a message, but here you are, with your hair all weird. I was worried, and you were taking rich girls for walks? I told you not to trust them!"

I dug in my pocket and typed the words—my first words to my first friend. "She is my chaperone."

Rat jumped away, glaring at the source of the strange voice. "The hell is that?"

I beamed, holding it out. "TalkBox; she gave it to me."

"You sound like a robot. A crappy robot."

I stuffed the device back in my pocket. Shame crept up my neck, hot and sickly, and I couldn't look up from the gravel path. I thought he'd be happy for me. No more worrying about me. No more defending me from everyone. I could tell people off myself.

Rat poked a bony finger into my chest. "Leave that girl and her kind alone. The rich and powerful stink on her is stronger than her perfume. Tower City kids like her have no clue how we live in here and don't want to know even if they say they do. Don't trust her, and don't take gifts from her! That's what they want! They want you indebted to them!"

The TalkBox seemed to grow heavier in my pocket, and my hand twitched to reach for it, but Rat crossed his arms over his chest and raised a brow. A frustrated growl rolled up my throat, and signs flew from my hands. I'd gotten used to everyone around me understanding. "Why can't you make anything easy?"

Rat offered his open palm as a surface to write on. "You think you're better than me now? Better than what worked for us for so long? We did just fine, you and me."

I pulled Rat closer and traced, "Y U?" with my finger on his palm.

"Why did they ask me?"

I nodded.

Rat shrugged and rubbed his palms together. "Word got around that I would get them people to speak at their little shindigs. They give me a cut, and I find them people who will say what they want them to."

My writing surface jerked out of reach, ending the conversation.

Rat wouldn't look me in the eyes. "I'm not smart like you are, but I'm not too stupid to see exactly how this place works. I'm just doing the best I can to make sure I have enough saved up to grease the right wheels if I need to when the time comes. If you had half as much common sense as you have smarts, you'd do the same instead of dreaming about girls that are walking tickets to the cells underground. Just because they say we're equal don't make it true, and that's never gonna change. I might as well make a few bucks off of the ones dumb enough to think different.

"It's not about equality." Imma's lip trembled, but she took Rat's glare. "The Tower provides equity and fills in the gap between what different people are capable of and what is expected of them. If equality was the goal, then everyone would be in the Tower. Instead, it's a leg up to level the playing field for those who have a hard time with the cut-throat society in the city."

Rat grinned, the single most unkind grin I'd ever seen. "Is that what they teach you in the fancy schools out there? Those are just pretty words. If that was true, city folk would be banging down the Processing gates to get in here. Look out there. The razor wire is to keep people in, not out. This place is here to keep us where they want us, out of sight. The difference is that we all know what we are. They get you all high on power and spending cash. You people think you're free? Do you know anyone who has left?"

Imma cheeks blushed red. "Not personally...."

"No one does. We're all stuck here. It's all a lie. None of us can leave. So, who's really the victims? The guys doing an honest day's work in return for housing and food? Or the sad sacks out there, working themselves to the bone just for stuff that don't mean shit once you realize you're stuck here, and it's all a hoax anyway." He turned his fury on me. "And you think you want to be out there, one of them and ditch the people who have always been there for you because the first person you meet has a pretty smile and thinks it's cute that you don't talk? That's bullshit. And you are too. Some friend you turned out to be, ditched for the first pretty face that pays you two seconds of attention. I see how it is."

"You manipulative jerk! How dare you! He shouldn't have even been there! He didn't want to go. He went because you badgered him, got hurt, and where were you?"

Rat's face blanched. "I was..."

"You were saving your own hide! You left him even though you knew he needed you to be identified!"

"How do you…"

I forgot about that. I couldn't fall apart so close to making it back out.

She smirked. "When no one ever tells you the truth about anything, you get good at finding it for yourself."

"All those resources shoulda gone to making changes, but your people snarf them up for your own benefit."

"Don't you dare turn this around on me! We're talking about you. Talk about a defining moment as a bad friend." She turned, and something about my face drained the fervor from her. "We need to go. You…"

"What did you do to him?" He turned to me, "Talk to me, 'Lo!"

A roar of frustration ripped through me. A few minutes before, he told me not to talk, now he wanted me to, so I did. "You left me! You did this to me! I'm not like you; I belong with them. They gave me my own voice." Imma stood next to me with her mouth agape. "Tell him! Interpret!"

"No. You tell him. That's what the TalkBox is for. Use your voice."

"What is the problem here?" a cold, slick voice demanded. Rat and I pressed our backs to the wall and turned our palms out to show empty hands. I held my breath. I swallowed back bile.

Commander Escher's cold eyes latched onto me.

"Nothing, Sir," Rat gritted, still glaring at Imma.

Escher looked Imma up and down. "Miss Pressman, I almost didn't recognize you. These residents aren't giving you any trouble, are they?"

"No, sir," she answered cheerily. "Just a misunderstanding." She looked up and met his eye, though, she kept her face haughty and her mouth firm. "And it's Pressman-Persaud, Commander Escher. Just because you dislike my mother doesn't mean you can erase her. Trust me, I've tried." She wore all of the arrogance of her social standing like a coat. "Now, if you're through insulting my family, my friends and I will get back to our discussion."

His finely cut jaw ticked. "Of course. My apologies for interrupting; I'd hate for something to happen to you on my watch.

"I'm not on your watch. I'm here on Embassy business. If you have any questions, you're welcome to call my father. Or my mother, since we both know how fond of each other you are." She smiled that soulless smile and the Commander excused himself.

▭

RAT'S EYES held no less disgust, but he'd stopped looking at her like she was prey. "You're gonna ruin everything." He glanced at me. "And you're gonna stand there and let her." He turned, but called over his shoulder, "Glad you're not dead."

"Hey!" My voice stopped Rat. He turned and stared at me like I'd grown a second head. My voice had power, but I couldn't harness it.

I pulled the device from my pocket, but my fingers felt clumsy and too big. They flubbed all over the screen words, and the wrong words in the wrong voice combined with the screech in my head reached deafening volume. The box flew out of my hand, and the unmistakable crack of fractured glass and cracked plastic stopped everything.

Words crawled up my throat of their own volition. I pursed my lips, covered my mouth. Shouting 'hey,' was one thing, jabbering like a drunk mockingbird was another. I ran. Gerald and Imma shouted at me, begged me to stop, but if I stopped, the noise would get out. All the things I wasn't brave enough to say pounded against my skull and fought for a way out.

Other voices overpowered my friends.' I barreled through the stanchion toward the turnstiles and the freedom of the world outside.

"Resident. Freeze."

My body wanted to obey, but the words stuck in my throat. They pressed toward my mouth with only my hand to hold back the waterfall of meaningless noise that would get me locked up and labeled incompetent.

Ten steps separated me from the life that didn't involve the Tower.

"Final warning. Stop, Resident!"

I made it another two steps before they pinned me to the ground with one knee on my neck and another at my back. I went limp, happy that the wind knocked from my lungs also knocked the words out of my mouth.

All of D ward stood at the atrium glass. Marta had Rats arms locked behind his back and whispered in his ear, but he fought and struggled against her.

"I told you not to come back here." I'd only known Guinn for a few moments, but his voice had burned itself into my brain. My muscles tensed. I fought to turn.

He jerked me back, put more pressure on my neck. "Don't look at me. It was stupid of you to come back and even stupider to run out like that. You can't leave without out-processing, and you know it." He huffed out a breath and gave me a little extra room to breathe. "I'm gonna let you up. Act real scared like some dumb Citizen kid who didn't know any better and don't pull this shit again. Riley will kill me if anything happens to you on my watch."

He hauled me to my feet, and a Warden rushed over with a Biometric scanner to check my prints.

Guinn pressed my hand to the glass.

I held my breath. The tips could have peeled or fallen off entirely in the struggle.

"Jonah Cooper," the Warden read, "non-verbal, twenty years old."

Imma rushed over. "It's my fault. He's my chaperone, and he wanted to try on TowerCloth. He'd never seen it before." Her mouth chastised me, "I warned you not to mess around like that! Honestly. Pretending to be an escaping criminal while we're here. It's despicable," but her hands said, "I'm not going to ask what is going on. You're upset, and I'm going to guess this is all Laurel's doing."

I wanted to melt into a greasy puddle on the ground.

Guinn, like he had during the Border Day rally, gave nothing away to his peers. "You know this person?"

"Yes, sir—Jonah," she glanced my way, and the hurt in her eyes felt worse than all of the boys' from my Ward ogling us, "came with me on business for my mother. If you allow him to unzip his coveralls, you'll see that he is in an NVL uniform. He's a sweet boy, just maybe a bit misguided. For my sake, for my mother, Senator Persaud's sake, let him off with a warning."

A voice called out of the crowd of kids from D ward, "Awwww, Glitch got himself a girlfriend! Good to know that mouth is good for something!"

I always wilted away from their catcalls, but not anymore. Guinn's hold on my arms kept me from lunging forward. His grip dug in.

A yowl rose. Marta held Rat the same way Guinn held me, only Marta wasn't as strong; she struggled to keep him back. "He ain't a glitch! Don't call him that! He is a dirty rotten liar, though!" He surged forward, but she was ready with a single shot syrette of tranquilizer. The needle jammed into his neck, and he dropped to the floor. Everyone's attention turned to Rat.

Guinn jerked me over to the exit turnstiles and hurried me through, getting me out of the coveralls. "Get out of here and be more careful. Next time it might not be me on duty." He shoved me out into the street.

Imma followed. She wouldn't meet my eyes but held out the TalkBox.

"I'm sorry."

She glanced my way but started walking. "I'm not the naive moron that my sister and everyone else thinks I am, you know?"

"I know."

"Does my mother even know I came here today, or am I going to be in trouble with her too?"

They gave her more to worry about for my sake. She already spent so much energy on worrying about her mother's opinions, and I made it worse. "Laurel set it up with her office."

She wrapped her arms around her waist. "Thank goodness for small favors, I guess." Deep brown eyes flicked up. "You don't have a real release, do you?"

I wasn't supposed to tell her. She wasn't supposed to be involved.

"You don't have to answer that. I'm sure Laurel and Seb threatened you up and down to make sure I stay out of it, but they involved me."

"No one would question you being at the Tower. Your father...."

"I suppose it would surprise you to know that this was my first time there?"

I chuckled at the strange, sheltered pair we made. No wonder she was so interested in where I came from.

She frowned and stomped ahead of me. I caught up and grabbed her arm. A shocked little squeal burst out of her that scared me back a step. Patrol officers seemed to appear out of the sides of buildings. They surrounded us. "Miss, are you all right?"

She smiled, and it almost lived up to those camera smiles I saw back in the atrium, but her sadness showed through. "I'm fine. Arlo snuck up on me. Thank you, Officer."

She walked away, and they didn't stop me from following. We walked a few blocks in silence. "I know I must seem very silly and precious to you."

"I laughed because the day I met you was my first day outside the Tower. We're the same."

Her lips turned up, but her eyes didn't share the expression. "Come on, we better get back and explain what happened so Seb can smooth it over."

Chapter 13

A few more weeks and a few more visits to the Tower with far less fanfare passed.

I always came back exhausted. Lying to Marta, hiding as much as I could from Imma, and staying away from both Commander Escher and Rat wore me thin. Imma had gone to her room to grab something while I went straight to the dining room. I sat at an empty table in the dining room at dinner and moved the meat and fresh vegetables around my plate. The hum of trays sliding and chairs scraping and the presence of the language that I finally felt was mine let me relax.

A tray slammed down, and Jack slid into the seat opposite, smirking. "So, back from the Tower, High Rise?"

The old me whispered in my head not to take the bait and cause trouble. I couldn't afford more problems. "Don't know what you're talking about."

He chuckled and leaned across the table. "Sure, you do. I saw you and Imma's passes, Jonah." Two tons of panic buried my confusion." What I don't know is what you would need to go back for. Especially with a fake pass. Education release doesn't mean you're not still a Resident. You should only need passes to leave not to get back in."

Sweat broke out on my forehead. "Not your business."

Everything was different, especially me. I could not just stand with my head down anymore. Imma and Rae sat around us and picked up on the tension.

Imma glared at Jack. "I hope you're not being tiresome again." Jack rolled his eyes and opened his mouth, the zeal of the oncoming tirade rippled off of him. Imma's boredom stamped out his fervor. "Stop it with your conspiracy theories and go away."

Rae snorted. "We're all bored with you and your nonsense."

Jack turned on a megawatt smile, fitting the political position his internship would put him in line for. He looked like Imma did, smiling for the cameras, except he believed everything he said. It was a part to play for Imma. He lived and breathed taking down the Tower System. "We don't all have a big estate and a mother and father in power, like you. There is crooked stuff going on in this world, and we all know it. You're the only one who doesn't seem to get it! You think everyone is doing your bidding in the research library because you finally made friends for the first time in your disgustingly privileged life? Wrong. They're all just kissing ass because you're damn royalty as far as they're concerned! You might not think so, but the rest of us have had it shoved in our faces since you rallied the whole intern staff to dig up every piece of dirt you can find on High Rise here!" A hot flush climbed the back of my neck. I searched their faces for the truth. They all looked away except Jack, who's grin grew more poisonous by the moment. "What? He doesn't know that you've been scouring every government record that you could buy a hack into to find dirt on him. Some friendship you got there."

Imma's already wide, round eyes grew wider, and her cheeks drained of color. The others still wouldn't look at me. "It's not what it sounds like."

Jack cut her off, "It's exactly what it sounds like. A few days after you got dropped on our doorstep, she started a full-scale investigation into all things' Arlo No-Last-Name Towerward.' When she didn't find answers she wanted quick enough for her liking, she roped the others into searching with her. Everyone who sits at the table knows just about everything about your life since you were surrendered."

Heat and tightness filled my middle, a spring coiled, and ready to snap. Her pleas bounced off with no effect. "Arlo, please, listen to me. I just wanted to have answers for you before I said anything."

Jack kept going. "She used you to get us to do what she wants the same way her parents do. It's all she knows: using other people." I didn't know who I hated more at that moment: him or Imma.

Rae went to Imma's side and wrapped a protective arm around her friend. "Leave her alone. She can't help who her parents are any more than you can help who yours aren't."

Jack's glare turned from condescending to dangerous. "Don't."

Rae grinned. "What, you don't want Arlo to know that while you sit there and call him High Rise and torment him, you came from the same place?" Rae smirked. "It sucks when it's you who gets their dirty laundry put out in public."

Rae rolled her eyes, but Imma tucked into herself. Tears ran down her cheeks. "I'm not my parents." She shoved Rae off and stormed out, leaving the interns and me in shock.

The others went back to their lunches, more subdued than normal. I couldn't believe they pretended nothing happened.

"Crazy, isn't it?" Jack spoke low so that the sounds of plates scraping and silverware clattering covered the sound to everyone but me. "They go back to business as usual because this is all that they know. We know different. Don't you ever wonder why they are so afraid of people that they seem to think beneath them? They're terrified of becoming us…" He kept talking, but the noise in my head and the heat overpowered his voice.

I slammed Jack up against the wall and held him there with an arm across his throat.

"Lemme go!" Jack squawked. "I wasn't trying to start anything!"

I blinked and took a breath and for a moment couldn't remember where I was or what he said that made me so angry. I let him go, and he scrambled away, looking over his shoulder. But it all came back.

He tormented me. He made me see Imma for what she was. She betrayed my trust and kept secrets from me. She was just as bad as the people who put the implant in me. I was done being lied to. I let him have a few steps and pounced on him again. The pain blazing up my arm from my fist felt amazing. His cries for help joined the never-ending noise in my head. All of the vertigo and freedom and power and guilt I felt watching Gage beat that other little kid to a pulp came back, and I struggled to stay up. My arms turned to wet noodles flapping at my sides, flailing against Jack's curled up body.

Arms wrapped around me and hauled me up, dragged me out of the cafeteria and into an empty classroom. They dropped me into a chair, and Seb came around to my front, a disapproving look on his face. "He's an asshole, kid. Assholes will always be assholes. You can't let him get to you like this."

I hated that I had disappointed him, but Jack deserved it. "Did you know he's from the Tower?"

"Of course," Seb signed. "The first Tower-raised kid to get an internship in decades, and he chose to be placed here."

"Is that why they all hate him?"

He shook his head, and a sad smile curled his lip. "They hate him because he takes out his anger about his own lot in life on them, especially Imma."

I scowled at her name.

He pulled a chair up, knee to knee with me and waited for my full attention. "So, he finally ratted Imma out, did he? He's been threatening for weeks."

"How long has she been looking into my files?"

"I resisted for a while, but she kept coming back. I set her up with a station in the Research library and gave her open access. Imma came to life looking for the real Arlo. No more mousy, dreamy, stupid rich girl. She had all the interns in the research lab the other day following orders like her personal staff. She could find anything and anyone she wanted, given the way she attacked it. She's insatiable, unstoppable because of you. Everyone downstairs was so relieved that she wasn't blundering around that they let her be."

I scrubbed my face. "I didn't do anything to change her."

"You didn't have to. Everyone deserves to know their own story, and you don't even know your whole name.'"

"Everything before doesn't matter. They didn't want me. They were ashamed of me." Pain radiated from my teeth into my head and down my shoulder. "No one asked me if I wanted to know."

"No, but no one asked you if you wanted to forget either."

<hr>

THE TOWER BLOCKED out the dawn, a void of black in the East surrounded by the red haze of sunrise. I wanted back into the void where things made sense.

"May I sit with you?" Imma's voice called through the door.

"How did you find me?"

"You told Gage that you liked to be in the greenhouse to be alone. This garden is the closest we had to a greenhouse. I know you wanted to be alone, but I'd like to explain what I did. I won't force myself on you; I've done enough of that."

No one asked my permission before, not about my hair, clothes, or even my presence at the NVL. Everything was done to me, and it was my job to deal with it. Implanted, it was easy. I had no connection to my emotions, but I had more than I knew what to do with since the rally.

With my consent, she sat next to me, tucked her legs underneath, and edged closer. Her hip touched mine, and her warmth seeped through my uniform and into my skin.

"I wanted to help. How are you supposed to know what to do with your future if you don't know your past? Good or bad, you deserve to know where you came from, and the years that you don't remember are the ones that I have the happiest memories of. I didn't want to tell you unless I found something that made a difference."

"Nothing to find."

"And I would believe that if you remembered it! But I remember the flavor of the cake and the color of the icing at my fifth birthday party. I remember my nanny's face when I got in trouble, and I remember the names of the other children at nursery school."

I sat, running those words over and over in my head. Cake. She brought me cake my first day, and my fifth birthday cake was chocolate with strawberries. I didn't know the names or the faces of the other children. "Why is this important to you?"

"The Founders thought this was the best of both worlds, but our system traps everyone. Those in the Tower are beholden to the state and the system with no hope of changing once they go in. People like me who can't or won't fit into the pegs we're expected to fit in are trapped between duty and misery. We look for a way to make it through the day without completely losing a sense of ourselves. I'm just as trapped as you are. We both deserve the freedom they promised us, and so does everyone else like us. You and I together, we can make things happen that Laurel, Seb, and Jack only dream of with their rallies and pamphlets. If you never showed up, I'd still be the Embassy nuisance, and you'd still be hiding in a greenhouse, hoping no one would notice you."

Guinn made that decision for me. He made sure I was there, but she couldn't be connected with Guinn. "Together? Why?"

She ducked her head. "There are things that I know that not many others do. I'm not really supposed to know, but I think they assumed that it wouldn't mean anything to me without context. I probably wasn't really supposed to read the files they gave me to organize, but it was so boring!" She stopped, stilled, and stared at the sun. "Your file keeps me up at night. It's nonsense—like someone recreated it from the scraps of something else." She sat back on her feet, her palms resting flat on her knees. "I'm still looking for one thing. Once I find it, I will tell you everything, for now, will you take a walk with me?"

I wanted to know what she found but left it alone. She told me more than anyone else in my life had.

The sun came up as we walked a few blocks to a large building whose facade gleamed, one solid pane of glass. Inside was cold and silent as a tomb. Imma's face, blank and pristine, stared from the few austere pictures on the wall. She led me through the stark residence and never let go of my hand.

At the center of a great vaulted room was a grand piano finished in buffed black lacquer. My fingers gingerly touched the keys, afraid to break the silence in the house. "Play for me?"

A sad melody flowed from my fingertips and echoed in the empty house. She sighed; her eyes turned away. She stopped me and said, "Come on." She led me out a set of large glass doors to a green lawn. She kicked her shoes off and ran barefoot through the manicured garden, leaping onto a wide, uneven tree stump.

Her eyes sparkled as she danced around. "When I was little, too little for school, this was a huge live oak. It was my playhouse, my castle, my secret fairy realm, my whole world." Her face turned dreamy and tilted as the warm breeze caught her hair and swept it into her eyes. She looked free. "It was over a hundred years old. I climbed up into her branches, and she held me up, let me be whoever I wanted to be until a storm came through. Lightning struck her and split my tree down the middle. My father had her chopped down and hauled away, and I cried on this stump for days." She lied down on her stomach but had to curl in her arms and legs. "Back then, I could stretch, and only the tips of my fingers and toes hung over the edges."

I knew every loose piece of drywall, broom closet, and utility port on the 47th. I knew every bedtime story Marta ever told by heart and the melodies to hundreds of songs, but everything before meeting Marta was a wash of feelings or flashes of disjointed scenes.

Imma hummed my song under her breath, her arms wrapped around an imaginary partner. Her tree became her ballroom, and I wanted a part in her fairy tale. Those black coffee eyes, heavy-lidded with the dream she created, raised to my face, and a lazy smile spread across her face.

Under her tutelage, we twirled around the large yard, and I pulled her into me. My hand released hers to graze up her arm. My heart fluttered madly the higher my hand traveled, up her arm, over her shoulder, her neck, and came to rest at her cheek.

I wanted to stay locked in that moment forever, but a throat cleared and broke whatever magic happened between us.

Imma scrambled backward. "Mother!" Like a cornered animal, her eyes darted to a woman polished to a lacquer finish in the doorway. The same suits and heels that Imma tottered around in fit this woman to perfection. Power radiated off her. My body threatened to assume the position it was trained to take when Commander Escher came through my hall.

"Mother, this is Arlo. He's—" she stalled, "He's one of my classmates at the embassy. Arlo, my mother, Senator Miriam Persaud."

"Nice to meet you." I held my hand out and tamped back the hurt at being just Imma's classmate.

Shock, disgust, and contempt laced together in the Senator's expression, but her eyes never left my open hand. "Imelda, go upstairs, we have guests for dinner."

"I have to sign Arlo back in; he's not an intern. I have other duties there."

"We both know that's not true, Imelda. I will return him to Laurel myself. Upstairs. Now." She turned her dark eyes onto me, and I wished I could disappear.

Chapter 14

The leather seats burned the backs of my legs, but I tried not to squirm. The car moved smoothly through the pedestrian-filled streets, and dark eyes so much like Imma's but with none of her bubbling enthusiasm, stared into me. Imagining Imma growing up under the thumb of such an icy woman in such a cold house made no sense.

She kept her face cold and impervious. "You aren't supposed to be allowed education leave."

Patrol didn't know, most Warden's didn't even know. No one was supposed to know, but she did. Marta's warning my first day and during my trip back to the Tower rang in my ears. Senator Persaud could end my time. She could end my life. She could end my friends.

The car stopped, and I scrambled into the sanctuary of the embassy. Laurel's office seemed miles away with the Senator's heels clicking on the buffed floors after me. "Sit there, don't move."

I obeyed and watched through the window in Laurel's door. The venom in her words bled through the feeble barricade. "What are you playing at, having that boy here? Do you know what he is?"

"Of course I do," Laurel smiled at me through the door and

leaned over a pile of papers, "he's a boy learning sign because he has a serious, undocumented speech delay. But I'd be careful what you say. The walls are thin, and his hearing is excellent."

The Senator slammed her hand down and shoved the file off Laurel's desk. "Don't threaten me! A boy like that has no business mixing with your students and interns, including my daughter?"

"You mean especially 'your' daughter, don't you? A boy like what?" Laurel, with coolness, smiled through the window. "He's smart, kind, keen to learn, really just a dream to teach. What problem could other parents, or anyone for that matter, have with that? We're lucky to have him."

"Don't insult us both by playing dumb!"

Laurel settled back, a smirk on her face. "I'm afraid I don't understand at all. What could possibly be hurt by extending a bit of goodwill to our supposed equals in the Tower?"

"Send him back where he belongs before you get yourself into trouble that neither your father nor I can save you from. Send him back, forget him, and don't look back."

"This has nothing to do with my father or with you. I can't just send him back. Arlo is my business and ratting out a kid who just wants a voice will look worse for you than harboring him will look for me. Stay out of it and keep your big mouth shut."

"Your principles won't save you once you've been processed and are waiting in the Underground. Don't destroy yourself for someone who can't repay the favor.

"I have a lot of work to do, and I'm sure your itinerary for the afternoon is full. Please do let me know when you're returning my intern to me; we wouldn't want your overbearing parenting to be mistaken for nepotism." She smiled and opened the door.

Imma's mother's eyes found me again. "Leave her alone."

I nodded and didn't move until the door at the stairwell closed. My heart hammered in my chest. "I'm sorry. I didn't mean it. I ruined everything." My hands shook, muddled the words. "Imma shouldn't be in trouble. It's my fault."

Laurel knelt in front of me. "I meant what I told her. You are worth it. We all want you with us. I won't be bullied." She stood; a cautious smile spread across her face. "Be more careful from now on, huh? Don't poke the beast."

I watched for the car that brought me back to return from my bedroom window. I fell asleep with my face against the glass and woke to a soft knocking on the door. My legs had fallen asleep. I stumbled to the door and wrapped her in my arms.

She felt rigid in my arms. "Let me go, please."

I stepped away, puzzled by her cold reception. "She let you come back?"

She nodded as tears fell from her cheeks. "Father made her. Laurel was right. It wouldn't look good for me to suddenly ignore my commitment to the embassy."

Her tentative sidesteps made me nervous; she wouldn't let me near her.

"She tells me to ask questions and make sure I am in control of the situation, but she doesn't mean it when it's her. I don't want what she does, and she doesn't care!"

"Tell me." I reached out. "You'll feel better."

Her look chilled me. "You won't." She stood. "I can't be here. Not anymore. I'm not allowed to have anything to do with you. Please, for both of our sakes, do what she says. Leave me alone." She turned and took off down the hall, but so did I. She made it to her floor, me still behind her. She slammed the door in my face; the bolt clicked into place, and her sobs filtered through the crack underneath. "Leave me alone!" The door rattled as something on the other side hit it, "Go away, Arlo!"

A hand landed on my shoulder. Rae smiled. "Go back to your room before we all get in trouble." She gave me a shove in the right direction, "I'll talk her down and see what I can figure out. She comes back from home messed up sometimes. It's not really about you. Go back to bed."

I wanted to pound in the door, demand answers but Didn't have it in me. I brushed the door with my fingertips one last time and turned.

"Oh, and Arlo?" Rae pointed a finger. "If I find out that you caused this—"

"I know.'" I feigned a punch to my jaw.

"That's right." She knocked on Imma's door. "Let me in. It's Rae."

That night went on for years. Without a word from either Rae or Imma, I fell asleep in my clothes. The alarm woke me in the morning, and I rushed to the door, but no messages had been slipped underneath. Going back to bed sounded better than facing the day, but I had to face it. And her.

I buttoned my shirt and pulled on my red vest. Rat warned me to leave Imma alone. I should have listened. I left the dorms with the other boys, but Rae cut me off at the dining room door.

She shoved a plate in my hand. "You don't want to do that." Her hair fuzzed and haloed around her head. "I just got her calm enough to come down and sit. If you go over there, you'll undo the last three hours. She hasn't slept, she hasn't eaten. Give her some space. Go eat outside or something."

"What did I do? I don't understand."

Rae rubbed her exhausted eyes. "She cried a lot, and you know what that means..."

I didn't have any clue. "Sad?"

She rolled her eyes. "She's angry! Don't you know anything about girls?"

My blank stare fueled her annoyance, and I winced at the shriek she tried to muffle with her teeth.

"You have to fight this, Arlo! Prove to her that she's wrong!" Rae's bloodshot eyes pleaded. "She's just confused."

When she checked up on me behind my back, it was for my own good. Now, it's not her fault? I shoved the plate back at her, turned, and walked out to the playground where the youngest kids were getting their energy out.

Chapter 15

Imma wouldn't speak to me. She would hardly look at me, and the other interns were forced to choose sides. They all chose her. I sat by myself like I had so many times in the cafeteria on the 47th.

They'd all shut Jack out after how he called both her and me out. Despite all the vitriol he harbored toward me, he still sat at my table. Being outcast by the others united us. We weren't friends; just fellow rejects.

A week into the new arrangement, he set his tray down on the table. "Seb wants to see you. Go see him then meet me on the playground. I have to go see my folks, anyway." I kept my eyes on my plate. "Did you hear me?"

I nodded and stalked away.

He called, "I don't like it any more than you do!" at my back.

Seb was waiting in the lab when I got there. He pasted on my prosthetic fingertips and went back to work without a word to me.

I rapped my knuckles on his desk. "I'm not going with Jack."

He pushed back and stared at me for a long time. "You need a chaperone, and he has a family function. You just have to get in and out of processing together."

"So he can use what he sees to make my life worse? He hates me."

Seb laughed. "You wanted normal and real. Imma turning on you and Jack not liking you because he's Jack is the most everyday thing that has ever happened to you. It's awful, but you don't start out knowing how to react. You have to work through it. So, go. Work it through." He turned back to his computer and waved me away.

He was right. I begged them to let me pretend to be as normal as I could be. Imma and Jack didn't know it, but they were making sure I got what I wanted.

I sat on a swing to wait for Jack and nudged myself back and forth with my toe. Swings only existed in storybooks until I arrived at the embassy. I kicked awkwardly until I got the rhythm. My body knew what to do, and I leaned in.

The swing next to me rattled as Jack sat and started to swing. We pumped our legs, climbed higher until our combined weight made the A-shaped frame rock. Jack let go and soared through the air with a loud whoop, landed in a heap, and bounced to his feet. I stopped my momentum and caught my breath, awestruck at what I just watched.

Jack chuckled and dusted himself off. "Takes a few times to get used to the feeling before you can fly. Up top, we didn't have any of this stuff." He gestured around the play yard at the brightly colored climbing structures and swing sets. "Room to run and kick-balls, but no climbing."

I nodded. "Nothing where our feet could leave the ground."

Jack sat back in the swing and doodled in the dirt with his toe. "Coming here, it showed me that everything that felt wrong in the Tower really was."

"Tower is all I know. You lived down here before."

His eyes drilled into mine. "How do you know that?"

I said, "I was at the rally. Heard you talk about your brother."

"And remembered it? One face out of a thousand you saw the day your whole world changed?"

I nodded. "Turned out to be an ass."

He hung his head. "Yeah, I know. C'mon. We better go."

Jack walked with his hands stuffed in his pockets and his eyes on the ground. He watched as I went through processing and didn't react when they called me Jonah. He wandered the Public Garden while I put on my coveralls in the shed.

To get to D Ward on the 47th, I would normally take the southwest Tube, but he dragged me over to the North hub and punched in Floor 154. The electromagnetic mechanism hummed to life and shot us upward. Gravity pressed against us, compressed our joints until I thought I'd just be a puddle when we stopped. It slowed as we neared the top, and a grunt snuck out of my throat.

He chuckled. "You didn't ever ride to the top, huh?"

The door slid open, and I took my first look at the upper floors. "We went to different green spaces, but never this high. I never understood why housing was up so high. Seems like people from the city trying to make a home here would want to be closer to what they know."

He shook his head. "No. they want to be as far as they can get from what they left behind. Whether they think of this as accepting help or accepting defeat, they don't want to be reminded of what they left behind. Besides, it's not a choice. We get processed and assigned, same as you. The closer you are to the prison, the lower you rank." The 47th wasn't even halfway up.

Instead of halls and dormitories, the upper levels felt like a miniature city. Walls had facades built over them to give the varie- gated appearance of a row of connected buildings. People gathered at various points, fixing things and trading goods. Doors led to small bartering shops and modest apartments. I tripped and stumbled through a street-like hall after Jack, too distracted by my surround- ings to pay attention to my feet.

Jack pointed. "I'm the one down there with the yellow door."

"All the doors on my floor are gray."

An older man pushed a mop. My feet caught on his bucket; it rolled across the smooth concrete and knocked the mop from his hands. The handle hit the floor and, the loud crack dropped the man. He covered his head, curled up next to his fallen mop, and trembled, whimpered like a terrified child.

I stepped forward to help, but Jack stopped me. "Don't touch him. He's scrambled. If you touch him, he'll freak out more. He just needs a minute for his brain to catch up."

"I'm sorry. I didn't mean..."

He shook his head. "It happens all the time. Loud sounds like that always set him off. It's probably not even the first time today."

That could have been me. Only luck stood between me and being curled up in the fetal position at every knock at the door or dropped spoon. I didn't belong there with his family

"I'll meet you downstairs. Go see your family."

"You're sure?" He looked between the scrambled man and me and nodded. "Okay, public garden, south entrance, in an hour."

▭

I WANDERED the halls of the 47th, and visited my favorite green spaces, unable to focus on the people I saw. Everyone looked like that man who I could become. I needed to feel like I had other options and the comfort of my red school clothes. The windows where I waited for Rat the day of the rally called to me. I sat on the floor with my head against the glass. The city spread out below me. For the first time, it didn't look like a model. I knew where the embassy was and Imma's house. I could discern streets I'd walked, and I wanted to be back down there.

Someone sat by my side, but I didn't look. "What are you doing back here?" Rat asked.

I shrugged and watched a group of birds fly in swirls and curlicues. A murmuration, Imma called it. I hated that her strange little tidbits of information wedged their way into my mind and reminded me of her when I just wanted to forget.

"Where's what' s-her-face?"

Tired and conflicted, I didn't want to pull out the TalkBox. I mimed a punch to my jaw. He always understood before.

"You punched her?" He grinned, and I knew he understood. "You had a fight?"

I nodded and made my hands into two puppets, acting out a silent argument.

He laughed but cut off abruptly. It was a first. Unless he was cheating at Roshambo or sniggering because I did something absent-minded, we didn't laugh. I waited to see what he would do, terrified that he would see how much had changed. He cleared his throat, and his eyes darted from me to his picked and scabbing fingers. "Girls are weird, man. Most of the time I don't think they know what they're thinking. How are we supposed to if they don't?"

Imma knew what she wanted, but her mother wanted other things. I didn't blame her for bending to Senator Persaud's will; I just wished she didn't have to shut me out completely to do it.

"Oh, shit. It's like that?" He stared at me, wide-eyed. "That's a 'deep shit' sigh. There's no coming back from that. What are you going to do?"

What could I do? Nothing. I had to suck it up, keep my head down and wait for my birthday so that Seb and his people could get me out of the city. Then I could make new friends and losing her wouldn't hurt so bad.

"Come home, 'Lo. You don't need them. You've got us." His confidence wavered. There was no "us," and he knew it. The others would still call me glitch. They'd be just as right about it for a whole new reason. I had him and Marta and Gerald the gardener if I gave up and returned.

I'd returned this many times, maybe I could make do.

"You've got me, at least. We've always done okay." For the first time, I saw the dull look of his eyes, compared to my friends at the embassy. Compared to the altered me, he'd always seemed so lively and full of wit. I only saw how incomplete he was once I had something else to compare it to. I couldn't return to the 47th. The secrecy and subterfuge of the visits weighed on me; I couldn't subject myself to months of it.

"Well, what happened?"

I reached for the device but stopped. If I told him why Imma's mother wanted her away from me, I had to tell him all of it. And I couldn't tell him any of it. Fewer words were better this time. I held my hand out, and his hand filled it, palm up. I thought the grin would split his face wide open. "Mother," I spelled, drawing the words on his palm.

He scoffed, and a knowing smirk filled his face. "Don't get me started on their mother's. If one more City girl tells me that her mother would never approve of her seeing a kid from the Tower, I'll puke. Say no more, Pal. Say no more."

Say no more. That would be the story of my life if I went back. I stood, and he followed. "Time to go," I signed.

"What happened to you, anyway? I take you to that rally an you're, well, you. You wouldn't let anyone touch you, and you'd rather be in that music room than meeting people. Then I lose you there." He wouldn't look up. "Then the next time I see you you're like a different person. You told me off. You threw that thing that talked for you, and you nearly got yourself killed trying to leave without out-processing. Now, you're here, and you're more normal, but we're talking about girls. We're talking. Something isn't right. Something changed, and it can't just be that you learned a way to talk with your hands. You could always tell me stuff. What's different?"

I pulled out the TalkBox. "The rally. I almost died. Had to change." I handed it to him instead of having it speak.

"I didn't mean for you to get stuck."

I tucked away the TalkBox and tapped my temple. "I know. See you next time."

I rode down to Central Processing. Jack was waiting for me. We made it out of the Tower without a hitch and began our walk back. While I made a beeline for the embassy, Jack stuck his hands in his pockets and slumped in the opposite direction. I jogged to catch up, grabbed Jack by his collar. "Wrong way."

Jack shrugged me off and straightened his clothes. "I got a stop to make first. It'll only take a few minutes." We worked our way away from Embassy Row through alleys, and side streets, and into the Industrial sector where Jack ducked into an old warehouse.

Inside, it was dusty and bare. "What are we doing here?" I stood my ground at the door while Jack walked deeper into the gloom and ignored me. A growl ripped out of him and turned into a ragged, "Hey!"

"Welcome to the home of the Resistance. Wait here," Jack called, "I'll be right back." He opened a door deep in the huge building. Lights leaked up the stairs he descended, and shadows of people milled about. Before I could see more, though, a hand wrapped around my bicep and a bundle of ropes hit me in the face. My eyes watered, I tripped and pulled and got my bearings when I was thrust out into the sunshine and blinked at Seb.

Seb held me still and gave me a quick once over. "You can't be here, not right now. How did you get here?"

"Jack brought me. Where is this?"

His lips pursed. "This is where the Resistance meets sometimes. I told him to bring you back first."

"Can I see?"

Seb rapped his knuckles against my scalp. "Only a few weeks ago, you had a full-scale electrical storm inside your head. You're too volatile to be trusted." Seb patted my shoulder, ending the contact with a squeeze. "Soon. When you're healed and don't feel like killing Jack every five minutes, I'll bring you back."

I tried to get another look around him.

He laughed. "Come on. Let's go get me some sound samples to work with so you don't sound like a machine to your hearing friends."

Chapter 16

Seb took me back to his lab. He opened up a program on the biggest terminal in the room, and the screen filled with graphs and meters that moved with every sound in the room. He clamped a microphone on a swinging arm onto the edge of the table and pulled it between us. The microphone stared back at me. It dared me to open my mouth and try out the voice that had been kept a secret for a decade. "I don't want this. I talked to Rat today. He understands me; he always has. I don't need this."

He sat down across from me and made adjustments. "You're not going back to your friends on the 47th when this ends, Arlo. No matter how the end comes, you can't go back. You have to be prepared for everyone else, and this is the only way I know to help you with that." He looked up from his settings and graphs. "Do you remember if you had speech therapy as a kid?"

No one had ever tried to make me speak on the 47th, not even Marta. "They just accepted it. So did I."

"I mean before." He faltered, and uncertainty flashed on his face. "Before the Tower, did your family get help for you?"

"I don't remember before." He saw the lie, and his frown dug in. "The memories are small. Pieces. Nothing that makes sense."

I'd never told him that the failing implant left me with fragmented bits of my old life. He leaned over the table. "But..."

I shrugged and let out a breath. "I remember little words. Baby words." I flipped through the strange half scenes my mind had let loose. They all involved the woman with blue eyes or just me and other kids except one. "Is speech therapy a doctor? She had a mask on her face, and I was strapped down. She had a needle."

Seb's dark skin turned ashen. "No. No doctor. No needles. This would have been someone who came to your home and tried to teach you how to speak. Dr. Zachili did a full scan of you when you arrived. There's nothing physically wrong in your mouth or your throat that's kept you from speaking. Whatever stopped you is neurological. They chose you for Project Livewire, so, Services knew that. Do you remember anyone coming to your home, asking you to make sounds? Repeat them?"

"I don't remember home." It gutted me to say. I pulled in a sharp breath and held it. How could I be homesick for something I had no memory of? "Before, in the Tower, I would remember small things: eyes, smiles, smells, but then there would be this noise, like a whistle or a scream that would stop them. The others called me 'glitch' because of it. I hear it whenever there's a spark now. When I think too hard, or something makes me remember now, it's bigger, but not enough to understand what happened."

"I don't think we'll ever really understand what happened to you. Even with the facts, I can't understand what would make people surrender children and have them implanted against the law. I don't think I want to understand people who would do that. But, you don't remember speech therapy. That's what we do know. Have you tried your voice out since that night?"

The night of the rally came back to me and the torrent of nonsensical sound that had poured out of my mouth when I tried to answer Guinn.

My burning face spoke for me, and he laughed. "So, it works?"

I shook my head. "Doesn't make sense."

"What do you mean?"

"At the rally, I tried to tell Guinn my name, but it came out wrong. The words in my brain and the sounds that came out didn't match."

His smile turned sad. "Then you really will be like one of us. Speech is the worst memory of my childhood. They made me sit for hours, repeating sounds I couldn't hear, slapping my hands when I tried to sign." A snarl crossed his lips. "When I said I didn't want to do it anymore, my family surrendered me, too. I never belonged with them. They signed to me the way you did when you got here: pantomime and made up gestures. They wanted to fix me. I was a ward on an education release, and this was my only family. I found my place here. I wish you could have that, but the truth is that even once you age out, without credentials, you will always be on the run from them."

Always on the run? That wasn't what Marta promised me. She said I would be out. That after I turned eighteen, I wouldn't have to worry about them coming for me anymore. "Laurel and Marta said–"

"I know what they said. I don't know if they couldn't think beyond keeping you safe for now, or if they planned to figure that next part out when we get there, but you deserved to know. I will find a way to get you out of the city. Many people live full lives out on the Frontier even without credentials. If you want that, you have to do your part and make it so that you have all the tools at your disposal to talk to people. Are you ready?"

"No, but I haven't been ready to do anything else, either. I can do it."

"Good answer." He moved the microphone closer to me and tapped something on his screen. "Start with vowels.."

I knew my vowels but wasn't sure if my mouth knew them.

He requested vowels, and I tried to give him the ones he asked for, but my mouth fought back. He switched to other sounds, and it got worse. I wanted to slide under the table and never come out. Hearing it when I was delirious at the rally had been bad, but dissecting each sound, knowing what it should sound like, and hearing the errant sounds roll off my tongue was worse.

He turned the microphone off. "I need a break," he said. Sweat trailed down his face, and his breath came in short pants. He hid his face in his hands for a long time, long enough for my thoughts to run away. He couldn't help me. I was too stupid. Too broken to teach anything. I'd be trapped out on the Frontier with a voice that sounded inhuman, and nothing would have changed except the place. Life would be the same as it was in the Tower.

He knocked on the tabletop. "Sorry. I forgot how much that takes me back. I don't like thinking of back then."

"I can't hear you, Arlo. The samples you gave me are nothing but readings to me. I know you're upset by what you heard, but I'm not ashamed. You warned me. We knew it wasn't going to be easy, but you did it anyway. I'll see what I can do with what we did today, and I'll tweak the program. We'll get it working so that it makes it a little easier on you."

"How?" I asked.

He grinned. "I don't know yet, but I'll figure it out. Maybe we can find a way to have my algorithm choose the right sounds and re-organize them. Then, no matter what sound you make, it's still usable." He rolled his chair over to the terminal he normally docked at. He checked over his shoulder and waved me over. "This is where I make your passes and your credential changes. You need to know how to do these by yourself, in case something happens to me."

The overhead lights flicked on and off. Laurel stood in the door-way. "He's in this deep enough without being held accountable for Resistance intel. Don't do that to him. Go back to your dorm, Arlo."

Time alone to think about everything was what I needed.

"Arlo," Laurel called, "I don't think you need to worry about making your own passes, but you need to be able to use your voice in an emergency. I'll work you into the speech rotation as soon as I can. We can't just keep avoiding it because it makes you uncomfort-able. That's what they did in the Tower. They went around it. We're done doing things their way, right?"

I couldn't hold still long enough to give her an answer. I could go the rest of my life avoiding the sounds lodged in my throat.

BY THE TIME my next Tower visit rolled around, I looked forward to having Jack as company.

Imma's voice bled out from under the closed door to Laurel's office, and the desperation made my heart stutter. "You don't understand!"

Careful to keep out of sight, I peeked through the window. She curled up in a chair with her face hidden.

Laurel focused on her paperwork. Her snappish response had me on my toes for more. "I might not know what happened, but I understand perfectly. This whole situation has Miriam's sticky little fingerprints all over it."

I waited for Imma's answer, my heart pounding in my ears.

"There has to be someone else who could go!"

Imma and I waited for the words, words that seemed to pain Laurel. "Everyone else wants to be here, Imma. They've made themselves necessary. I love that you found yourself in the library, but you aren't here to research Arlo. You're here as an intern, and that means you do what I say."

I didn't understand why she didn't drop her fascination with my origins when she dropped me cold turkey. It was as good of a time as any. I pushed in the door, resigned to my fate. Laurel wouldn't budge for either of our sakes.

Laurel sucked in a deep breath and plastered a charming smile on her face. "Right on time, as always."

Imma picked at her cuticles and did her best to pretend I didn't exist.

I pleaded with Laurel. "Don't make her do this."

She turned on her rich face, the face she showed me my first day, and turned it on Imma. "He has to go and needs a chaperone to do it. You can ignore each other for all I care, but you're both going!" I stood in front of the door, held it open, and waited for Imma.

"Laurel, please. You know my mother..."

"I'm done cowing to your mother and her demands. It's time

that someone made her deal with the consequences of her actions. He is not the problem. She is. Go."

Imma stood with force, and her chair toppled over backward. She stomped past Laurel and me.

Laurel stopped me and smiled. "She'll soften up. Be patient."

I followed Imma out of the embassy. She stomped like a child having a tantrum down Front Street to the tram stop and never let me within ten steps of her. I let her have her space. I didn't need to add chasing someone down a street to my rap sheet when her mother turned me in.

She sat across the aisle on the tram and jumped off before it came to a stop, but her pace slowed, and her fists unclenched. Maybe Laurel was right, and she'd soften, but she still wouldn't speak to or look at me.

We entered the Tower without a hitch and rode up the Tube. Her silence wore on me. Rat greeted me at the 47th floor tube station with a smile that turned sour when Imma followed.

"Go away." His reverse snobbery was on full display. "I know how you treated him; he told me last time when you couldn't be bothered to come. Go home to Mommy!"

"I can't," she smirked, taunting him. "You won't understand him without me. He didn't check out a TalkBox because you made fun of him last time." Her raspy voice raked over my skin. Something hid in those soft tones, a flicker of life that went missing that night she stayed home. That tiny spark, barely noticeable, had me hanging on every word.

"You weren't here last time, and we did just fine. We did just fine all the years before you, and we'll be just fine once you get your own life and butt back out of ours. Tell her, Arlo!"

I sucked the inside of my lip. Neither one of them deserved my loyalty at that moment, but it didn't matter. Rat was wrong and Imma, right. "I wasn't fine. I survived. With your help and Imma's, it will be fine."

Rat's eyes bulged in disbelief as Imma interpreted my signs. "You and Marta would be enough until I get out. Then the embassy will help me."

"You aren't one of them!" Rat growled. "You belong here with Marta and me! We stick together! You don't need them, you need us!"

Imma rushed between us and shoved Rat's chest. Through my confusion, warm pride filled me. She stood up for me moments after trying to hit me with a shoe.

"How dare you?" She shoved Rat again. "How dare you try to guilt him into staying for you! If you really cared about him, you wouldn't use him like you have! You'd lift him up and want what is best for him, not for you! You're just like them!" Her ferocity touched me, and all of the pity I felt for her on the street dwindled. Standing up to anyone was a step she needed to take.

Rat's face took on a feral hardness that made my gut clench. "You shack up with him for a few weeks and think you know him better than me? He's loyal as a damn dog and twice as stupid because of it. Sooner or later, you'll go back to your fancy life and forget whatever this is between the two of you. Him not talking won't seem so adorable when every conversation means more work for you. Where does that leave him? If he's dumb enough to listen to you and go it alone out there, it leaves him all alone out there with nothing and no one. Dump him. Break it off now before he gets any more attached to you."

I couldn't stand listening to them fight over who cared more while they both ignored me. Neither of them noticed when I stepped away to call the Tube, they kept right on squabbling.

I rode the Tube. I wanted to punch the stupid screen forever promising a better life through neural implantation. My life didn't feel better. I thought about going back to the embassy but didn't want to deal with Laurel. One Pressman mad at me was bad enough. I sat in the Public Gardens in the Atrium outside the Courthouse and let the soil and humid air calm me.

Imma came down, wandered in with her eyes turned upward to the suspended decks and greenhouses floating overhead. I watched her, wondered which Imma she would be before I stood and cleared my throat.

She turned and smiled. "Are you all right?"

I nodded.

"I have something to show you, will you go on a ride with me?"

"Where?"

"To see what you came from so you can make your own decision about who you want to be."

Chapter 17

The tram pulled to a stop in the outer suburbs. Identical brick houses lined the street like sentinels. Imma focused on one; its front gardens overflowed with rich black soil and thick foliage.

"This house belongs to Ira and Larissa Cooper. They have nine children. Jonah, Lori, Arlo, Grace, Ramsey, Maureen, Gray, Tallulah, and Graham."

My heart pounded. Jonah and Arlo. My name and the name I used for my Tower passes. The kids in the street all had black hair and blue eyes like mine. An ache formed in my chest as their black curls bounced.

Imma grabbed my hand. A woman stomped down the manicured lawn. Her hair was a tumble of salt and pepper, wild and untethered. "Services has no right to be investigating us!" The children dropped what they were doing and crowded around their mother, glowering at Imma and I. "They are allowed to play. You can't tell me there is any harm in that." Her blue eyes filled with fear.

Imma stepped forward and smiled. "Mrs. Cooper, I'm Imma, and this is Arlo. We're not from Services, and I promise we won't take anyone. I brought Arlo back. You've waited too long to meet each other."

My mother stared at me like I was a ghost. I guess I was, in a way, the child she gave up so long ago, back from the dead to haunt her. "My Arlo?" She stepped closer; her hand reached for me.

I gripped Imma's hand, the anchor keeping me from running, as panic bubbled up inside me. I stumbled back. Feelings that I didn't recognize filled my head. My skull filled to bursting. Words pressed up my throat and filled my mouth. Looking at my mother, I wanted to scream out words I knew wouldn't make sense.

She held a hand out. "You need to sit." She smiled, and for a moment, she seemed younger. Her hair was darker, and concern hadn't carved so many tracks around her eyes and mouth. I shook my head, the two versions of her separated and converged.

Overwhelming vertigo rocked me and distracted me from keeping the words inside. Sounds forced their way out. My hands signed, *"Don't touch me!"* but the sounds that broke the neighborhood's peace didn't make sense. An ice pick of pain drove from my temple to my spine. It dropped me to my knees, and I cradled my head.

Imma crouched next to me. "I'm sorry," she whispered. "I didn't know it would hurt you."

"We need to go inside," my mother glared at the surrounding houses, "They are all cowards and will call Services on you just for being here." She held a hand down to me. "If you come inside, I will tell you anything, answer any question."

Her warm, rough hand wrapped around mine, and lightning struck my brain. The stench of ozone and burnt feather engulfed me.

My arm was smaller and held up a flower to a younger mother than I'd seen. She sat in the garden, surrounded by plants that would keep us all fed with a toddler in her lap and a baby asleep on her shoulder. "Thank you, my darling!" She tucked the dandelion behind her ear. "I love the little treasures you find me."

Despite the compliment, I was disappointed. The lady who came to play with me every few days told me to make her say the words I wanted so I could repeat them. I wanted 'flower.' I reached out to touch the golden mane of the dandelion to show her what I needed the name of, but she pushed me away.

"You'll hurt the babies, Arlo!"

I stamped my foot and yelled. The noise that came out of had all the musicality of the other's speech, but she didn't understand. She never understood me when I tried.

The kitchen counters were high, but I was used to scaling them to get what I wanted when no one understood. Her plates and teacups had little pink, and blue flowers painted on them.

"It's not dinnertime yet, Arlo. You have to wait." Even at five, I could hear how tired she sounded, but I just needed one word!

"Un-nuh dat," my little voice grunted, pointing at one flower as I held the dish out to her.

I taught myself to change my sounds so they would understand that little sentence, and I used it enough that it didn't fight back inside my mouth.

She sighed and put two-year old Grace on the floor.

"Dat!" I said excitedly, pointing. "Un-nuh dat, Ma!"

She took the plate from my hand and put it back with the others and walked away. Too frustrated to cope, I grabbed the plate and threw it to the floor.

Air dragging into a dry throat replaced the sound of shattering china. Imma's soft hand squeezed gently at the dense rope of muscle that curved from my neck to my shoulder. I reached up and closed my hand over hers, pressing in deeper. My eyes felt weighted. I sat at the table— the kitchen around me exactly as I remembered it—with my upper body collapsed on the surface. I tried to pull myself upright but slumped over. My body protested; my muscles too shaky to control limbs that felt leaden.

A hand raked back the wet curls from my flaming skin. "It's going to keep happening now that it's started," my mother soothed. "Seeing us fried the implant."

"You're burning up," Imma tried to move away, but I held fast to her hand until she whimpered and cradled the bruised appendage.

"They say the nickname scramblers came from that." She chuckled at Imma's disbelief, "Scrambled eggs when the implant fries."

"And a smell of burnt toast that won't go away," Imma dug her fingers into that muscle at the apex of my neck and shoulder. The pressure in my skull released momentarily, and I breathed out in relief. "You're bleeding."

My mother brought a steaming mug and a towel to wipe away the blood that trickled out of my ear. I shoved myself up–propped my upper body against the edge of the table–and brushed the tip of my finger against the familiar pink and blue flowers on the side of the cup. "Un-uh dat," I mumbled, dragging my heavy arm back to my body to sign 'flower.' My brain knew those words, guttural and infantile, and didn't have to fight for them. I felt more slow and languid by the second.

Mother mopped my face. "As they turn eighteen, we'll see more and more of them. They'll be conscripted, without ever knowing what is inside them."

"There were others like him?"

"Hundreds. Boys and girls alike with different issues that forced their parents to go to Services for help. We signed stacks and stacks of papers, and never knew we were signing away our parental rights."

I reached for Imma, and she put her hand back in mine and used it to focus my mind and will my eyes to stay open, but the ozone and burnt feather smell pulled me back to the haze. Over and over, the memories hit with a flash of light and a burst of heat. In between, I fell into a state of rest, less sleep than sucking paralysis. The fits and spurts slowed, the periods of rest grew longer until my mind moved back toward the world where soft hands pulled me upright to clean my face with cool water that wanted to sizzle when it hit my skin.

They tipped my head back and poured something hot and acrid in and then smoothed down my throat to make me swallow even though I sputtered and choked.

"That's it," my mother cooed, "he's coming back to us now."

I hissed. The burning cold of an ice pack pressed at my temple and another at the back of my neck.

Imma's slender hand wrapped around mine. "Open your eyes, Arlo."

I fought against the tarry hold my brain held over my body.

My mother's hand slid across the table toward mine but pulled away. "There wasn't enough of me to go around. We got a recommendation that Central Services might be the only way to get all the help he needed. I didn't know when I made the call that it would mean ending up without him."

Imma ruffled her short hair. "I couldn't find a diagnosis in the files, or even an explanation."

"His brain turns the outbound language cues around, the same way a person with dyslexia turns incoming signals. He knows what he wants to say, but his mouth associates the wrong sound with what he thinks."

My eyes felt sticky, and my mind full of fog. "Stop talking about me like I'm not here."

Imma grinned and sniffled back a fresh set of tears. "You weren't doing it."

Tears filled my mother's eyes as I signed, and Imma interpreted. "The neighbor kids ganged up on me. They went after Jonah, and I panicked and attacked them."

My mother nodded. "First, they sent doctors and therapists. We were so grateful for the help that we didn't even notice the problems. They expected so much of him, and he wanted to be fixed. He was already so frustrated, and when the neighborhood kids went after him and my oldest, he fought back. One of the mothers called in the disturbance, just like the doctors told them they should. Retainment broke the door down at three o'clock in the morning, and he was gone."

Imma whimpered. "They sent Retainment for one little boy?"

"We fought to get you back, and they came back with threats. We had to cease and desist, or we would end up in the Prison, and your brothers and sisters would join you in the Tower. We had to choose. Not choosing you has haunted me for twelve years."

"Ten years." I clung to the hope that my file was wrong.

Mother shook her head. "You turn eighteen in four months, and you were five and a half when they took you."

Imma smoothed her thumb over my knuckles. "There's still a missing piece?"

I nodded, and Imma's face warred between anger and grief. "So much just to make one little boy obey, but why?"

Mother chuckled, but the sound had no joy in it. "I used to call you my hellion, my wild boy, my feral child. I imagine it took a little extra muscle to strong-arm that will."

"Marta called me a rebel, but I always thought she was teasing. Maybe she just saw me. Before."

The jealousy on her face hurt. "Marta? Is that who took care of you?" All color drained from her lips.

I nodded and pushed my hand across the table, reaching for her for the first time.

A real smile, not a hesitant half-smile, graced Imma's face for the first time since we'd arrived. "She's been his warden since he was seven. She really cares about him and the others, but I don't think she replaced you."

I used my free hand, and tapped my heart, thanked her for saying what I couldn't.

▭

MY MOTHER BROKE DOWN. Tears streamed down her face, and her eyes pleaded with me. "I failed you. I tried so hard, but I didn't know how to help you. You tried so hard to tell me what you wanted, what you needed, but there were so many of you and only me."

Two of my youngest siblings who watched from another room. They were around the same age I was when I was taken. "I wanted…" The emotions were so clear even after so long. I just wanted her. I wanted her to look at me and be proud like she was when one of them did something ordinary. She looked at me the same wounded way she did when I was five and threw her dishes. "I wanted you to see me like you saw them."

"I saw you, my Darling." She held her hand out and led me away from the kitchen. She sat at an old upright piano. "Do you remember this?" Her fingers brushed the keys. The ebony and ivory coating had worn off from all the play it had seen. "This was where I could see you best. I spent hours here with you. Your father would come home to a house where nothing and no one was clean, the gardens were full of weeds, and he would just take care of it because you and I were at this piano, talking to one another. He knew better than to interrupt. All of them did." A familiar melody filled the room and brought hot tears to my eyes.

"That's your song, Arlo," Imma said from the door, "The one you play for me."

Mother scooted down the bench. I sat, and my fingers joined hers. I played the part I played for Imma. Mama broke off into a harmony. For the duration of the song, everything fell into place. Everything felt right. The last chord rang out, and she turned to me. Her eyes dripped with happy tears, and her cheeks grew rosy. Her smile did me in. I ran from it and shoved out the back door. I couldn't breathe in the warm light of the happy picture postcard life that was supposed to have been mine. My deep breaths turned to screams that turned to sobs with edges like knives. Noises so harsh, they cut my throat as they barreled out.

A hand pressed into my shoulder, comforting and heavy. Its owner didn't talk or soothe, just weighed me down until I calmed on my own. "Not so little now, are you, little brother?" Seeing Jonah was like looking in a mirror. I jumped to my feet and hugged a brother I didn't know I had. Memories flooded back. Jonah was the only one who never seemed upset by me. "When Ma said you showed up, I nearly got fired trying to get here. I looked for so long. Lori and I almost got ourselves locked up trying to sneak past Processing over and over to look for you." Jonah pushed me back and smiled, holding me out at arm's length. "Are you going to talk to me? You used to tell me everything; I could always figure you out."

I shook my head. I wouldn't know what to say if I could.

Jonah circled his arm around my shoulders and led me back

inside and steered me to one of the seats as my mother came in with the last dish. I was used to big tables, but the one my mother set to feed the family seemed huge even by institutional standards. The younger kids stood behind chairs at the massive table. Same black hair, pale skin, blue eyes, all looking at me. There were two empty seats.

"Imma, you can sit in Lori's seat." Mama beamed with joy. "It will be so nice to have a full table again at last."

"She won't mind?" Imma asked.

"Lori has another year on her conscription," Jonah answered.

Imma smiled; her respect plain on her face. "But you set her a place every night? And Arlo too?"

Mama nodded. "To remind us that while they can't be with us, they are still our family and always in our hearts."

My two youngest siblings crawled under the table and into my lap. "What's your name?"

Imma rested her forehead in her palm. Exhaustion slumped her shoulders and pooled under her eyes, but she smiled at the little ones. "He wants to know your name."

My little sister turned. "I'm Lulu, and he's Graham. You look like Jonah. What's your name?" She kept her eyes on me, didn't look to Imma for the answer.

Imma giggled when I looked to her in awe. She signed, "Go on, tell them."

"A-R-L-O." They mimicked the letters and wanted to know their own.

My mother smiled, but her brows knitted together. "You were always so good at helping with the little ones."

"He still is." Imma sat up. "The entire primary school follows him around like a row of ducklings. They adore him." She saw through my smile and frowned as she brought her fork to her lips. "You need to eat."

"Can't." I looked at the food and swallowed down my gag reflex. Even at its quietest, the world was a roar of anger and regret, sadness, and joy inside my head. I didn't know what to do, so I held tight to my siblings' wiggling bodies and let their laughter dampen the worst of it.

The front door closed, "Ma, I'm home." She sat in the empty seat, her blue and white Junior Warden Society uniform spotless, and never took her eyes off Imma and me. "Who is that?"

My father, quiet and reserved, smiled. "Your brother, Arlo. Arlo, this is Grace."

Grace nonchalantly cut into her food as she spoke as if her cold words were small talk. "You shouldn't be here." No longer the toddler from my confusing memories, she was a beauty with an attitude to match Rae's.

My father pounded his fist on the table, and all of the china jumped and rattled. "Grace, not now!"

"He was taken away for a reason, Dad! Why can't you all accept that our lives are all better because he's gone? He went for the benefit of us all. He should go back with his own kind."

"He is your brother! He is our kind!" Mother stood, and her chair scraped on the floor.

"Please, elaborate." Imma stayed calm, let that cold, soulless smile mask her face. She batted her eyelashes over gleaming eyes. "What makes a person one kind or another?" Her tight-lipped voice sent a chill down my spine, and I pulled Tallulah and Graham closer to my body, hiding behind them to watch. "We are all equal, even though we're separate, aren't we? Surely it isn't becoming of a Junior Warden to be heard speaking like that."

"The Tower gives the help those struggling need, but it can't help Residents if they aren't there. Nothing good can come of him being here."

Imma's calmness unnerved me more and more the longer she kept it up. "I used to use the 'level playing field' to rationalize it too. The only leveling your brother needed was a language he could speak without his mouth, and the Tower didn't provide that. He is intelligent, kind, calm, and well-adjusted despite what the Tower did to him. Where does he fit in your black and white assessment of the way our world works?"

"He has the chance to test out in a few months, and if he does, then he can come home. He shouldn't be here now, and you should know better, being the daughter of one of our representatives."

Imma's eyes blazed with anger when they met with mine. "My parents' sins will follow me to my grave. I will die still trying to atone for what they stand for."

"Go to bed, Grace," my father intervened, "You're insulting your brother and all of us with your opinions."

A growl vibrated out of my throat. "I want out." Grace's words weighed on me, and as much as my parents looked ashamed, as much as they assured me I was wanted all this time, they just sent her to her room. They wouldn't get rid of Grace. My newfound anger flared at the injustice of it all. The toddlers in my lap squirmed to escape my grip and reached for their mother. Their mother. Not mine.

"Go," my mother said and pulled the children free, "I understand, but we don't share her feelings. You belong with us. You always have."

"I don't. She's right." Imma put her hand on my elbow. Her presence helped me stay calm. "They took me away from you and you away from me. I don't belong here, and I can't fix that."

Mother nodded and kissed my cheek. My skin burned under her touch. "Come back when you're ready. We'll be here."

Chapter 18

We walked past my mother's garden plots, and Imma stopped with a sad, faraway smile on her face. "Your love for greenhouses and people who like to grow things makes so much more sense now." She stared into my eyes, searching, but I didn't know what for. "Are you mad that I brought you here?"

Everything made more sense, but nothing did. I had all the answers I thought I wanted, but they didn't change anything. "No. You showed me everything I was missing. You showed me everything I never knew I wanted. We should get back. Laurel will worry."

We caught a tram and rode back into the city. Imma stared out the window. The tram rambled slowly into the city center. I tapped her shoulder, but she didn't turn, too deep in thought. "Uhmmma." It sounded close to what it should. She turned shock and delight in her wide, dark eyes.

"Did you just say my name?"

I blinked, still in shock, and nodded.

"Do it again."

I had too much on my mind and signed instead. "Later. Will you help me?"

She turned in the seat and sat crossed-legged. "Of course."

I had to do something. I couldn't fix what happened to my family. "Can you find other people the way you found my family?" Something in me screamed to take care of Gage and to make sure he felt heard. After Imma introduced me to my family, I knew I had to help him and his family the way no one helped mine.

"Who?"

"Gage's family." I needed to make sure he remembered them and that someone was setting a place at their table in his honor. "Gage and I are the same. They didn't mean to give him up."

She wrapped her arm around my elbow and leaned against my bicep. "Arlo, I was there the day they brought Gage in. Laurel went to his house herself. You and he are not the same. He was removed by Services." She sighed but hugged me closer when I tried to pull away. "I know you don't want to believe that, but it's the truth. He came in ragged and dirty. They took him and brought him to us to see if his parents could take care of the two younger children who were hearing. His mother had never taken him to a doctor. She didn't know what was wrong with him, just that he screamed and didn't listen."

We rode in silence for a few blocks, and she stood up a stop too soon. "Come on. I think we could both use a walk." I followed her down the tram steps but stayed a step behind her. "I understand that you feel like reuniting Gage with his mother will save him from what you are going through, but you have to see the difference between your situation and his."

"I thought we were the same."

"From what I saw, you are not and never have been the same as anyone. You are one of a kind, Arlo Cooper. My mother chose you for the project by hand. That's why they all want us kept away from one another. She promised to leave you be for as long as she can. You're no good to her now that you're deactivated, but I had to promise not to talk to you. There is too much attention on me."

I stopped. "Your mother chose me?" I was sure I heard her wrong.

She hurried ahead. "We need to keep moving. Surveillance will get curious if we stop." I jogged to catch up with her. "Yes. My mother chose all of you. Marta told you that the first day you were with us, remember?"

"How do you know that?"

"Laurel heard her. It took knowing what I found for her to make sense of it. Arlo, you are a secret. If Tower City, if anyone found out about you and the other kids on the 47th, my mother and father would be under a legal magnifying glass."

"So, you want me to shut up? Keep my head down? Stay out of trouble?"

She grinned. "For right now, yes, I do. I'm still following a trail of breadcrumbs in my mother's files to see how deep this whole thing goes, Arlo. Until we have all the facts, you can't do anything stupid like trying to take Gage home. Promise me."

"It's not stupid!"

"It's not smart!" She stopped short, and I readied myself for a fight. Her focus locked on the motorcade limousine parked outside the Embassy a block away. "Drat. I forgot about her stupid campaign dinner. She'll be madder than a hornet." She fidgeted and worried her fingers through her hair. "You need to get inside without her seeing you, Arlo! Go around back."

I refused to put my head down and my back to the nearest wall. I stood tall. "Who?"

"My mother." She shoved me back and around the corner. "You can't let her see you. Go! Back around the play area!"

A shout rang out as I ducked inside the gate. The Senator's crisp voice cut through the air. "Imelda Amiek Pressman-Persaud, in the car. Now."

I winced at the distinct sharpness.

She stood on the Embassy steps, as regal and well-appointed as a fairy tale evil queen.

Laurel ran down the steps. "Miriam, go home." She snapped her receiver into place and grimaced as it squealed to life. She tried to put herself between her step-mother and sister.

The Senator yanked Imma out of Laurel's grip and shoved her

into the waiting motorcade. "Shut up, Laurel. You are out of your depth!"

Laurel stepped up closer than I'd ever seen anyone get to the Senator. "Imma is my depth. She has duties and responsibilities here, and you can't just come and pull her out whenever you feel like it. She isn't just a student here. She is an intern and is subject to the rules of her position!"

Senator Persaud opened her mouth, ready to give Laurel a piece of her mind, but the car door opened, and Imma pushed out. "Mother! I'm not going anywhere. I'm going to stay and finish my commitment, and then I'm going to conscription. I'm sorry I'm a disappointment, but I can't keep pretending to be someone I'm not. I'd make a terrible politician, and I have to follow my own path like Laurel did."

Laurel held her hand out, a lifeline, and Imma reached for it, but her mother pulled her back. Imma wrenched her arm from her mother's grasp and darted into the door of the Embassy. I turned, ran in from the back, and hoped like hell I could find her and help her hide.

Her mother's aides and bodyguards were in every hall I tried to search. I darted through the halls, ducked into empty classrooms and offices, but couldn't find her. Students flooded the halls looking for an explanation for the strangers in their home.

Jack caught my arm. "What are you doing?"

"Finding Imma!"

He pulled me back and into his room. "Yeah, well, so are they, and you and I both know you can't afford the kind of trouble that will come from helping her get away from them. That phony education release and pass of yours won't fool them for a second. Go wait in your room. Imma handles her mother better than most of the Senate. She's got it. Stay out of their way."

I hated to leave her, but Jack was right.

I lay awake for hours. Every time I dozed off, my leg twitched, or a loud yell jolted through my mind. The sheets tangled around my legs and held in the heat radiating out of my brain, and I couldn't take it anymore. I pulled a soft undershirt on and left my room. The darkness in the Embassy hallways toyed with my mind. Catcalls echoed from every shadow, drafts, and breezes made me shiver in my fevered skin. I needed answers, and the only place I could get them was the Research Terminal.

I used Imma's password and searched: Neural Implantation in children.

That search came up with nothing but explanations of the laws concerning implantation and studies on brain development in children, but a line caught my eye:

Implantation cannot be recommended for children or teenagers. Though the surgery is safe, coping skills could not develop normally if emotions or memories were switched off. If the implant malfunctioned later in life, the patient would be unable to process emotions correctly. Desirable subjects should be older than twenty-five and in good mental health before implantation is recommended.

The article was written by Miriam Persaud.

Imma's mother was somehow an integral part of why I was the way I was. A sour taste I couldn't seem to swallow filled my mouth, and I knew I should stop, but I couldn't.

Search: missing children.

A few reports came up, but they were mostly kids who wandered off and got lost.

Search: Children removed from family.

The list went on, pages and pages. A filter narrowed it down to only children with medical issues, but the list was still endless. There were hundreds, if not thousands, of us. I couldn't look anymore. I needed out.

I BURST out the rooftop and pulled in a deep breath of cool night air. My heartbeat quieted enough for the sound of rustling in the plants to catch my attention. Curled up under the wide leaves of a collard plant, Imma hid between two planter boxes, fast asleep.

I hated to disturb her, but eventually, her mother's anger would turn to worry. A dangerous woman like Miriam Persaud worrying would lead to trouble for all of us.

Now that I knew the song belonged to my mother, it didn't sound so sad. I whistled, gave the song a lively tempo, and a smile graced Imma's lips as she woke. "Is she gone?" She sat up and shook dead leaves from her hair. "Did Mother leave?"

"Why did you do that?"

"Because I'm not going to do what she wants just because she tells me to anymore. My whole life, she has controlled every move and every stitch of clothing on my body. I won't do it anymore. I'll be an adult in a few months; I'll take my conscription and go my own way. I'm tired of her ruling my life."

She would give up the time she'd already put into working her way out of her conscription for the chance to make her own choices. I almost laughed. My only want before being scrambled was to get out of conscription so that I had a say in what I did with my life.

She looked over the side of the building. "Her car is gone, but a few of her aides are still probably lurking." She wrapped her arms around her middle, squeezing tightly. "And it's a beautiful night. Someone once told me gardens were a good place to hide." Her eyes stayed on the Tower, but I didn't need to see her grin to know it was there. The wicked lilt spiked her words.

I hopped up on the wall so that the lights from the Tower and the other buildings would let her see me. "I never said that."

She shrugged and leaned on her elbows, resting her chin in her hand. "Maybe not, Gerald must have. He keeps me company while you do the things I'm not supposed to know about. He told me you hid in the ones in the Tower when you wanted to be left alone. Anyway, it worked. They came up here, but only looked around the edges of the gardens."

We sat in silence. The dark made signing difficult, and I didn't have a TalkBox with me. I reached out and motioned for her to follow me. She took my hand, and as I led her to the kitchen, she whispered, "You make me feel the comfortable kind of quiet. Like when you've found a story that speaks to you, and you're silent and still for so long that people start to worry you've died." We snuck in, and I sat on the counter. She jumped up next to me. "Will you talk to me?"

I shrugged. "I am."

"No, like you did earlier. I've heard you yell, but you spoke, and I understood you on the tram. Talk to me."

I shook my head; my hair slapped me in the face. "I sound stupid."

"But you're not, and I know it."

I sighed, staring upward. "Don't laugh."

"Never." She took my hand back in hers and squeezed.

I couldn't look at her.

My mother's huge table came to my mind. She set me a seat every night for more than a decade, to keep me in her heart. Marta's warning before she left me that first day echoed in my ears. My heart had taken Imma's shape. I tried to say, "Marta says your first love changes the shape of your heart, and it hurts." What came out sounded like a foreign language, one I didn't speak. Like my mother said, the sounds in my head didn't come out like I knew they should. I put her hand over my chest and covered it with mine for a moment. She smiled, even though she didn't understand the mush of sound I made. "I feel it whenever you're around." I clapped my hand over my mouth. I had to stop any more from spilling out. Words and feelings pressed in my throat, my tongue, and even the front of my skull. So much to say and no way to say it all. I almost wished for the implant to work again. When it worked, I didn't feel the constant pressure of the words.

"Arlo, don't be ashamed. I liked it." Her cheeks flushed.

I cupped her cheek in my hand, ran my thumb over her lips, "Un-ah dis," and dove in before she could protest. Her kiss was warm and soft. Neither of us knew what we were doing, but the connection stole my breath away. She pulled away after what felt like only a moment and a lifetime all at once.

My stomach rumbled, hungry for a dinner I'd missed. Imma looked between us. I took a much-needed breath; she stifled a giggle. "I didn't have a chance to eat much before we left the Outer Rim, and I don't think you ate anything. Do you want to eat?"

"Do you like eggs?"

She smiled, "I do, but I don't know how to cook them."

"I do...I think."

A searing pain flashed my brain and doubled me over.

I stood on the seat of a chair with a wooden spoon and stirred golden eggs in a hot pan with Mama pressed to my back, her hand over mine, humming in my ear. The egg sloshed over the sides and onto the stovetop, but she never scolded me. She kissed my temple and kept humming.

"Arlo," Imma patted my face, "come back to me." She cradled my upper body in her arms and somehow kept us both from falling off the counter.

My hands shook, "Always."

"Always?"

"Come back to you."

She smiled, her lip trembled. "That's just the implant talking. You don't mean that."

I tipped her chin up. "It doesn't speak for me anymore."

A grunt of laughter tickled my skin. Every whisper and murmur from her affected me. I slid to the floor and gathered tools and ingredients. She kept her place on the counter and watched me crack and whisk eggs. "Do they teach you to cook in the Tower?"

I shook my head and put down my tools. "Mama taught me."

Her lips tightened, and she looked away. "So, you understand what I told you about my cake and my tree?"

I nodded and tipped the bowl of yellow goo into a waiting pan. They scorched the moment they hit the heat. Steam and smoke rose in a sulfurous haze. I scowled at her giggles and started over in a fresh pan. The second set of eggs hit the pan with less fanfare. She put a steaming bite into her mouth and fed me bites while I cooked a second serving.

Dishes washed and bellies full, I flipped the dishtowel over my shoulder. She lost herself in the deep well of her mind, staring at something I would never see. I was afraid she'd fall off the counter she perched on. The snap of the towel against her silk-clad knee drew a startled squeak, and I grinned, thoroughly proud of myself. The kitchen clock read three in the morning. "We should get some sleep. We have to be up for breakfast in just a few hours."

"I don't want to." She took my hand and pulled me to stand between her legs and rested her head on my chest. "I don't know how much longer she'll let me stay before she decides I'm incompetent and locks me away in her campaign office again. I don't want to waste it."

She moved torturously slow, one fraction of an inch at a time until our lips touched.

I froze, thinking of the rally, but this was different. The soft tips of her fingers traced along the veins on the underside of my wrist. My skin rippled with goosebumps. I wanted to stay locked in that perfect moment and fell headfirst into kissing her instead of standing still and hoping I'd disappear. She sat tall to press one more soft kiss at each corner of my mouth before resting her forehead against me with a feathery sigh.

She enveloped me, pulled her sweater around us, kept us warm, and rested her head against me. "Close your eyes," she stroked my neck, clutching me with a loving hug. I danced my hand over her hair, holding her to never let go. No amount of words or signs could explain the whirlwind in my skull.

I pulled away so she could read my sign, "Talk to me; my brain is loud." She chuckled, her voice groggy and slow as she started to doze. I pinched her side, made her squeal. Her happy sounds broke through the storm.

She yawned, sleepiness slowed her words. "Someday, I'm going to leave Eidolon. No more names to live up to, no more expectations. Just me, living my life."

I pulled her body closer to mine and tapped her nose so she'd open her eyes. "What about me? Where will I be?"

She chuckled. "You can come, too. Be alone in your garden while I solve the mysteries of the universe. Just us." She let out a happy sigh, and her words petered off to a mumble. I kissed the top of her head, settled into her embrace, and let her slow even breathing lull me into the abyss.

Chapter 19

Everything changed after meeting my family. Something in me came out of that last long battle with the failing implants different than it went in. I could feel it inside of me but didn't know what it was.

At breakfast, Imma pulled her chair next to mine and sat. Her warmth pressed in on my thigh. I threw my arm around her shoulders and dragged her in closer. I wanted her in my lap, her lips on mine, her arms wrapped around me. I wanted everyone else in the dining room to know that she belonged to me. I belonged to her. I needed everyone to know that.

Rae raised an eyebrow and sat across the table from us. "You two look chummy again all of a sudden. I'm glad you two finally got your acts together and stopped ignoring one another and throwing tantrums like children." She winked at me. "It's nice to have the group all back at one table."

Her teasing hit a nerve. I pulled Imma closer and dropped my fork on my plate. It wasn't my fault that Imma shut me out. She did it because of her mother, not because I did anything wrong.

Imma squirmed. Her hand rested on mine that sat on her shoulder. "That hurts." I heard the pain in her voice, the way she clenched her jaw and the desperate squeal below the surface of her words, but my hand didn't react. "Arlo, let go. You're hurting me!"

Rae rushed us. She pried my hand open and pushed me away from Imma. My chair screeched against the floor, and my feet stumbled. I didn't mean it. My breath sawed up and down my throat. Rae inspected the bruised skin on Imma's shoulder, but Imma pushed her away and followed my retreat. "It's okay, Arlo. It was an accident. I know you'd never hurt me on purpose."

"It's not an accident when he doesn't let go on his own, Imm," Rae said. "That's a choice."

Imma smiled and held her hand out to me. "Rae, you don't know what he's going through. I said it's fine." She stepped forward. I pushed back. Something was wrong, and until I knew what it was, I couldn't be trusted. "Arlo, look at me." I forced my eyes up, and they got caught in hers. "Are you all right?"

My hand shook. I pulled the collar of her shirt aside to see the deep bruises forming across her shoulder and upper arm. "I don't know why I did that." A tiny whimper leaked out of my throat. "I'm sorry. She teased me, and I got angry, but I didn't mean to hurt you."

Rae watched us, ready to pounce in if I made a wrong move. Imma pulled my attention back to herself. "You know she was teasing me, right? I was the one throwing a tantrum like a spoiled child. She made sure to tell me that at every meal the past few weeks." Her eyes filled with tears, and I wanted to comfort her. My fear held me in my seat, though. I'd hurt her once; I could do it again. "This isn't like when you were little. I know those memories feel like they just happened now that they're free, but they're old. No one here wants anything bad to happen to you. No one here would call Retainment on you. We're your friends."

A knife twisted in my gut. She could see what was happening in my head before I did. I took Rae's teasing as a sign to get ready for a fight. I'd been ready to protect Imma the way I'd protected my brother from the kids on my parents' street when I was five.

Her hand wrapped around mine. "Come on." She tugged me to my feet. "I think you need to tell Laurel what happened yesterday.

Or I could sign you out, and we could go back to the Tower and tell Marta."

I stopped. "No. Marta will worry. She might send people to the house to make sure they won't say anything. You saw how nervous Mama was when we showed up. Laurel will call Marta."

"Seb, then? Arlo, we have to tell someone."

I agreed to her dragging me to Seb though I didn't want anyone knowing how far Imma had forced herself into the situation I was supposed to keep her out of. Seb was unlocking the lab door. He opened it for us and ushered us in ahead of himself. "Shouldn't you two be in class?"

Imma looked at me, but I could hardly move. Everything in me felt cemented in place. She threw her arms around me. "You have to tell him part of it, but I'll get started, okay?" I nodded, and she kissed my cheek. She took a deep breath and started signing. "Something happened yesterday, and I should have come straight to you or Laurel afterward, but I didn't. It seemed like everything had worked itself out at the time, but now I'm not so sure."

Seb waved low, but I couldn't pull eyes off of a crack in the flooring. "Did something happen at the Tower? Do I need to look through the security footage?"

"I took Arlo home."

Seb's hands dropped to his lap. His eyes blinked rapidly.

"I…I thought if he could see where he came from…" Her voice petered out under his dark glare.

He moved his chair forward and waved again. "Arlo. Look at me."

"He collapsed, and his face turned red. I think the implant in his head scrambled when he saw them."

Seb froze; his eyes locked on her. "You know about the implant?"

She smiled, but it looked like it hurt her to do. "Thank you for not playing stupid with me. And yes. I know about them. He doesn't have one; he has five. I think all of them have scrambled but one. He had an outburst this morning in the dining room, and I'm worried. He wouldn't agree to tell anyone but you."

A bomb went off inside my head, and anger billowed through me. "Rae was being a—"

Imma pushed my hands down before I could finish. "She doesn't understand, Arlo. She was being protective of me, just like you were."

The anger grew and had no boundaries. It wanted to hurt everyone who had hurt me. Even her. "How can she not understand? You had them all looking at my records without telling me. How can they not all know what is happening to me? Everyone knows but me!"

"Because I was very careful." She kept her voice cool and calm. She refused to buckle under the weight of the emotion that threatened to crush me. "I blacked things out or cropped them before I let the other interns read them so that they couldn't see names. When I couldn't do that, I just had them running searches and then narrowing them down. Jack was the only one who caught on. I don't think the others had any clue what they were really looking at. Those files read like technical manuals. If you don't know what you're looking at, you don't get much from them. We were in my mother's private archives, Arlo, I couldn't very well let them loose. We'd all be in even more danger than we are now."

Seb stood. "Go back to your classes, Imma, and don't mention anything to anyone. If the others ask about him, just tell them he had a rough visit to the Tower and needed some counseling."

She stepped away, but I grabbed her. "Don't leave."

She hugged me tight. "It will look bad if I don't go. I need to make all of them feel like everything is fine. You stay here and calm down. We'll figure it all out. You trust me, right?"

I nodded but held her in. If I let her go, I wasn't sure I could keep myself in check.

Seb's hand rested on my shoulder. "Let her go. We need to talk."

⊏⊐

IMMA LEFT me stuck toggling between emptiness and anger, with no clue how to break the cycle. Seb walked across the room to something covered in a thick blanket. "Imma had me bring this down here a few days ago. I kept waiting for you to notice and ask about it, but you were pretty withdrawn. Maybe this will help you think." He pulled away the blanket. The piano that I played for Imma and Gage hummed, and I ran for it. I needed it. It didn't matter that it was out of tune or that the pedals didn't work. With the hum in my chest, everything else felt tolerable.

Seb left me alone with the music until I stopped on my own. Tears ran down my face and splashed across the keys. His hand rested between my shoulder blades, and his face turned drawn and weary. He sat beside me on the bench. "Do you want to tell me what happened?"

"No." I skipped my fingers up the keys and back down. "Why is this here?"

"Imma came to me last week and asked me to have it moved here. She said you looked so alone and you deserved an old friend by your side. At the time, I told her off. I told her that you wouldn't look so lonely if your friend hadn't deserted you. She said, 'It has to be this way. My mother knows Arlo. She made Arlo, and when Laurel refused to send him back after she caught us at the house, she made me promise to stay away. Arlo deserves the chance to learn and be among people who understand him more than he needs me.' I think her mother made some threats that scared her. She was protecting you. Now, tell me what happened this morning."

"Rae made a joke, and I got scared and angry. I couldn't control it. I hurt Imma."

"But it was an accident?"

"I would never hurt her! Why couldn't I let go?"

"Marta said that you and your ward mates were implanted with extra impulse control so that you didn't need as much adult supervision. Maybe what went out yesterday was that one. You're running on your own brainpower now. You're going to have to be careful and think about your reactions."

I slammed the cover over the keys. "I always have to be careful! That's all anyone says to me anymore. What was the point of getting me out of the Tower if I'm always going to have to look over my shoulder?"

"The point was, and still is, that you are free to make your own choices as much as anyone else in Eidolon can." He looked tired again. "But that's the real problem. None of us has much say. Our lives are planned out for us. Freeing you is important because if we can free you, then maybe we can free the rest of us. If you want any part in that, you're going to have to learn some self-control."

It took me a moment to understand what he was saying and why he wasn't being plain. He offered to let me help with the Resistance, to let me see inside the warehouse Jack took me to. "You said I couldn't," I knocked on my temple, "remember?"

"I said you weren't ready yet, and you're not, but that doesn't mean you won't ever be. Prove to me that you can be trusted. Now, sit down. I have equipment to get ready. We have work to do."

He brought out all of his recording equipment, and I knew what he wanted to work on. I already felt myself tipping off the ledge of sanity.

He adjusted the levels and waved me over. "I figured out a way to change the algorithm. It will choose the sounds it needs and layer them with the stock voice." I hadn't moved. "Will you help me test it? You could help others like you who don't have normal speech sounds."

"Fine."

"One condition. You have to keep your cool. Any outbursts and we stop. We call Laurel and Marta and let them decide what the next move is. Prove that you're better than a little bundle of burnt-out wires."

I wanted it to be easy. I wanted to be better than my implant, but every sound from my mouth, every dip, and rise of Seb's instruments grated me to shreds. When I was ready to scream, Seb pointed to the side of his head. "I can't hear you. I sound just as bad when I try. No shame." He pushed a piece of paper toward me and a pair of headphones. "The headphones will block the sound. It will make it easier. Read the words on the page."

The world inside the headphones was so peaceful. I read the

words on the page, and he watched my mouth. I could remember sitting in the back of the classroom on the 47th listening to the others read aloud when we were little. I didn't remember a time when I couldn't read, but I remembered the instructors whispering with Marta about me. They didn't know how to test me. They grouped me in with the slower readers until I could prove to them that I understood everything they put in front of me.

Movement in the room pulled my attention up from the paper Seb gave me. Jack stood in the doorway, face blank and eyes wide. The headphones fell, and Seb followed my glare.

Jack swallowed. "I figured you had a stutter or an emotional thing that kept you quiet. I expected just about anything but that."

Seb blocked my view. "Prove it to me." He smiled at Jack. "What do you need?"

I swallowed back the fight in me, but it refused to go down.

"Arlo's teacher asked if I would find him when he didn't show up for his class." He grinned. "Why didn't you tell anyone that you had a secret weapon hiding out here with us?"

"This isn't a good time. Go back to class. I'll send Arlo's teacher a message right now."

"He could be the best thing to happen to the Resistance since we first got the wards to come in and talk! Arlo is a bona fide case of how far Services can miss the mark. People will eat his story up like candy!"

I stepped around Seb. "You want me to talk at one of your rallies?"

"No," Seb said, "Jack doesn't know what he's asking."

"Don't you see? They'd love you!"

I took a marker off of the writing board on the wall and pulled the piece of paper close. Jack hung over my shoulder while I drew. A scratchy and smudged little Arlo took shape with a sign held over his head. "Can you hear me in the back?" his sign read.

Jack laughed. "Yeah, but you'd have your TalkBox, or someone could interpret for you. It would be great."

"So I could be the laughing stock of the whole territory? No, thanks." I shoved the picture at him, crushed it against his chest, and pushed past. Seb caught my arm, but I yanked out of reach. "I don't have to prove it. I don't want it! I don't want anyone to hear that or to look at me! Find someone else to help people."

I ran for my room but got sidetracked by a large group of small kids crowded in one corner of the yard. Gage stood at the center. He held one of his classmates up against a wall by his neck. He saw me, and a big smile spread across his little red face. He turned back to his victim and slammed him up against the bricks. I wanted to keep running until I got to my room, but I couldn't let him hurt someone the way that I hurt Imma.

I pushed Gage aside. The crowd of spectators looked up at me like I was a monster. "Get out of here and take him with you!" They scrambled. Gage wiped his face and beamed up at me, oozing pride. I wanted to shake the kid. We made so much progress with his temper, and he threw it all away." What are you smiling about?"

His pride fell away, and confusion took its place. "He was messing with me, called me stupid. I'm not stupid! Not my fault I started later than him!"

"So, you held him up against a wall? Like a bully? Like him?"

He shoved me like he hadn't since the first day we met. "Like you!"

Like me? I would never do that unless…unless Jack caught me at a bad moment. I took a step back. "Stay away from me. Play with kids your own age. I'm bad for you. Bad for everyone."

"No," he grabbed my shirt, "we're friends. We're the same. Don't leave me!"

I pulled away. "Don't say that. We're not the same. You don't want to be the same as me." I shook him off, and he lost his balance. He fell to the pavement and yelped. "Don't follow me. Stay away!" I ran. I left him on the playground with a scraped elbow and tears running down his face.

I hid the rest of the day with my back against the door. If I didn't see anyone, I couldn't get into trouble.

Chapter 20

The daylight was fading before anyone came looking for me. The door rumbled behind my back. "Arlo? Are you in there?" Imma asked.

My knuckles rapped on the slab. It hummed as she slid down, back to back with me, and a soft wave of her perfume plumed up from the space underneath. Her fingers bumped into the back of my hand like she knew just where I would be without seeing me.

"Everyone missed you today," she said. "Gage was beside himself. Laurel had to put him in a classroom alone. He couldn't calm himself down and kept trying to barge up here to find you. Jack doesn't understand what he did, but he knows that he set you off." I turned my hand so that my finders could slot between hers. "Let me in, Arlo."

My throat hurt after reading to Seb and using my neglected vocal cords. My voice rattled. "No."

Her fingers twitched and clamped down on mine. "Why?"

She knew I didn't have any more words to answer her with. I'd have to open the door to talk to her. Whatever was wrong with me, the times I was with her were worse than when I was with Seb, Jack, or Gage. With no one to stop me, I didn't want her near me.

"Are you afraid?" Her whisper seeped through the door and into my chest. "You don't want to risk a repeat of what happened at breakfast to happen while we're alone?"

I squeezed her fingers.

"Arlo, I trust you. I know you won't hurt me. I'm not some precious little flower. I'm not going to die from a few bruises. Please. Let me help you." I wanted all the good things I felt before I self-destructed that morning. Losing the connection between our fingertips made my chest ache. I knew that I would get more within moments, but I still had to brace myself. The lock slid open, and she flew into my arms.

I held her close until her spine let out a few loud cracks, and I dropped my hold, hands up, and shaking. I did it again! I kept hurting her!

She closed the door and stepped in. "It's okay," she said, "That felt good." She held her hand out to me, but I stepped back. She followed. "Gage said you told him to stay away from you. Are you going to keep me away, too?"

"I'm bad for him. He shouldn't watch me." My chest heaved, and I chomped down on my cheek to hold the tears in. "I can't keep doing this."

"Doing what?" she asked.

"Hurting people, running away. I can't wait until my birthday. I can't stay here."

She wiped the traitor tear that ran down my face with her thumb. "Where would you go? Nowhere in Eidolon is safe for you."

She stumbled back, and it took me a moment to realize that I'd pushed her. "I'm not safe! You're not safe with me! Your mother broke me. You found enough information to find my family, and Mama found some of the other families. Isn't that enough to stop her? I don't want to have to hide anymore. Do you understand that if things get worse, Laurel will have to send me back? They will lock me up Underground. My freedom depends on you. Why haven't you done anything yet?"

She sat on the edge of my bed and tucked her hands under her thighs. "Do you know what you're asking me to do? Fighting for your freedom means I might lose mine. I want my mother's trials shut down. I want you and the others free and allowed to live normal lives, but exposing her secrets won't come without consequences." I didn't want to hear her excuses, but she pushed my hands down when I went to argue. "She isn't working alone, Arlo. She didn't redact her own files on the public record. She has Services backing; she has to, or you would have been kept at Persaud BioMed, not the Tower. Going against her is going against Central Services itself."

She sat in the chair at the desk, and even though I was mad at her, I didn't like her sitting there like she did when she was a stranger. I wanted her close to me. "You aren't alone; you have help. You have Seb and Laurel. You have Marta and me. You have your family now. Things might have ended strangely the other night, but I have no doubt that your mother would fight to the end of the earth for you. If I take them on, I will be going against the people who have been my support system. I will have no one because everyone who loves me will go down because of you! So, yes, I'm dragging my feet! I'm terrified. I don't like my life or what I've learned about Eidolon since I met you, but I'm still not sure I can give up everything I know for a boy I met a few months ago!" She clapped a hand over her mouth and stared at me with wide, shocked eyes.

The silence sat between us, weighted and dense. I hadn't thought of any of that, only of myself.

"I shouldn't have said that. I'm sorry."

"Did you mean it?" The fact that she considered giving up everything for me even for a moment shocked me. The fact that I expected her to made me sick to my stomach.

"That I'm scared? Yes. I'm scared of losing you if I don't act and losing everything that is supposed to make up me if I do. If it was as easy as turning my mother in, calling Retainment on her and reporting her, I would do it in a heartbeat. Laurel and Seb would take me in until I turned eighteen, and it would be fine. But it's not that easy. They would bury me and any evidence I found the same way they will bury you if someone tells them you're not where you're supposed to be. I would be a traitor and nothing would happen to any of the people responsible for what happened to you and your family."

There was no way out. Every possible solution had consequences that I couldn't live with. "Hopeless."

She stood. Concern made her look older. "No, it's not hopeless, Arlo, but it needs to be handled delicately. We can't just go blundering in and hope for the best. We'll need help, and I'm still trying to sort out the people who have the kind of power we'd need who might be trustworthy. I'm trying my best, and I'm sorry you're struggling, but so am I."

"I'm sorry." I wrapped my arms around her, and she melted against me.

"I can't help anyone if they cart me off to one of my Father's prisons, and I refuse to leave you like that. You've had enough people taken from you. Please, just try to be patient."

She let me walk her to my bed without letting her go. We fell back against the pillow together, and she curled into my side. "You're doing it again, walling everything up inside of you. It's not good for you—for either of us. You let me ramble on about nothing to let it out. I want that for you. Talk to me."

I shifted, but she pushed back and made herself weigh more than she did.

"Tell me. Let it out." She looked up at me through her eyelashes. "They're all sitting there—all those hopes and dreams and fears— waiting for you to break. Tell them to me, so you don't."

I didn't want to, but I couldn't stop myself. I told her everything. I talked for hours until my throat felt full of sand, and the words fell apart before they fell off my tongue. She didn't understand any of it, but she reacted as if she did. She followed the tone and volume, the mood and intonation, and held me closer. She never laughed. My voice wore out as she ran her fingers through my hair. Her nails scraped against my scalp, and her lips rested against my neck.

"Sleep now," she whispered. "Everything will feel better in the morning."

I woke with my mouth pressed against the soft skin of her shoulder. Dawn wasn't far off, and her warm, clean smell tickled my nose. I pulled her closer and kissed everything I could reach.

She hummed in contentment. "S'early." Dark eyes opened and stared from under heavy lids. Her thick lashes fanned over her cheeks in slow flutters of morning recognition. Her smile affected me like a drug. I dove into kissing her and lost myself in the swirl of sensations. Her hands tangled in my hair and gripped. "Arlo, stop."

Her words said one thing, but the purr that came out urged me on. I chased a moan I could feel lying in wait just below her surface. Her tugging at my head directed me back up to her mouth, but I couldn't stop. Her hands pressed against my chest.

"Stop!"

With one final shove, she rammed her forehead into my lip, and I fell to the floor. My eyes and nose and mouth all wept together. Blood and tears pooled on the floor in front of me.

The door slammed, and her footsteps hurried away.

Bitter salt and iron burned in my throat. Rage shot through me like a geyser. I dragged myself onto my knees and rested my aching head on the edge of the mattress. Her perfume and her soap, her unique smell plumed out of my pillow. I hated that I wanted to bury my nose in it. I hated that it smelled like she was still there, and I hated that I didn't understand why she wasn't. I swung the pillow through the air; the hollow *thwap* landed on the mattress felt right. Over and over, I swung until I couldn't lift my arm, trying to dull the roar in my head to a more bearable volume.

Chapter 21

Dressed in my uniform, I stalked into the dining room with a fat lip and dried blood clinging to my nostrils just as the lights flashed to signal the end of the meal. Rae blocked the door. "No, you don't get to go in there. Not like that. I don't know what crawled up your butt and died, but we are not doing it this way. You need to go somewhere else and get your head straight before I let you anywhere near my friend."

Rae's short stature let me see over her head and into the dining room. Everyone had started cleaning up, but Imma sat at our table watching Rae, and I face off. Her face was bruised, and her eyes were red and puffy. "She's my friend, too!"

"Friends don't hurt one another. Friends don't do what you did to Imma today or yesterday. She said no, and you ignored her. Look at her face. Friends don't do that; abusers and criminals do. Is that what you are?"

In my head, I could see Seb telling me to prove that I was better than my implant, that I could be stronger than my impulses, but I wanted to shove Rae out of my way. I wanted to tear her apart for suggesting I was a criminal, but acting on that would prove her right.

Imma snuck out the back door with a last, teary look over her shoulder. Rae watched her go and turned back, looking smug. Her expression shifted to something uncertain. "You're my friend, too. I don't know what is going on with you the past few days, but something changed. The way you were before was good for her, but you can't be around her or any of us like this. You need help, Arlo."

I did. I needed help, but I didn't know what that help should look like. It wasn't like when I first arrived, and I needed as much exposure to Sign as I could get. I didn't know how to fix the hurricane inside of me.

Jack came over and stepped between Rae and I. "Let's go take a walk. Knowing Imma, Laurel already knows you're having a rough morning. She won't mind."

A walk wouldn't fix me.

Nothing could fix me.

Like the previous night, when Imma coaxed me into talking until I passed out hadn't made anything better.

I needed to get away.

"Arlo—" Jack's hand reached for my arm, and then he was on the floor with his hands over his face, and I had my hand clutched to my chest.

A whimper pulled my attention up from the ache in my wrist. Gage stood just behind Jack. Rae blocked him with her body, but she didn't need to. I ran. I didn't remember hitting him or even thinking about it. My heart drummed in my ears.

I wanted my mother, but Laurel was all I had.

Imma sat at a computer station outside Laurel's office. She saw me coming and stood. "Arlo?"

Too ashamed to face what I'd done to her, I plowed past and into Laurel's arms. Sobs replaced breaths. Once I started, I couldn't stop. She tried to push me back to see my face, but I wouldn't let her. "What's wrong? What happened?" She tensed in my grasp, and I knew I was hurting her. "Arlo, talk to me."

The words poured out of me, and even I didn't know what they meant.

She struggled and pushed. "Imma, call Seb. Tell him we need Marta."

"Arlo?" Imma called.

"Not now. Draw the blinds, close the door, and call Seb." Laurel patted and soothed my back. "It's just us now. Marta will be here soon. Can we sit?" She eased us down.

My knees hit the floor, and I let her go. The mumbled tirade stopped, and I crawled away to the corner farthest from her. "Help. Help me," I signed. "Put me Underground."

"Help is coming," she answered. "We're okay, Arlo. We're in this together." I wouldn't let her near enough to touch me while we waited, but she stayed as close as I would let her.

Marta arrived, and they whispered together. They snuck glances my way. The weight of their attention felt like it would crush me, and I wrapped my arms over the top of my head. I wanted to go back to being the nearly invisible glitch if it meant that no one whispered and stared anymore.

Marta knelt with a worried smile on her face. "You want to tell me what's going on?"

She wanted to help. She cared about me. Somewhere inside, I knew that, but looking at her, knowing what my mother and Imma told me about what was done to me, all I felt was anger. "Don't tell me what to do! You're not my mother!"

Laurel interpreted for me.

The hurt on Marta's face gave me a sick jolt of satisfaction. "Tell me what happened."

"I met my mother, and she's beautiful and plays the piano and wanted me. You kept me trapped when I had a family who never meant to send me to the Tower!"

Her hand poised over her pocket. I recognized the stance; she came armed with tranquilizer syrettes, ready to take me down if I didn't maintain control. She'd drop me like an animal. Her eyes darted to Laurel. "I warned you this could happen. I gave you explicit instructions. This is why we want them in a safe environment. They've never learned to deal with their own emotions. Arlo was never going to be one who could control his without help."

I could have used the syrettes on her and ran…but what then? Then I'd never see daylight again. Attacking a warden was a serious crime. I had to prove that I had some control. "Are we all stolen? Or was it just me?"

"Are we all—" Laurel interpreted, but stopped short, "–what do you mean stolen?"

Marta's freckles stuck out on her white face. "I can't promise much, but I will answer what I can." She turned to Laurel. "Do you have one of those talkie…walkie…." She churned the air in an attempt to dig the word out of hiding.

Laurel pulled a TalkBox from her desk and tucked it in my hand. "Use it to call Seb or me if you need us."

I didn't trust Marta or my own corrupted brain. The dictation function winked up at me, and I hit it. I wanted to be able to hear her explain it over and over. My fingers punched at the words on the screen, thumping the glass. "Tell me how to make it go away."

Her hand reached, but I moved away. "You just have to ride it out; it takes time." She threw herself into the nearest chair. "What do you want to know?"

"Everything."

She barked out a laugh so caustic my ears burned. "Everything would take days, and none of it will make either of us feel better."

"Everything."

Elbows on knees, head cradled in her hands, she gave in. Tears filled her eyes, but she turned away to wipe her cheeks. "I knew there was something wrong from the beginning, but more parental surrenders came in. Most didn't know their own names." Marta's sadness fell over me like a wet blanket, cold and smothering. "You were one of the last when they first brought you to me."

"What do you mean, first?"

Marta smiled, and her pride cooled the fire I'd been fighting for days. "You wouldn't break the way they wanted you to. It took five tries to get you to go more than a few weeks without disrupting your implant. They brought you up that last time, just a little shadow of yourself, and I knew I couldn't go anywhere. You needed someone on your side." She chuckled as I typed. "Such a chatterbox now."

The normalcy of her teasing let me breathe. I thought she would punish me for questioning her and her motives, but she took it in stride. "What happens after my birthday? Age out?"

Her brow furrowed, and she straightened things that didn't need straightening, avoiding eye contact. "He triggers the implants, puts them—you—through a series of challenges to put those emotions they never let you acclimate to into overdrive. The 'hope' is that with those emotions permanently disabled, you would be able to do your duty as a Retainment Officer with as much logic and reason as possible and little interference from emotion or morality. Those who fail but live end up as adult wards of the state below ground. Those who pass go into Retainment. I don't want that for you."

My heart clapped against my ribs like a flat tire, a deflated flap of rubber that slapped my ribcage with every beat. My brain scorched in my skull.

Laurel's voice broke through the dull buzz of my brain boiling itself. "Give her tonight to say goodbye! I know you think this has been a waste, but she made friends, Miriam! Don't make her leave without a word."

Marta and I both stood and moved to the window. Marta flipped one of the blinds up.

The Senator, in all her unsettling perfection, stood nose to nose with Laurel. She straightened her suit and smoothed her hair. "I warned you to send the boy back, Laurel. Imelda is done here; this little experiment that you and Dell came up with is over." She turned to Imma, her manicured brow raised, and her lips pursed. "Get packed. A car will wait outside. You have an hour, none of this hiding nonsense you tried last time. If you are not in that car on your way home in an hour, the consequences will be more than you are willing to sacrifice. Choose wisely." She swept out of the room.

"Yes, your majesty," Laurel signed at her step-mother's back, along with a few other choice obscenities.

Imma locked eyes with me, her grief and anger palpable. Our time was over. She curled her lips in a sad attempt at a smile. She didn't open the door, just put her hand on the glass. I slid mine under the blinds and matched my palm to hers.

"I won't sacrifice you. I choose you. Please be smart." Her lower lip trembled, and she went to pack.

Marta tugged at her uniform and jittered with nervous energy. "Dr. Persaud knows about you?"

I picked the TalkBox up off the floor. "She caught me weeks ago. Imma made a deal with her. She would let me stay as long as Imma stayed away. Imma couldn't do it anymore."

Her hands splayed on her cheeks. "I have to go and make sure that things are taken care of in case she decides to teach us all a lesson. You be careful. If we all make it through the next few days, I promise to tell you everything I can." She reached for the doorknob but stopped. "When you feel like you're going to blow, remember that they want you so overwhelmed that you stop feeling. They want your heart and mind so overloaded with feeling that it forces you to shut that part of you down in the name of survival. Don't give them what they want. It's okay to feel all of it. Your survival depends on you staying with every one of those feelings." She wrapped me up in her arms and squeezed and then ran out the door.

Chapter 22

I startled awake late that night. "You talk in your sleep now." Imma sat on my bed with her legs pulled up. She wrapped her sweater tails around them. "It's just me."

I turned the lamp on and rubbed the sleep from my eyes. Her short hair frizzed and stuck out oddly, and her skin glowed from how hard she scrubbed at tear tracks.

"What are you doing here? It's not safe, Marta said it just takes time. I don't want to hurt you like I did this morning."

She burrowed into my shoulder and clung to me. Her anger made my hair stand on end, but I let her hide. Impatience built in my gut.

Her thumb pressed over my lips, her index finger wrapped around my chin, and her eyes fixed on mine. "I think I handled the situation well." She ran her thumb over my split lip, with a cocky smirk.

I winced at the sting of her touch and the dusky bruise on her forehead. "I don't want you to have to handle me."

A smile spread her lips, but her voice was hoarse from arguing. "Father is going on campaign in the Territories at the end of the week. They've decided that I'm going to work as a staffer on his campaign so they can keep a closer eye on me." She pulled away, glaring down at my bedclothes.

"What do you want?" I grinned at her confusion. No one trusted her or asked her opinion; she did what was expected of her no matter how unhappy it made her.

"I want—I don't want to go!" She raised up on her knees, her face glowing with excitement as she shuffled around until she straddled my legs. "I want to stay with you, but I can't. I want books and computers and information and a thousand stories to tell. I want the whole world just as it is instead of Eidolon on a silver platter."

She had Eidolon on a silver platter, and she knew it while I just wanted to live–even if I could never leave Eidolon–with half of the freedom she took for granted. Rage and anger percolated in my head, but I had to keep it at bay. I couldn't risk another outburst. "Tell me."

"Tell you? Tell you what I would do if I could get out of here?"

I nodded.

She went still for a long time, and a slow smile spread across her face. "I think I would travel for a long time. I want to see everything I can. I would stop in as many of the territories as possible and stay for a while, a few months, maybe a year, and really try to learn what each of them is all about. Then I would move on to the next. Once I had my fill, I think I would come back here and use what I found to try to fix this. How can anyone know or learn or do anything when all we know is each other and the way things always have been. There has to be other ways of doing things, doesn't there?"

I didn't have an answer for her.

She cuddled in again. "What would you do?"

I knew exactly what I would do. "Live. Get a violin and a piano. Grow plants. Have a home. Belong somewhere."

Her confusion and protest danced across her face. "But you could…" Her face fell. "You can't do any of that now, can you? I keep forgetting."

I wondered what it would be like to forget that people like me might have the basics for existing covered but that we had to trade what made living exciting for those necessities.

"What if you could come with me, instead? We could get a violin–it would travel well–and go see the world. Once we find a place that feels like home, you could have your garden and your music. We could have a house, and we would belong to each other."

Belong to each other.

I'd always wanted to belong somewhere and to someone. When I was little and still lived with my family, I could remember watching them all play together and sing. I knew I was different. I heard how their words sounded different and saw the pain on my mother's face when she couldn't understand me. At the Tower, Marta and Rat made sure I was included, but I never belonged. It bothered me, but the implant kept me from wondering about it too much. Even at the Embassy School, I was older than most of the students, and they knew I had my own classes that I did away from them. I wasn't a student or an intern. I just wanted to feel like I was the same as someone–anyone– else.

"Would you go with me, Arlo? Would you come on an adventure with me and stay by my side forever?"

I would. Her smile turned warm and wide, and I kissed it.

She giggled before her body turned rigid and her face soured. "She'd hunt me down. Mother would never let that happen. It would hurt her precious image. Wouldn't that be wonderful?" Her eyes glowed and met mine. She lunged, capturing my mouth in a frantic, hungry kiss.

I wanted nothing more than to let her continue her assault, but pushed her away, held her back when she fought and waited until she stilled. I stared at her soft, manicured hands. "Don't use me to hurt her."

Her behind dropped onto my legs. "Don't you know you're more than just some ploy to make my mother mad?" She looked up. "I would never use you." A smirk twitched at the corner of her mouth, "But it would be fabulous if our happiness also made her squirm... just a little."

I smiled, pulled her down to me, and leaned my forehead against hers. Anything that made Miriam Persaud squirm would end badly for me, but Imma couldn't see it. I held her, that hunger simmering below the surface. Marta's words rang in my ears. Maybe I couldn't control myself for me, but I could do it to spite Dr. Persaud and Commander Escher and anyone else who had a hand in Project Livewire.

"She controls everything she can," Her voice turned to a growl. "She'll never let me go. I wish I could be someone else. Someone who was free. I'd go out there, and I'd start all over." Her eyes grew owlish. She pulled away from me and wrapped her sweater around her again. "That must sound terrible to you. I am—or I should be—one of the freest people in the territory, and you are one of the most shackled. But here I am whining about how I want freedom. I'm sorry I'm so awful sometimes."

She was a bird in a beautiful cage and had a luxurious looking life. The anger in me wanted to agree with her. It wanted to put a stop to her whining because she didn't know anything about what being imprisoned looked like. That didn't make her any less of a prisoner. "Not awful."

"Elections are just after my birthday." I'd prove Marta wrong. I refused to end up underground, or as one of Retainment's Goon Squad. I made it through the disruptions; I had to make it through the after-effects. "Promise you won't go without me."

She nodded. "I can make it for a few months. We can make it a few more months."

I nodded and wrapped around her for a long, languid kiss that threatened to send me out of control. Her lips were so inviting, her body so warm. "You need to go back home; I don't want to wake up to you headbutting me again." I rubbed my aching nose.

She kissed it and tucked in closer, grabbing fistfuls of my shirt. "You asked me what I want. I want my last memory of this place to be waking up in your arms. Happy one last time."

I chuckled at her melodramatics. "I'm not safe for you now, but by the time you come back, I will be."

"Just sleep. Please, Arlo? One last time?" She put her head on my pillow, her eyes locked on me, begged me to give in.

I sighed and wrapped around her from behind. The soft skin behind her ear begged to be kissed, and I chanced it.

Her fingers raked through my hair. "Sleep."

Chapter 23

I checked out a TalkBox from Laurel, and Seb pasted on a set of Jonah's fingerprints. I took comfort in knowing they were my older brother's and that he wanted me to have them.

Once we were outside, Rat started looking over his shoulder. Every patrol officer and warden he saw made him jump. He kept up a constant stream of nervous chatter. "See? We could do this again." My disinterest in answering him seemed to bolster his confidence. "Everything could be good again once you come back home, and things go back to normal."

I didn't have the energy to argue.

"Once all of this blows over, you'll see, Arlo.

Life will be good. Like it used to be."

We entered in the open maw of Central Processing and wound through the maze of stanchions. "Next!" the warden called.

I took a step toward them, but Rat held me back. "I'll go first and say your name for you."

He couldn't check me in under my own name. I'd never checked out. I pulled out of his grip and shook my head. He watched while I went through on my own and gat called a name he didn't know. I didn't wait for him and stepped into the supply closet to change as he entered the Public Garden.

He glared at me. "What are you playing at? You've got TowerCloth stashed in the gardener's shed, and they called you a new name!" His cheeks flushed. I knew his mind was hovering around the truth like mine used to. He rubbed his ear against his shoulder like there was a fly buzzing in it.

"Education release. Things are different now," the TalkBox answered blandly. He followed me to the Tube, the same compartment we rode together the day of the rally.

Locked in a box with him, I understood why Rae brought pepper spray to walk me down a hall. The air around him crackled. "They've really done a number on you, haven't they? They got all the way into your head. You think you're something different now, but you're not. You're just Tower trash, like me and Marta and Beryl and all the rest. You always will be, too. You're not one of them; you're one of us."

I started typing. I knew I shouldn't do it, but the anger took over. "I was never one of you. There is no us. We are just misfits. The only thing we have in common is what was done to us. They took us, stuffed our heads full of circuitry, and now they're going to set us off. They want soldiers, mindless goons. I'm not a mindless goon."

His skin flushed deeper, and sweat beaded on his upper lip. "What the hell are you talking about? Who stuffed us full of circuits?"

"Escher and Persaud BioMed put implants in everyone on the 47th. They want to scramble us and set us loose on anyone who tries to get past the borders."

Rat scowled, but his skin turned gray, and instead of a quick quip, he stammered. "Bull. I ain't no lab rat! Those dummies in the Resistance put you up to it. Or was it Imma, using you to make mommy mad?" His narrow frame shook, and his hand gripped at his neck. He slumped to the floor.

Just knowing the truth could blow any of them at any moment. I held power and watched him writhe, not just in pain as the circuitry flared, but from the knowledge I lived with. Our lives, past, present, and future didn't belong to us. I knelt and dug my fingertips into the meager flesh of Rat's boney spine until he stilled and took a full breath. He panted and rested his cheek on the polished concrete.

"It's bullshit. I'm not an experiment."

Marta rushed forward. "Arlo—you didn't—"

Rat stumbled to his feet. His words slurred and lagged. "You're a liar, and you can just stay gone." He ran, footfalls echoing.

Smudges welled under Marta's eyes, and the spark of humor was missing. She closed her eyes, wrapped her arms around her waist. "You were supposed to be aged out before you knew about any of this. You are—" she smiled and rubbed her forehead, "and always have been, an anomaly. We have to make it a few more months of you being the lit candle sitting on top of a stack of firecrackers. We're going to have to lay a few more ground rules. Ones that we come up with together to keep everyone safe."

I pulled the TalkBox out of my pocket. "What am I supposed to do? Hide from everyone? I'm different, even if you aren't!"

She said, "It has to be the same here, even if you're not. If you disrupt the system, they will find an excuse to send you to Juvenile Confinement until your birthday and then Mental Health. I don't want that for you."

Boots stamped up the hall toward us, and my stomach heaved. Men in green uniforms blocked the hall on either side of us. Guinn to my left and another nameless man on my right. Marta stood at attention in a way that moved her body in front of mine. "Back to the wall." She spoke so quietly, it was just a mumble. "Sirs, Sergeant Wofsy, Ward D leader. How can I help you?"

Guinn stood toe to toe with her without sparing me a single glance. "An anonymous report has been placed concerning you and your ward. The report states that one of your wards may have been absent without a pass for an extended period of time. The commander would like to speak with you."

She smiled. "Been a long time, Teddy."

For a split second, I thought I saw his neck turn red; the flush was gone instantly. "Don't make this worse for yourself, Sergeant. Commander Escher is waiting."

"By all means, lead the way, Captain. I'd be only too happy to answer any questions he has."

He held up restraint ties. "Downstairs, Wofsy."

A pathetic bleat rushed out of my mouth. I grabbed her hand, afraid that If I let her go, she'd be gone for good. She squeezed back and caught my eye over her shoulder. "I'll be okay; go with your friend. Be good, Kid. Remember what we talked about; try not to light up any fireworks, okay?"

I bit my lip to keep it from trembling and pushed a traitorous tear away with my shoulder. Guinn restrained her, placed her between himself and his partner, and gave me a sidelong sneer. "As you were, Resident."

I stared, frozen. If Escher knew someone was missing, he had to know it was me, but Guinn made no move to detain me. "I said beat it, Kid."

I walked away as calmly as I could. Her words about doing everything in spite of them helped. I couldn't be what they wanted. Jack waited around the first corner with a chalky face that made the black eye I'd given in him the day before stand out.

We stayed quiet until we were safely closed in the Tube. "What did you hear?" I asked.

"Everything. I was on the Tube right after yours. Rae was worried you'd lose it again and take the other kid out. Was that bull, like he said? Or do you actually believe that you are being held here as an unwilling lab subject?"

An ad for Persaud Biomed blinked onto the wall screens, and it took everything I had not to punch one of them.

Rae stared at the ad. "Better life through biomedical implantation. That's why your pass isn't real; they can't let you out. You're an asset."

I nodded.

His eyes locked on the ad screen, and his head nodded, but he couldn't bring himself to say anything. His head rocked on his neck until I wanted to knock it off so it would stop moving. I crossed my arms and tucked my hands under my elbows to keep them from doing anything stupid. I couldn't afford to come unhinged again. Not while I was inside the Tower. He took a deep breath, let it out, and his eyes came back into focus. "We need to get back to the Embassy. Laurel will hide you."

The wall thumped against my back, a slow, deep cadence that soothed the fire running through my veins. "I've been hiding the whole time you've known me. Services doesn't let science experiments out on education leave." A deep ache settled under my sternum. "They just arrested my warden in front of me. Imma's mother knew what I was and where I was. They will go to the Embassy next, and I can't be there."

The door opened, but he didn't exit. "We can't just wander the streets, Arlo!"

We couldn't. Patrol would question us if they caught us loitering. We needed somewhere safe to go. Somewhere Retainment and Commander Escher and Senator Persaud wouldn't think to look for me. I caught the door as it closed and held it open. "I know a place we can go, but it's a long tram ride."

▭

OUTSIDE THE TOWER, we boarded a tram and used the emergency fare card Laurel gave me.

Jack dropped in the seat next to me. "Where is this place?"

I pulled my knees up. "Outer Rim. My family will hide me. If I have to, I can run for the Frontier."

"You're a ward. I thought that meant you didn't have a family."

"They took me away when I was five like they took your brother. They just wanted help with me, and Services took me away. Imma found them." I rested my head against my knees and wrapped my arms around them.

We stayed silent, but my brain was loud. My time out of the Tower was over, but I still had so much I wanted to do. I promised myself I would help Gage. What would happen to him once I disappeared into the Underground or out onto the Frontier? He needed me.

I tapped Jack. "Will you do something for me if I don't get back to school?"

"Sure," he said. No arguments, no teasing, so bravado. The stakes had sunk in. He knew he was riding the tram with someone who wouldn't exist anymore soon.

"Talk Laurel into letting Gage see his family."

He snorted. "You might never see daylight again, and you're worried about a little kid seeing his mom?"

The rage flared, but I tamped it back down. He didn't have to understand, he just had to listen, and as long as he listened, I could stay calm. "He deserves to know what happened to him, for better or worse. He didn't understand what was happening when they took him, and he acts out so that Laurel will get fed up and send him back. He needs to know—"

Jack cut me off, pushed my hands down. "You're not the same as him, Arlo. It wasn't the same. I know you two bonded over being new and messed up at the same time, but what he went through before they removed him isn't something he should understand. He doesn't need a chance to go back now that someone can explain it and see that the losers who gave him up didn't care enough to even notice that he couldn't hear. I won't promise to put him through that."

My heart sank down through the tram seat. It fell so low that I was sure it was bumping along the road under the tram floor. I couldn't make any of it better for anyone. "Promise you'll look out for him, even after you finish your internship."

"That kid doesn't know me from any other stranger off the street."

"He knows you." I grinned. Gage knew him as my enemy. "He might try to punch you at first, though. He can hold a grudge."

"I seem to be getting that a lot lately." He took a deep breath and blew it out. His eyes searched me, and I turned away from the scrutiny. "Is that what you did when they took you? You acted out so they might get fed up with you and send you back?"

I braced myself for the burn and the pain, but it didn't come. I remembered arms wrapping around my body and pinning my arms to my sides. "Shhhhhhh," a kind voice said in my ear. She pulled my back to her body and sat on the floor. "It's all right, Little Rebel, you're safe with me." Her voice was soft, quiet, and low. Something about her warm arms, her calm heartbeat thumping steadily just behind my racing one, and that soft voice in my ear quieted all the fight in me. I crumpled back against her. Hot tears welled up in my eyes and began spilling down my cheeks before I could stop them, and the heavy, wracking sobs followed. I hid my face in her shoulder and cried. I cried because my parents gave up on me, because I was so angry, because I was lonely and hungry and tired. She smoothed my hair back and rocked me gently, never loosening her grip on me. "There now," she said when I was calm, craning her neck to get a better look at my face. Her smile was wide and bright, and her hazel eyes sparkled.

I cleared the tears out of my grown throat and wiped my streaming eyes on my shirt. "Maybe."

The tram driver interrupted us, calling, "Last stop."

Jack and I shuffled off the tram and walked through the streets at the Outer Rim. Suddenly, I feared that I wouldn't remember which house it was. They all looked the same, but Jack stopped in the street. "That's a little creepy." He pointed, and I laughed. My brothers and sisters were out in the street playing like they were when Imma and I arrived. "It's like half a dozen tiny Arlo's. How many are there?"

"So many that they had to get rid of one." I felt bad as soon as my hands stopped moving. I knew it wasn't true. They wanted me. They looked for me.

"But you said–"

I waved him off. "Nevermind." I knocked on my temple. "Scrambled eggs, remember? I can't keep it straight sometimes." They played, and I thought about how they swarmed around Mama when she noticed us watching from inside the house. If I got any closer, she would protect me. She felt so bad about what happened to me that I knew she would, but I didn't want her to anymore. "Let's go. This is a bad idea."

"But we just got here," he said. "I thought you were going to hide out. I can come back tomorrow and let you know if the coast is clear. If it's not, you can try to get out onto the Frontier. Maybe one of the Farms will take you in until you can get to the border."

"They already watched once while I was dragged out by Retainment in the middle of the night. Even the ones who weren't alive yet are affected by that night. Hiding with them is asking Retainment to come back and do it again."

"How would Retainment even know you're here? They don't know you remember."

A weight settled on my shoulders. "They have Marta. As soon as she tells them that my implant is deactivated, they will go to the Embassy, then they will come here."

"Why would Marta rat you out after she worked so hard to help you stay with us at the embassy?"

"She won't have a choice. They will make her tell." I didn't know how I knew that, but it made my chest ache and my stomach flip.

Little voices called my name. Lulu and Graham had seen us and broken away from the others.

I stepped back and turned. "We need to go. Now."

He followed me the few blocks to the tram stop. When another tram wasn't visible, we started walking for the next. I needed to put space between myself and my siblings. I had to keep them safe like I knew they would do for me this time.

Chapter 24

I woke alone in my room with her scent on my pillow. This time, I breathed it in and tried to memorize it. I dressed and ventured through the halls to the girl's dorms. Her room was empty. Her mother removed every trace of her from the Embassy. I sat at breakfast but couldn't make myself eat. A soft hip bumped my shoulder, and I whipped around, but the eyes that smiled back, full of knowing sadness, were the wrong color. Imma's eyes sucked me in, velvety and dark like black coffee, but Rae's glowed warm amber. Imma wasn't coming back until the train returned from the campaign tour.

"Imma asked me to check on you before she left." She sniffed, and I knew she didn't trust me. "She said that something happened to you the other day at the Tower and that you had a reason to need a little extra slack." She grinned. "She also said that if you don't shape up, I get to kick your butt."

I couldn't drum up an ounce of care.

"Laurel also wanted me to tell you that you have a visitor waiting in her office. She wanted me to walk you down there."

I wanted to tell her that I didn't need her to babysit me, but I knew I did. I stepped around her to discard my dishes, brushed my hands off on my pant legs. "Let's go." She kept her distance, and I couldn't blame her.

I gave no thought to who might be waiting in Laurel's office. Common sense said it would be Marta back to finish what the Senator cut short the day before. Apathy smothered any caution I should have felt.

The shades were drawn on the office windows, but she stepped out as we approached as if she was waiting for us. Annoyance pinched her brows. "He has a pass with Marta's code on it and says he knows you."

What he would know where I was, and why would Laurel let anyone but Marta in without warning me? My heart drummed in my chest.

Rae sidestepped across the room. "I've got pepper spray this time, Arlo. I won't wait for you to hurt someone else."

Laurel put a hand on her shoulder. "He's just a kid. I don't think he's a threat, just a little rude, but we can call Patrol if Arlo thinks something is wrong."

A fist banged against the inside of the door. "He can hear you all talking about him, too!"

I would have known Rat's voice anywhere and pushed past my new friends to see my oldest one. "What are you doing here?"

His scowl dug deeper. "You know I don't understand you now."

Laurel patted Rae on the back. "Why don't you stay and help the boys out. I don't think Arlo can stand to wait for a TalkBox interpretation today. You need more service hours, don't you, Rae?"

She sputtered. "Yes, but…you're just going to leave me with them? What about Arlo? You saw what he did to Imma!"

Laurel's eyes met mine and flicked to Rat. She signed, "I'm trusting you with her. Can you do it?"

I nodded. "She can pepper spray me and beat me up if I mess up." I turned to Rae. "You trust me?"

"No, but I'll try." The smile she gave was watery and unsure. She and I went into Laurel's office and shut the door. Rae took a deep breath and pulled herself up to her full five feet before facing Rat. "He wanted to know what you're doing here. I'm Rae, by the way."

Rat snorted and walked around Laurel's office with his hands in his pockets. "I came to see him, of course."

"You,” Rae corrected. She threw me a wink. "I'm just here to interpret what he says into your language. You talk to him."

His brow quirked. "He and I do just fine. We speak the same language and always have.”

"If that was true, he wouldn't be here with us,” she sneered.

After watching Rat with girls before, I knew he liked what he saw in her. "Fine. Have it your way. I'm here to see you, Arlo. I hear your little girlfriend finally got called back to the real world.” He kept moving, looking at the certifications on the walls and the open files on the desktop. His hands never left his pockets. He couldn't and wouldn't touch anything but would stick his nose into everything he could see. "That mean you're coming home too?”

The tiny lilt of hope in his voice cut my apathy open and exposed the raw anger underneath. "The Tower isn't my home or yours."

Rat spun on his heels. "It's the home we got! Don't tell me the Resistance morons got to you! Or was it her?” Rat faked a lunge at Rae and smirked appreciatively when she sucked her teeth and lifted her brow at him in boredom. He slunk around her in a slow circle. "I bet you and me could be the hottest thing to happen in this place since the last time the Resistance set the dumpsters on fire."

She snorted and rolled her eyes, but the color in her cheeks darkened. "My mother taught me not to bet unless I knew I could win.” Her eyes traveled slowly up and down his narrow frame. "There is no winning with boys like you."

Rat grinned. "Nah, it ain't you. You're too smart to fall for that shit. This phony wearing my best friend's face,” his finger swirled all around my face like an annoying housefly, "has Imma's perfect little fingerprints all over it.”

"Don't talk about Imma.” Rae struggled to keep up interpreting my rapid signs. "This is me! The wet blanket I was before was the lie.”

"I didn't come to start a fight. I came to get you. Marta said that she wanted you to come back for a little, but she couldn't get away. I just want to walk you over there. She said someone else had to walk you back."

Rae narrowed her eyes; confusion pinched her face. "Why wouldn't she just send a message to Laurel, then?"

He put a poisonous smile on his face and made his eyes wide and dewy. "What do I know? I'm just Tower Trash, following orders."

I nudged him with my elbow and shook my head. "Fine. Let's go. I don't want to be here anyway." I needed to walk and think about what needed to be done. With everything going on, I hadn't been able to make a plan to help Gage like I'd wanted to. My time was running out. If I was going down, I wanted to go down doing something I was proud of. I needed Jack's kind of brave, radical, vigilante radicalism.

Rae put herself in my way. "You have stupid written all over you today, you know that? She'd want you safe. Imma wouldn't want you to do anything stupid, and if that guy is involved," she glared at Rat, "it's stupid."

"It's fine. My warden was just here yesterday and doesn't want Services questioning excess communication between her and the Embassy. She wants to keep them out of our hair. Will you tell Jack to meet me in the Public Garden in an hour?"

She sighed but nodded. "Yeah. That's what friends do. Tell you you're stupid, but help you anyway."

⬚

AFTER THE TRAM caught up to us, and we were on our way back into the city center, Jack said, "I know where you can go." We got off a few stops too early to be going back to school. I didn't recognize where we were until the door closed behind us. He took me back to the same warehouse he took me to the last time we went to the Tower. "Come on, we'll wait downstairs. They know we're here."

"Seb said no. I'm not ready."

He smiled and clapped a hand on my shoulder. "You're not

ready to help, but you don't need to give help to get it here. That's why we all do this: to help."

He went down the stairs, and I followed. Our footsteps echoed in the room below. My mind teased and tormented me, telling me that he had led me into some kind of trap. I had to remind myself that I'd seen the bustling movement myself. Seb had been there. I couldn't panic and let my broken brain run away with me.

"Where is everyone?"

Jack laughed, and it rolled through the huge space. "Being one of us isn't a full-time job. Last time I brought you, some of them were meeting, and I wanted to catch what they were saying. They have lots of places they meet to keep the goons confused. This is just the one I know about." His face turned sheepish, and his shoulders shrugged inward. "I didn't understand what Seb was doing for you then, but I thought I did. I thought it would be fine to bring you because I knew that the others knew you were with us. I thought you were either one of us or a spy sent by Services to keep watch on us."

"So, you brought me to a meeting?"

He rolled his eyes and grinned. "I didn't think you were a spy anymore by then. I thought you were someone like me. Everything about you started to make sense just a little while ago in the Tower. I'm sorry I judged you wrong…multiple times."

I shrugged. I might not have many more chances to apologize. "I'm sorry I punched you in the face."

"You didn't know what you were doing, Arlo. The scrambles do that to you."

I shook my head. I didn't want it excused. I wanted to own it. "I have to be better than what they did to me."

"And you will be, but cut yourself a little slack on the first one. Next time I'll punch back."

"Keep telling yourself that."

The door at the top of the stairs opened, and the lights turned on. "Jack?"

"Down here, Percy," Jack answered. "This is Arlo. He needs our help."

Percy came down the stairs, a sheen of sweat on his dark skin. "Seb's kid, Arlo?"

Jack shoved me and knocked the awed gawp off my face. "Yeah, that one." He sobered quickly. "The warden who was helping Seb hide him was arrested about an hour ago at the Tower. They're on to him, and he needs somewhere to go."

Percy took to his HHD, tapping a frantic cadence. He looked up with deep grooves across his brow. "Smuggling someone out of the city is no small feat. Getting them to safety across the Frontier isn't any easier. You need to know before we do anything else that there is a bigger chance of failing than succeeding."

"It's worth it," Jack said. "He's been through too much to go back now."

More people filed down the stairs. More lives, more risks, all for one kid who didn't exist a few months before. Imma, my closest friend, was afraid to turn her life on end for me.

No one should have had to.

I put my hand up to stop them. "I have to go back to school and turn myself in before they start looking for who helped me. I won't put anyone else at risk."

"Arlo! No."

A spike of anger drove through me and forced a grunt up my throat. I needed him to listen. I'd been manhandled through every other situation in my life. I wouldn't let him take my choice away. "I was scared when I left the Tower, and they brought me to school. I let people put themselves in danger for me. I won't do it anymore. I'm going back. No one else is going Underground to hide me."

Percy nodded, his face full of resigned admiration. "Seb would kill you if he knew, but he'll be damn proud of you in the end."

I thanked him and climbed the stairs. Jack trailed behind. My hand rested on the door. Jack said, "I can't believe you're giving up now!"

We stopped outside and let our eyes adjust to the bright sun. "I'm serving the greater good. If they found me leaving the city with your people, they would put the whole movement in danger. The people need the Percys, Sebs, and Jacks of Eidolon to keep fighting and helping those who really need it. Let me do this. You wake the people up to what Eidolon really looks like."

He stopped, and I kept going. If I stopped, I might not make it there. I might turn around and hope that the people were still in the warehouse. The few blocks from the warehouse to the school's back door took only moments. We turned the last corner and stopped short.

Retainment officers, a field of green uniforms armed to the teeth, stood in formation on the NVL steps.

Jack stopped, grabbed the back of my shirt. A million scenarios ran through my head, and none of them ended well.

I held my hands up in surrender.

The leader of the squad jumped to action. "Arlo TowerWard! Get on the ground with your hands behind your head."

I obeyed, dropped to my knees, and put my hands behind my head. A boot connected with my back before I could drop prostrate and knocked the wind out of me. I fell on my face in the street. My face burned from gravel and dirt. The boot pressed heavily between my shoulder blades, grinding me into the ground. "You are under arrest for identity fraud, leaving Central Services custody without a pass, and willful endangerment of yourself and others. Confirm that you understand."

I nodded, despite the lack of range of motion from being mashed to the road.

"Confirm that you either understand or need an interpreter, or your silence will be considered an act of defiance."

"He's non-verbal!" Jack rushed toward me. "You're at the NVL; he can't answer you without his hands!"

If the officer acknowledged Jack, I couldn't tell with my face on the road. The boot dug in more and answered any question I had about whether they would take it easy because I surrendered. "Confirm that you understand or need an interpreter." They wanted me guilty, whether it was the truth or not.

A panicked roar of syllables left my mouth in answer, sounding nothing like the "Help, interpreter," I hoped for. The boot lifted for just a moment but then crushed down further.

"Your willful defiance will be noted on the record of your arrest. You will be taken to Central Processing and detained in the prison until a court date can be scheduled to try you for the accused crimes."

The boot between my shoulders slid back to my hips. A knee took its place on my spine and pressed the remaining air out of my body. Impulse took over.

I became nothing but an animal fighting for my life. Arms flailed and punched, feet scraped against the road, trying to make purchase and run. I felt every blow, every tug at my clothes, not as pain, but as obstacles. The duplicity of not knowing where or when I was that I felt when this implant started to fry returned. The rally, the day I was taken in at five-years old, the day when the neighborhood bullies surrounded me and the current moment wove together into a confused tangle of yells, hits, and kicks. A bolt of lightning sizzled up my spine. I hit the asphalt, aware but unable to move.

It took a few moments, but as the officers shackled my hands behind my back, feeling came back to my limbs. My skin felt too tight, and everything hurt. One eye was swollen shut, and my cheeks felt full. I pulled my knees to my chest and groaned, but they wouldn't let me rest. Arms clad in rough green uniforms hauled me up and dragged me to a waiting van.

Through the closed doors, the crowd yelled, but I couldn't make out the words. Fists banged on the metal, and I curled up to weather the ride to Processing.

The latch on the double doors clicked open, a shadow fell over me. The cargo area floor vibrated with every hefty step. Commander Escher knelt. Instead of his normal, cold indifference, he watched me, bloodied and bruised on the floor, with unguarded interest. I moved away in fear. I couldn't survive a second round of beatings.

"You've managed to escape our notice for three months. I know Wofsy had something to do with it, but you had to have had other help. Tell me how you did it and who aided you, and I will get you back to the 47th as if none of this happened. I won't reimplant you, and I'll waive your conscription. We could get you an apprenticeship with the Atrium staff like they told me you were doing all this time."

I tried to move, but my body protested and fell back to the floor with a groan.

He knew I had no way to answer him. "One knock if you want to tell me who helped you, two if you'd rather be processed and tried."

Broken knuckles bent and rapped three times on the floor. My eyes never left his.

"One for yes, two for no, Arlo."

Three knocks, three raised fingers.

"You have a third alternative? Do tell."

I smirked and rolled so he could see my hands and let him see the single finger salute I'd been hiding behind my back.

His mouth pursed in disappointment. "Have it your way then. It's much easier to monitor you underground, anyway."

The butt of a stun gun came down on my temple, and the world went dark.

Chapter 25

Weeks could have passed, but it might have only been hours. If my eggs weren't scrambled from the implant, the blows to the head finished the job. My mind rode a wave back and forth, in and out of reality. Sometimes the ebbing tide brought me into a quiet room, cold and lit with unwavering white-hot lights I could see through closed eyelids. They kept me away from waking up. Somewhere in there, I knew that if I opened my eyes, I'd wake up below ground.

From time to time, the lights would still burn, but the room wasn't so silent; familiar voices spoke in low tones around me. Rat stayed with me the most, mumbling to himself. The silence clawed at him, so used to the din and chaos of the 47th. "You're famous, you know." He spoke around his thumb, gnawing at his cuticles until they bled. I thought he kicked the habit. "You're all anyone talks about anymore. Someone hacked the security cameras nearby and posted the footage of you surrendering and how they surrounded you."

He cleared his throat and shifted in his seat. If I didn't know how often we were treated for vermin like lice and bedbugs, I would think my friend was infested from the symphony of creaks and scuffles around him. "I—uh—got asked to talk at another rally."

Their dumb parties couldn't change anything, but Rat's whole demeanor changed as he continued. Warmth filled his voice, and I fought to break free from the heavy sleep. "It was gonna be huge, but someone caught wind of it and sent Wardens to stomp it before it could start. We've got 'em running scared, Arlo."

Discomfort stirred in me. Nothing that didn't directly benefit Rat got him that excited.

"The Resistance isn't a few quacks in a basement trying to work kids up to fight their fights anymore. It's in the streets and hallways now. People are talking about the system instead of assuming it works. You started something big. So you gotta get your lazy ass outta this bed and see it. You can't sleep through this. Please, Arlo."

Another time, Imma's voice raised me up from the depths to shallow awareness, and I fought my way up, but couldn't break the surface. "Make sure he gets this, please. As soon as he wakes up."

"Why don't you do it?"

"Please, Rat. I know you don't like me, but can we put that aside for right now? The campaign train leaves in a few hours. Will you give it to him or not?"

"You're still leaving? I thought you liked him! He wouldn't leave you if it was you lying there!"

"You made that perfectly clear when you said he was loyal as a dog, but it's not up to me. I'm not supposed to be here now, but I couldn't go without seeing him." Her lips pressed a warm, soft kiss to my cheek and then to my ear. "Come back to me."

I wanted to keep my promise. I wanted to answer, but all I managed was a deep sigh and a hand twitch that left me powerless to the sucking void of sleep.

She chuckled and squeezed my hand. "I know you will."

I gave in to sleep.

When I woke next, the lights were dim, and my eyes agreed to open. Rat sat alone in the chair by my bed. "Arlo? You there, Buddy?"

"Mmmmmma."

The rough vibration of my voice put a scowl on Rat's face.

"She's not here. She's gone, remember? She had to go to the territories."

Female voices filtered in from out in the hall. The Senator's haughty sneer sent chills rolling down my spine. "I know she was here!" Life trickled back into my muscles, dragging the pain of the beating I took behind it.

I wanted the dark tide to take me back to sleep. Nothing good happened when the Senator was around, but something in her words kept me there. The only 'She' we had in common was Imma. For Imma, I would try to stay awake and take the pain.

"We checked the visitor logs at Central Processing. She came to see him."

Rat jumped from his seat and slammed it open. "Lady, the apocalypse could have dawned in this room, and he wouldn't know it."

My lips twitched and tingled with a smile that couldn't break the surface.

"He's been out cold since those goons got a hold of him! That's four days without any sign that he's coming back." His voice cracked. Rat didn't cry.

"He knows where she is!" Senator Persaud looked wild, dark hair whipping around a red face. The cool facade fell, and in her rage, she looked so much more like Imma.

Rat pounded the heels of his hands against his temples. His jaw clenched, and I wished I could say or do something to make it better. "He doesn't know where he is!"

The Senator's breath caught, and she froze. "Another one." She tried to tame her hair, straightened her posture, and smiled Imma's camera smile. "Of course, he doesn't. My mistake."

Laurel caught me watching them and smiled. "Have you seen her?" She kept her signs small and discrete.

My head felt too heavy, but I managed to shift it from side to side. I swallowed, but my dry mouth caught on itself and gagged me.

Rat put a straw to my lips, and I winced at the sensation of water running down my throat; everything ached, even drinking.

Feeling came back to my hands, but weight pulled against them.

Restraints secured me to the bed and kept me from signing. I tried to speak, but all that came out were pathetic squeaks. Hot tears stung my eyes, something heavy and cold pressed down on my lungs, kept me from taking a breath.

Laurel pulled her back by her arm and held tight. "He doesn't know, Miriam, look at him. He's just as distraught as we are."

Rat smashed my face between his palms and slapped my cheek. "Breathe, damn it!" His voice broke whatever held my lungs in stasis, and I gasped in loud breaths as my vision started to cloud and waver.

He stared into my eyes.

"Un-ah...." It was a rasp, two pieces of paper rubbing together, sandpaper on wood. What did I want? Would he even understand? "Un-ah nnnno." I pushed the thought out at him, begged him to understand.

He nodded. "Tell him what happened. He deserves to know why you're here."

"She jumped." Laurel moved forward so I could see her. The unflappable headmistress wore rumpled clothes. Her hair fell over the shaved side of her head in strings.

Gray surrounded my vision. It popped and rippled. A loud sound filled the room, the two women jumped away, and I realized that sound came from me. I wailed, I screamed, and I pulled against the restraints with all of the strength I didn't have. Rat's shouts joined mine, but I couldn't stop.

A sting in my neck stopped the noise. The burning liquid filtered through my body, and my muscles went slack.

Officers escorted Senator Persaud and Laurel from the room. Drool and tears fell down my face, my head lolled on my shoulder, too heavy to hold up. My eyes grew heavy, and the sea of sleep pulled at the edges of my mind. Rat sat, his chair in my limited vision. "I'm sorry, 'Lo. I didn't mean it. I just thought they'd bring you home. I didn't know they'd hurt you. This is all my fault. All of it from the beginning."

THEY WAITED until I stayed awake for an hour at a time before they rolled me, bed restraints and all, to the tubes. The smooth electromagnetic mechanism whirred to life. My body lifted up from the thin mattress, tethered only by the straps on my wrists and ankles. The doors opened with a rush of cold recirculated air that smelled like dust. The warden's unlatched the straps, transferred me from the hospital bed to the cot in the corner of the cell, and the door slid closed. Plexiglass walls left me enough space to walk ten steps in any direction with a toilet and sink in one corner. I curled up on the bed and waited for whatever was to come.

I slept in Resident Health for eight days. After six more in the glass room, my door unlocked, and two Wardens, their uniforms covered with rubber sanitation suits stepped in. Without a word, they hauled me up and dragged me out of the cell to an empty bathroom. "You've got visitors. Either clean yourself, or we'll do it for you." He pointed his gloved finger at the room full of shower nozzles.

I pulled the hospital gown around myself.

"Get in and do it yourself, or we do it for you." The second one tapped the long wooden handle of a bristled brush on the cement floor.

I didn't move, not when they threatened, not when they prodded me with the brush, not when one straddled my legs, pinned me, and the other knelt on my neck. Stripped bare, the water drilled into my back like needles, and the brush and detergent stung as they scrubbed. I lied on the ground, unmoving. My fight was gone.

As quickly as it cut on, the water stopped. A towel dropped on top of me. "Clothes are on the bench. Put them on. You have a meeting with legal counsel and visitors waiting."

They watched me from the door. "Get a move on, inmate."

Inmate. No longer Resident, my stupidity and impulsive actions got me demoted to a prisoner.

The grey jumpsuit was made of the same fabric all Tower clothes were cut from, woven on-site, full of nubs and little flaws, but soft. I pulled it on, slid my feet into the canvas shoes, and held my hands out to be shackled. They led me right back to my glass room.

The man waiting for me sat outside the box. He wore neither the crisp starched clothes of the city nor the soft, baggy homespun of the Tower. His shirt was white, not bleached, and gleaming; his collar hung unevenly, and his trousers faded. He shuffled through the papers in my file, and the deep wrinkle that sliced through his brow sunk deeper and deeper. "I don't know who you pissed off son, but whoever they are, they have a lot of power on their side. They tried to make it look like you kidnapped that kid who was with you when you were arrested but couldn't find evidence to support the claim. All charges against you will concern your failure to return to the Tower upon the expiration of your pass, re-entering the Tower with falsified documents, and resisting arrest." He waited for some kind of reaction from me, but I didn't move.

Saying anything in my defense would incriminate others. Seb, Laurel, and Marta did good things. Without them, kids wouldn't have good people to learn from. Gage would lose yet another person, and the Resistance would suffer. He shoved a worn, older model TalkBox across the table.

"Guilty," the voice garbled.

"You didn't make those identification documents or prosthetic fingerprints to get you through processing as your older brother." He shoved the evidence across the table. "Giving them someone else will take some of the heat off of you."

"I took my brother's papers. Easy switch."

The counselor sighed. "Fine. This is the sword you want to fall on, that's your call. Is there anything else I can do to help?"

"Make sure I have an interpreter. Are we done?"

"You have other visitors waiting." He shuffled his papers and gathered them back into their folder. "Good luck, Arlo. For what it's worth, I think this whole trial reeks."

I curled up on my bed. A soft tap on the glass pulled me out of the void in my head. Marta took the visitor seats, Guinn standing guard over her, but I felt nothing.

I felt empty, and her smile didn't spark in her eyes.

"You don't look as bad as I thought you might."

I didn't care that neither understood. "I wouldn't know. They just scrubbed me like a toilet and shoved me out here."

She reached out, shackled palms pressed to the glass. "I needed to see you for myself, but they kept me away until now." Her voice cracked, but she cleared her throat and put on a brave smile.

"They want us both to see where all our trouble got us."

Some emotion, something that hid between sadness and anger, glowed hot in her eyes. "They aren't going to let you go down this way. Stay calm and strong."

Guinn kept up his unflappable act but met eyes with me a moment before his neck twitched. A nod.

"They who? My own legal counsel knows I'm going down."

Tears rolled down her cheeks. Before this, I would have thrown myself against the walls to keep her from crying.

She sniffled. "You have people on your side. You're not alone." I put a faltering hand against hers, wanting nothing more than to believe her. Warmth sank from her skin to the glass and into mine, but it lent me no comfort.

I pulled away and pointed at the door.

"I'll go, but please believe me."

Guinn knelt at her feet and shuffled her shackles. "There's still a fight to be had here," he muttered, not looking up from her canvas shoes. "You can give up because you have nothing left to fight for, or you can fight because you have nothing left to lose, but so many others do."

I rolled over so I didn't have to see them anymore and when I looked again they were gone.

Chapter 26

The mahogany-paneled walls and marble floors in the Tube from the prison to the courthouse told city dwellers and upper-level Tower residents alike a charming story of the kind of money and care the city spent on their inmates. Only inmates living in a world of bare concrete and steel saw the sharp contrast with the luxury materials used for show in the visitor accessible levels. I rubbed my toe over a gray vein in the marble between my shoes. Marta's words about people being behind me rang in my ears. It was a load of crap. Escher and Senator Persaud took everyone who cared about me. Anyone who thought of me as a spokesperson or poster child deserved to be locked up in the Mental Health Ward.

The door slid open, a smooth, soundless whisper, bathing the guards and me in beautiful natural light. It burned my eyes, but I stood as long as they let me, soaking in the warmth and delaying what came next. The Wardens at my flank shoved me out. My hair hung in a single, solid mat, a shield against the world.

"Tower City Justice and Central Processing versus Arlo Cooper."

I hadn't heard my name with any surname besides TowerWard in years.

The man stood next to a judge with a clipboard full of cases for the judge to hear. "On the charges of willful endangerment, failure to report back to Central Processing on the expiration of a temporary pass, falsifying documents and impersonation, how do you plead?"

The air in the room hung like a living entity, it hummed with heat and vibration. I convinced myself that my extended stay in solitary confinement made the presence of others more overwhelming. My grief and injured addled mind played tricks on me, made their stares and whispers cling to my skin like spider webs. I ducked my head until I could only see my own toes, forced the Wardens to guide me to where I needed to be instead of looking up.

The judge opened a file; I stole a glimpse through the tangles as the older man with tiny gold reading glasses peered down from his podium. "It says here that his primary language is Non-Verbal Linguistics. Can this kid even hear me, or am I talking to myself? Where's the interpreter?"

"Sir."

I tilted my head toward Laurel's voice and disguised a relieved sob as a shaky exhalation of breath. I didn't know how badly I wanted her there until she spoke.

"Arlo can hear every word you say."

The judge leaned over his bench with a stern look. "Miss Pressman, am I to assume that the NVL couldn't drum up a single more suitable interpreter for this kid? The lead administrator for their school was the only person available."

Laurel pasted her Politician's daughter smile on her face, charming and lethal all at once. "Absolutely not, sir. A man of your stature should never assume anything, should he? It's a judge's job to listen with an impartial ear and decide what is right based on our laws, not his own assumptions." The glowing smile she flashed at the judge had all the charm of a shark about to eat a minnow. "We had more interpreters fighting for the honor of being Arlo's voice today than we knew what to do with." Laurel turned to me, her smile softened; her eyes begged me to believe her.

I turned away, scanned the room, and choked at what I saw. The heat, the stuffy air, and the rumble of noise I attributed to my rattled mental state weren't in my head. A crowd stared back, filled every seat in the room, and the standing room in the back.

The judge cleared his throat and frowned at the crowd with their signboards and banners. "You lot are still in this room by my good graces and will only be allowed to stay if you give this court the respect it commands."

"Show us that it deserves our respect!" The girl who kissed me at the rally shoved her poster in the air. "Not guilty!" Her fellow protestors roared in agreement, and the judge banged his gavel and bellowed to silence them.

Perplexed, I drifted over the crowd, searched for something that made sense. It would break their tender hearts when Senator Persaud's connections crushed their idealistic hopes and dreams about changing things. They grew louder as Patrol officers pressed them toward the doors at the rear of the room, but quieted when Laurel's voice rang out from the front. "Arlo has a special place in my heart; I take great pride in having been able to be a part of teaching him and watching him become the person he is now. I wouldn't be able to live with myself if I didn't do my part to return that pride by doing my part to make sure he goes free and returns to school, back to the NVL where he belongs."

With a disgruntled humph, the older man behind the podium shuffled his papers and straightened his reading glasses. "Fine then." He glared at the more subdued and muttered crowd at those in the back. "Quiet down, or I will order the Patrol Officers to escort you to Processing for your own trials!" The crowd trickled to a hush, holding their breath. Their posters and signs rippled and flapped, but the judge nodded in satisfaction before turning to me. "Do you understand the charges brought against you by Central Services and the City at large?"

I raised my chin, allowed my shield of hair to part.

The judge's shock widened eyes rose over the tops of his glasses.

"I hear. I understand." My nerves ground against each other, as Laurel interpreted. "Counsel said that the charge of kidnapping was dropped. Why did the officer announce it if no one is pursuing that charge?"

As Laurel translated, the judge looked more and more confused. He shuffled through his documents. He scanned a page and stood. "Remain in your seats. Mr. Bainbridge?"

The man who read the charges stood, his face turned white and dripped with beads of sweat.

"My chambers. Now."

They exited the courtroom together, and excited hum swelled as the crowd whispered.

Most men in his position would have ignored the word of a Tower resident if it went against the official court document in front of him, but I couldn't relax. My heart raced, and my palms sweated.

An entire row of black-haired, blue-eyed people caught my eye. My mother's eyes, full of tears, shortened my breath to sharp gasps. My wrists fidgeted, clanking the chains holding them together as she stepped into the aisle. Grace sat with them in regular clothes and no sign of animosity. The corners of her lips turned up in a strange smile.

His mother moved closer. "She had a change of heart. When we saw the video feed, she asked to see you, but we're still locked out."

My hands shook the restraints. I didn't want them putting themselves at risk for me.

"Don't worry," she put her hand on my elbow and stroked up and down, "this is a public hearing. They can't keep us," she tilted her head toward the protestors, "or any of them from being here to support you."

She smiled at Laurel. "You're Imma's sister. I hope she finds her way home or at least to somewhere she can let you know she's safe."

Every breath I took felt like glass. "She can't find her way home. She jumped out of a train!"

My mother squeezed my arm. "They didn't find a body or even any blood. She hit the ground alive and moved away on her own two feet."

Imma could have been waiting for me in the territories. My eyes flicked toward the door.

"No." Mother shook her head.

Laurel's arms wrapped around me from behind, held me up. "I need you to think about you right now, not Imma. You're no good to her locked away forever."

Mother pleaded with me, stroked my face. "Why would she jump, if not to make her way back?"

The door was so close. My muscles tensed, ready to run.

Laurel's arms tightened. "If you're both lost, you'll never find each other." The tip of an injector prodded my neck. "Please, Arlo, not again. Sit down."

I threw her off and booked it for the door. I didn't care that my hands and feet were shackled, that I wore a prisoner's suit, wrist, and ankle shackles and would be captured immediately. I had to try. For Imma, I would always try.

Something hit me from behind and dropped me to the floor.

The judge's voice carried over the noise filling the room. "Subdue him and bring him to my chambers."

I tried to catch my breath and scramble to my feet, but before I could, a cattle prod buzzed behind my ear and jolted to life. Every muscle flexed and went limp. My body hit the cold marble, but my mind kept falling.

▭

NONSENSICAL MEMORIES STROBED through my thoughts. One moment, oversized restraints lashed across my body; the next, they were gone. I screamed and fought against the straps. Whimpers took the place of screams, and I watched through clouded vision as doctors with their faces covered came toward me. A common thread of blinding pain in my skull wove through all the disjointed scenes.

The blaze of memories like sparks along the wick of a firecracker slowed and stopped. I startled awake on the floor of an unfamiliar room. Ice packs surrounded my head and neck. "Welcome back." The Judge sat behind his desk. "Come sit up here with me once you get your legs underneath you again. I had some food brought for you; it will help you shake off the effects of the stinger."

"It's a prod for cows; don't dumb the name down to make it seem less inhumane."

The judge sat behind the big desk watching with blatant interest, but it didn't make me uncomfortable the way the crowd did. He didn't inspect the sniveling criminal through the normal myopic lens of a citizen of the city. Disgust and mistrust had no place in his expression, and their absence put me at ease.

I stumbled to a deep couch. It coughed up a new plume of dust motes every time I moved. I filled my mouth with decadent food, street-level food, city food. Vibrant fruits and vegetables and heady spices I couldn't get enough of.

"Slow down, there's more where that came from." The judge hadn't moved from his seat. "I don't suppose it will be offensive if you talk with your mouth full, so I'm going to ask you a few questions while you finish up."

I swallowed and wiped my mouth on a napkin, annoyed that the man seemed impressed. "You sign?"

The judge slid a TalkBox across the table.

I scrambled to my feet, snatching the device before it could be taken back and retreated to my couch. Dust billowed up and filled my nose, but I swallowed the sneeze back. I couldn't afford to drop my guard, even to close my eyes while he sneezed.

A note filled the bootup screen:

If there was any time you needed the extra boost this offers, it's now—S&L

"Would you mind?" The judge gestured at the chair opposite his own.

I clutched the Talkbox close for a moment, weighing the situation. "Name?"

I nearly dropped it. The voice wasn't the same animatronic monotone of the one I borrowed from school. The voice sounded scratchy and hoarse, the sounds weren't perfect. It was my voice.

The Judge smiled like it flattered him that I saw him as a person. "Judge Arturo Rodan and you?"

"Arlo Cooper." I paused, scraped my nails against the plastic casing of the tiny computer, stuffed one last mouthful in, and went back to typing. "I'd say pleased to meet you, but I'd rather be anywhere else."

Judge Rodan chuckled. "No offense taken. Will you come closer?"

I stood. Something in me resisted his kind smile, but he seemed to want to help. I didn't take the seat he indicated but moved closer.

"Services has put together a strong case against you. The fact of the matter is that you did break the law. You didn't come back at the end of your pass; you knowingly used fraudulent documents to both remain out of the Tower and to get back in without triggering alarms."

"Then why are you bothering to talk to me?"

"Because you know more than you let on to your legal counsel. You have a voice but won't use it. Why?"

"Senator Persaud doesn't want anyone to know about me or the others. They want me silent. They hold all the chips."

He nodded. "There have been rumors of the trials at Persaud BioMed being unethical for years, but they couldn't be substantiated, yet here you are, plain as day." He took his glasses off and set them on the desk. "It seems to me like everyone took your incapacitation as an opportunity to slip things by, like that nonsense with the bailiff. They will lay their version of the events out and try to make sure they have the upper hand. If there is anything you haven't told us, now is the time."

I couldn't give up Marta or Laurel or Seb. They did what they did for me. Laurel needed Seb. The Resistance needed Seb. The kids at the NVL needed Laurel. Marta was already paying for her part. I could give up Guinn, but he was perhaps the most important one of all, someone nobody expected. Laurel didn't believe me when I told her a Retainment Officer told me not to go back, it would just add to the case for me not being fit to be a Resident.

Imma's words whispered, cut through my head. "All those questions are going to escape one of these days, and where will the rest of us be? Drowning in a lifetime of unspoken hopes and dreams. Tell him."

"My friend got a pass. I never used to leave. I didn't feel." Anything. I didn't feel anything back then. It feels like ages have passed since then. "Safe outside my ward, but I let him convince me. We went to the academic district. Rat had a scam going to Resistance rallies. They paid him to talk, but he didn't believe in their cause. He just wanted extra money. I didn't like it. I hid in a music room. Came out when Retainment showed up. Surrendered, but they didn't understand." I had to hope he'd ignore me leaving out my lack of fingerprints for the biometric scanner. "My Authentication says I need a verbal sample, but I couldn't. Took me to NVL, and I asked to stay."

"Why would the Tower assign a voice recognition identification to a Non Verbal person?" Judge Rodan asked. His anger at the situation seeped through.

"To make sure I always came back."

He slumped in his chair and furrowed his brow. "You didn't orchestrate getting yourself back in the Tower or hacking into the school system by yourself. Tell us who helped you, and this all goes away."

He wanted someone to pin it on, but I wouldn't give them up. Those people were all I had left. There was only one person who wouldn't suffer from helping me. "Imma helped me. Showed me the research terminal. Everything is there. Imma found my records. Imma found my family. Imma showed me where to look. Why couldn't I have done it on my own? Because I'm just some dumb kid from the Tower? They kept us away, so we wouldn't know we were different."

Skin pale and clammy, Rodan put his glasses back on. "Imma Pressman-Persaud?"

I nodded, satisfied that he didn't expect my answer.

"Well then, if you're feeling up to it, we'd better move this along." He stood, but sat again, leaned over the desk.

Media officials with cameras filled the back half of the courtroom. Protesters yelled, pushed and shoved. I took my place, and Laurel stood at my side. "I can do this." I winced at Laurel's shocked expression. "I have to do this alone. You have to let me."

Her reluctance aged her, but she took her seat. "If you need me, I'm here." The signed words from across the room bolstered me.

Shoulders straight and head high, I faced Judge Rodan with a nod.

He looked away, the facade of camaraderie ended with the rap of his gavel. "We'll resume now. All charges against Arlo Cooper have been dropped due to insufficient evidence. After a short debriefing, Mr. Cooper will be returned to his place as a resident ward of the state to await age-out testing and conscription."

The crowd voiced the outrage I couldn't. Bailiffs approached, and panic filled me. Not again. I didn't want to go back to the hospital. Neither my body, my mind, nor my heart could take another round.

The judge put a hand on my shoulder, and my hand flew back. I narrowly missed his nose, but he caught my flailing fist and held it. "Go with them, son. They will return you to your commander." The pity in his eyes told me everything I needed to know.

"You sold me out. You told them how much I knew!"

"I don't know what you said, but I think I got the gist. Just go. They won't hurt you unless you move first."

Chapter 27

True to Rodan's word, the officers kept their interactions gentle and escorted me back to the Tube that took prisoners from the Justice Center to the Underground. The doors slid shut. My guts bubbled and rolled. The compartment mechanism engaged and dropped us so fast that I thought I would be sick.

The doors opened, not back on the prison levels, but on Resident Health. I couldn't go back to being implanted. I wouldn't. The warm mahogany against my back was the only comfort I had, and I pressed into it.

A hand ensnared each of my biceps. "Let's go. They're waiting for you."

I pressed back further against the wall; my heartbeat drowned out their voices. My feet dragged against the floor, and I dug my heels in to slow them down. I grabbed the doorframe and tried to pull myself back into the compartment. It was no use. They were stronger.

Blind panic enveloped me. I scrambled and kicked, did anything I could to save myself from what I feared. I had to get back into the compartment and back above ground. A pinch in my neck stopped my protest and quieted my mind. They dragged my slumped form through halls and around corners until I grew dizzy and sick from watching the floor slip by and closed my eyes.

I came to on a table with a thick strap over my chest and arms. Another strap lashed over my thighs and a third over my ankles. The screens on the walls showed pictures of heads and brains. I got the sinking suspicion that they were all mine. "He's coming around now. Arlo, can you hear me?"

I knew that voice. My body writhed and fought the holds of the restraints. I had no way to answer her.

Senator Persaud stood over me. She shone a light in my eyes. "Nod your head if you understand me, Arlo."

I nodded.

"Good. If I free your hands, can I trust you to remain calm and talk to us?" Her eyes were sad and tired looking. All of the cold distrust had fallen away. I nodded, and she did what she offered. She undid all of the restraints and handed me the TalkBox I'd had in my pocket from the trial. The head of the table raised until I was sitting. She put her hand on my chest when I moved to sit up. "Give yourself a minute. They gave you a big dose of tranquilizer."

The screen on the TalkBox blurred and moved. I let the device fall out of my hands. My mind was still soupy from the drugs, but I had questions. "You gave me up. You called Retainment on me," I signed.

"I didn't. I was going to keep your secret for the sake of testing you. You are too valuable to throw away, no matter how many implants you disrupt."

"You understand me?"

Her smile was tart and prim. "I came into Laurel's life after she was already in school. Sign was hard for me, the expressive movement doesn't come naturally to me, but yes, I do understand so long as you don't go too fast. I didn't even know it happened until after she jumped, and I went to question you. Laurel was with me because I went to the school to find you."

She'd been the enemy in my mind for months, always standing between Imma and me. Confusion turned to fear, fear to anger.

"Why am I here? This is Resident Health. No one said anything about having to come here."

She pulled a chair up next to me and sat down. "I had you brought here to run some tests and check the state of your implants. We like to have you closely monitored when the implants are triggered. I'm sorry you went through that alone."

I swallowed, the questions that I didn't want the answer to but needed to know the answer to sat below the surface. "Did you put in a new implant? Am I going back to the way I was?"

Her eyes moved from scan to scan on the wall. "My collaborators want me to. It's the only way to ensure the security of the project, but I can't. You already had five different implants running at once, and all five of them are now inactive. The scar tissue and damage they left is considerable. If new implants took in the damaged tissue at all, I couldn't guarantee the results. I couldn't guarantee that they wouldn't kill you. I don't know what would happen. It would be unethical to try under such circumstances."

Escher snorted; he slouched in the doorway chair like a petulant teenager. "Your eggs just won't fry, and not for lack of trying." We held eye contact, and the connection seemed to draw him upright like a cobra.

"I know."

The Senator leaned forward. "How do you know that? You remember it?" For the first time, I saw a bit of Imma's kindness and compassion in her.

"Wofsy." Escher said her name like it was a curse word. "Stupid, sentimental..."

I picked up the TalkBox from my lap. I needed him to understand me. "She confirmed my memory. She respected me enough to tell me the truth."

Escher's face went deep red, and he jolted out of his chair, but the Senator planted herself between us. "It's in the past. What matters now is what we do going forward."

Escher paced the room, but his eyes stayed on me. "For the remainder of your time on the 47th, you will return to your previous schedule to ensure you are prepared to contribute."

The voice, my voice, rang out of the little speaker with an air of calm I only wished I felt. "The law says I'm entitled to technology, interpreters, and language courses for my peers. No one ever offered me a lesson, let alone anyone else. You denied me the use of a Talk-Box." I held up my new one. "Things are different now; I won't sit quietly anymore. You will approve daily passes for me to return to school at the NVL."

His lips rested on steepled index fingers. "Come on, Kid, make your move."

A twitch started in Escher's eyelid. His crow's feet dug in deeper, and his lips grew white. Despite the front he put up, a chink in his armor showed. The facade of power had a crack. It wasn't much, but it was all I needed to worm my way under his skin. My hope grew with every note Escher's voice dropped.

Each step lower felt like a finger hold of control giving way. "You worked up this whole blackmail; You've stated your demands, so what is it you think you have over me?"

"I have Rat and all the others on the 47th. I nearly disrupted him the day you arrested Marta."

The commander kept his expression flat, unconcerned.

My heart rippled, too fast to discern individual beats. "He's ready; the pin in the grenade you made of his brain is barely still in place. What will you do if I pull it again? If you want to keep your future Retainment Officers subdued until they are old enough to go through your test, I promise, you want me here as little as possible. You will give me what I want, or I will tell the truth when they ask me about it."

A cruel smirk twisted the older man's face, and his voice dropped to a growl. "You don't make demands of me. You're not a Citizen or an official Resident. You exist because I allow you to. If you disappear, no one will know."

I had to choose the words carefully. "Persaud BioMed, Dr. Persaud, and all her financial backers in the senate might notice how quickly your test subjects are deactivating. Make me disappear; we'll see how many I can take down on my way off the floor. "

"How about if I put you two in a confinement cell together for a few days and make an Officer out of the one that is still standing when I return. Would you be the one at my side? Or the one I had dragged to Resident Health?" Sweat rolled down his forehead, and his hands moved from a pious steeple to gripping the edge of the desk. His nails bent and cracked from the force. "Like it or not, you are a lifer here, and I will always be a part of that life. Even if I agreed to your terms, the outcome would be the same. After you turn eighteen this coming year, you will go through the testing process, and one of three things happens. Most likely, you will end up in the fetal position in Residential Mental Care, crying like you did when we first got you in. You might be one of the ones who burns out in the process and dies. If you live, you're mine. You will be under my direct command as a Retainment operative. Your mind has been tampered with too much for us to just let you loose on the world."

The anger, my constant companion since the implant went out, fizzled away and, in its place, stepped pride. No one threatened that much unless they saw what they stood to lose.

Senator Persaud stood and stopped me in the middle of typing my response. "Too much to stay here. You can spend your days at the embassy, night's here. Rance, draw him up a daily pass."

Escher's cold eyes bulged, but he turned a sickly gray. "If your grades drop or anyone at the embassy posts a complaint, this is over. Any whisper of a problem, and I put you in Juvenile Confinement. You report to Miss Pressman at the embassy and directly to me here. Do I make myself clear?"

I nodded and signed, "Understood."

"Get out. I have arrangements to make. Go to your dorm and stay away from the others."

I typed one last demand and smirked as the voice rang through the tense room. "I'm keeping my TalkBox, too."

He lunged at me, but Dr. Persaud got in his way." Out of the question. Personal communication devices are prohibited for Residents."

"You mean for wards."

"No..."

I pounded the bed. I wouldn't let him talk over me with lies. "Yes. I've seen Residents with HHD's, they also have access to Information Terminals, but we don't."

Escher scowled at the Senator. "I warned you. They have to remain isolated!

She smiled, and a flicker of something akin to pride warmed her dark eyes. "And I warned you that it wasn't reasonable to think we would never have slip-ups." Miriam Persaud shifted, almost like she might reach out to comfort me, but thought better of it at the last moment. "You're not in any danger of being harmed by deactivation. I will authorize your TalkBox, but any modifications to give it city system access or the ability to message must be removed by Tower Technical Services before it leaves this floor." She turned to Escher. "Is that an agreeable solution for you, Commander?"

The commander grumbled in displeasure but agreed and stomped out of the room.

Chapter 28

With Escher gone, the air in the room felt calmer, more breathable. Senator Persaud sank back into her seat and studied me like a specimen. "You could have asked for so much more," Senator Persaud said. "Why didn't you?"

I took my time choosing my words and laying them out. "He knows now that I'm willing to use what I know against him. I don't want all the way out. I need to be here, but I need to be at the embassy, too. We are not separate but equal. We're just separate, and we will remain that way unless people are willing to bridge the gap between us. No one can bridge a gap if they can't see the other side. Now, I can."

"You need to be very careful, Arlo. Your freedom is tenuous, at best. Don't underestimate Rance Escher or those above him." She stood and gathered her few belongings. All of the screens cleared. "Some technicians will be in momentarily to fit you with new credentials. Your escape brought to light some of the weaknesses in our security. Please, let them do what they have to do." She made it to the door but turned back. "Please, if she finds a way to contact you, let me know. I just want to know that she is safe."

I agreed, and she left.

. . .

THE TECHNICIANS HAD me stand with my arms crossed behind my back. A burst of light and a flash of cold on my forearm startled me. "Your mark can never be removed or altered. It is detectable by any Services security scanner. The mark will heal in forty-eight to seventy-two hours." The only sign that they'd done anything was a red scorch mark. One of them held a scanner over the top, and a series of blue numbers appeared. They held the light up again. One of them twisted my hair aside, and the cold flash snapped against the skin just below my hairline on my neck. "Please refrain from scratching."

They tagged me like a dog to make sure I couldn't run away from home, but I got them to concede. They gave me a way to speak, and they took away my need for a chaperone. I could push and get my way and knowing that it was worth the pain of a little burn.

They released me from Processing and sent me upstairs to meet my new Ward Lead. I refused to meet them as the boy Marta knew. That boy would live only in memory thanks to the barbershop on the 40th floor. I'd always refused to step foot inside before.

My hair was all I could control, so I would use it to say something. I had someplace to be, something and someone to stand for. I sat in the chair and hit play on the explanation I'd typed on the trip up. "Cut it all off. Shave above my left ear. "

The barber smiled. "Are you getting an implant? Or are you just letting people know that you're NV and Proud?" My mouth hung open. I knew that lots of the friends I made had the same haircut, but it never occurred to me that it meant something to them. He chuckled and twisted my hair back into a tail behind me. "I have a niece who works at the embassy over there. She told me it started because the kids who's parents implanted them had to get their hair cut this way, and the others did it in solidarity. Then it became a show of defiance. NonVerbal, unimplanted, and damn proud of it."

"Damn proud of it," the TalkBox answered.

He nodded. "Good for you." He shaved one-third of my scalp

clean, and both of us needed a moment to look over the lines on my skin. Markings like a bolt of lightning ran from the implant site over my scalp and down my neck. I hadn't noticed them before. Lichtenburg figures. The stamp of a person who survived a lightning strike. Imma was right. I was thunderstruck and would forever bear the mark.

The barber's voice came out choked. "I guess that tells me all I need to know about why you're proud to be unimplanted." He cut the rest of my 'beaver dam,' as Rae called it, into a simple but clean style with plenty of curls left up top to fall in my eyes.

I paid him, signed my thanks, and rode the Tube up to my old ward. I stopped at the floor to ceiling windows that I used to stand at and stare over the top of Eidolon. Far below, Citizens moved like birds. A smile twitched my lips. A murmuration, that's what Imma called it. The people, like the starlings she told me about, moved in patterns, flowing and ebbing. The smallest coincidences threw her absence at me, like a punch in the back. I never saw them coming.

Rat's haggard face reflected in the glass. He stood behind me, stooped and weary. "It don't make sense."

The delay went on too long as I tried to get the right words lined up, and Rat kept talking.

"I don't want what you said to be true, but what they say don't make sense neither. They said you made it all up, just like I did, but if you made it all up, why take Marta away? And why are you so different? I'm not some lab rat, but you're a different person all of a sudden. I mean, you were changing, but then there was just nothing left of the 'you' I know. What the hell happened?"

"It won't make sense, no matter how you try to make it, and I'm not allowed to confirm anything but the official story."

"Why the hell not?" He gripped his head and dropped to a low crouch. "That damn noise! Anytime I get mad, my ears squeal! It hurts!"

I sat, let my legs stretch out on the floor to tap against Rat's shoe. I pointed to my ear and nodded. I knew that squeal well.

Rat panted, gripped his ears, and peeked at me out of the corner of his eye. "You hear it?"

My hands moved before I thought. Talking to Rat came easily. "Not anymore. Before."

Rat surprised me. "Behind? Past? Before? Before what? Give it to me straight, Arlo."

I exhaled, blowing through my lips, and picked the TalkBox back up.

"No, just tell me. Like you used to."

I shook my head and started tapping. "This is me now."

Rat took a few deep breaths, his head hung between his knees. "How bad will it be when it happens?" He tapped his temple. "When they set this thing off, will it keep feeling like my brain is boiling?"

"Yes." I looked over my friend, my only friend for the longest time. He looked broken, haunted by what I told him. "You believe me now?"

He stared at the palm-sized tool in my hand. "So, that's what you'd sound like? That's your real voice?"

I shook my head, though I wasn't sure. It was mine, but it still sounded so foreign to me. "It's still a computer, just mixed with my voice. It doesn't speak for me, it gives my words noise. I speak for myself."

He tugged at his hair, heat poured off of him. "It was always my job to tell everyone else what you thought." Rat reached into his pocket. "She was real smart, huh? Imma?"

My face flamed. The words fought against my mouth, but I needed them out. "Is." It came out as a hiss, but Rat still paled at the sound. "Um-mmma is." My hands shook as I typed. "She's not dead. She IS smart."

He nodded and fiddled with something in his hands. "I should have given you this when you first got back, but I was just so mad that you ditched me for her. She came, you know. Imma. While you were out cold in the hospital. She sat with you for a few minutes but then had to go. It was the middle of the night. She asked me to make sure you got it."

Imma's face smiled, a few seconds in time trapped in a loop on a piece of computerized glass. My vision glazed over. On the back, in her hand, the words, 'Wait for me.' were etched.

"What did she say?" I forgot again, my hands formed words Rat didn't understand. I knew I heard her, but I couldn't wake up in time to see her. "Was there more?"

Rat's blank stare flipped that rage switch. I'd gotten better at controlling it, talking myself down, but with Imma's dark eyes glowing up at me, the fire burned hotter than ever. I roared in frustration, slammed my palms down on the floor. I wanted it to break, but it didn't.

"She said she had to go and that you wouldn't see her for a while, but that she'd come back with help."

Dizzy with memories and possibilities, I turned back to the windows and stared out at the Frontier. She said she would be back and we'd go together. She would make her way back to me.

Rat gnawed on his thumb, talking around it like a dog with a bone. "We've got to stick together now that Marta's gone. Something isn't right around here."

"Never was." And it never would be if I let it. What Guinn said to me finally made sense. I could roll over and die because they took everything, or I could stand up and fight because other people shouldn't have to lose everything. I needed out more than ever, but I needed to be in, too.

Chapter 29

Rat couldn't handle the side effects of his half-triggered implant. They took him away to the Underground halfway through the week and they made me wait to start back to school. Once my bruises were healed and the burn marks on my arm and neck faded, they gave me the clothes Laurel had sent over as soon as Escher got her word that a new agreement had been reached.

Dressed in my NVL uniform, I felt like myself. My new warden met me at the tube bank. He scanned my hand, and the blue number in my forearm lit up. "Here is your tram card. Your curfew is eight pm with a ten minute grace period. Your pass is in the system at Central Processing and will show up automatically. Commander Escher wants it made clear that any shenanigans involving your people at the NVL or you deactivating anymore of your ward-mates and this all ends. Is that understood?"

I signed, "Understood." He'd only been there a few days but had picked up the few signs that I used the most. I hated that I was impressed by it. I tapped a few words onto my TalkBox and handed it over. While I was glad to have it as a tool, the voice still gave me the creeps. "Is Rat OK?"

He read my message and handed the box back. "Stuart is recovering well. He'll be fine so long as you keep your part of the bargain and don't push him to remember again. Eight pm, sharp, Arlo. Don't be late."

I rode the Tube down and went through Processing. The warden there gave me the same scripted spiel about being back at eight. I made my way the few blocks back to the NVL and stood outside. I felt like a new student all over again. I guess I was. It was the first time I had my whole brain at my disposal.

Gage saw me coming from the playground and blocked the gate with his body. "Jack said you didn't mean to be mean. He said you were mad at other stuff, and it got bigger than you."

"You know what that's like, don't you?" I asked.

He nodded and dragged his toes in the dirt. "We're the same. Did it get small again while you were gone?"

"Smaller. I'm sorry I was mean."

He looked up at me, eyes full of hope. "Are you back for real? Forever?"

I sank down into a crouch, my face level with his. "I can't promise you forever. The people who took me away before will probably come back for me sooner or later, and I will have to go with them." It killed me to let him down. His lip trembled. "You don't need just me anymore. You have this whole embassy as your family now. No matter what happens to me, you have Seb and Laurel and so many others. They will be by your side forever, just like they were there for me when I needed them. Our family looks different than most, but that doesn't mean it's not still good."

Someone so little shouldn't have known so much loss. "Imma was gone, and you were gone, and Laurel was sad. I thought everyone left me again. Why does everyone leave me?"

"Imma and I didn't have a choice. The soldiers took me. Imma's mother took her. It wasn't your fault."

He crashed into me and hugged me through the iron bars of the fence. I laughed and pushed him away so I could get through the gate. He clung to me like he hadn't since he cried on me that first time we met.

I pulled out of his grip, but he kept a tight fist on one of my shirtsleeves. "Time for school."

He let go and led me inside. "Come on!"

I waved him on. "I'll see you at lunch. Be good." I needed a few moments to collect my thoughts and prepare myself to be in that building, knowing Imma wouldn't show up after lunch or any other time.

I walked the halls, and everyone I passed smiled at me with an awed look. They made a sign at me that I didn't know. Classes were starting, but I needed to know what they were saying.

Seb sat at his normal workstation but stood when I barged in. He made the same strange sign they did and wrapped me in a crushing hug before I could ask anything. He loosened his grip and held me at arm's length. "You look good. When they wanted to delay you coming back by a week, I was worried you would come back…not yourself."

"I'm fine. What is that word?" I made the sign. "You never taught me that word, and everyone keeps saying it to me."

He grinned. "That word didn't exist the last time you were in the building." I didn't understand what he was trying to tell me, and my heart was starting to race. "A-R-L-O. That word means you. 'Free' but with 'A' hands. They were just saying hello and acknowledging your new name sign."

I blinked. My heart slowed down. "I didn't know them."

"Everyone knows you. I made sure of it. Your name and face will be burned into people's brains for a long time."

"But why do they know me?" The crowd in the courtroom popped into my mind. I'd been too distracted with making it out of there to pay them much attention.

"I stole the security camera footage of Retainment taking you and pushed it out over the top of the next day's Simulcast. Everyone saw you surrender and follow directions. Everyone saw them beat you anyway. Services has come back and justified it, said your file showed you were aggressive and prone to violent outbursts. They never mentioned that you were five when those traits were documented."

"That's why all those people came to my trial? Do the people believe me? Or Services?"

He shrugged and offered me a seat. Neither of us cared that I was already late to my first class. "I don't know. People are scared, but they're talking about it. That's the first step. They stop pretending it isn't happening at all because it isn't happening to them. I do know that those of us who know you and know that you didn't leave those outbursts in the past are still on your side. You've started something, so what are you going to do now?"

"Go to class?"

His laughter burned for a minute. I wanted to stomp out and hide in my room. But I didn't have a room, and that was enough to make me stop and think. He wasn't laughing at me. He was laughing at the literal, small view answer I gave.

"What will I do now that I'm back?"

"Now that you're free? You have a few months before your birthday, and they can't put you through whatever experiment they made you for any more."

I was no longer eligible for Project Livewire, but I was still a Resident ward. Escher still had control over my life. I had a feeling in the pit of my stomach that Project Livewire would be back to take it's bite out of me eventually.

"You'll conscript and come back here. You'll have a normal life. What do you want to do with it."

No one in the Tower had ever asked me that. My wants hadn't mattered. When Imma asked me a few weeks before, I told her that I wanted a home and a family. I wanted to grow things.

But everything had changed.

Again.

And I wanted different things. "I want to know how you made them all see me on the Simulcast and how you made it, so no one noticed I was gone from the 47th. I'm not the only one like me. Others need help like that, and I want to help them."

He thought for a long time. So long that I worried he was trying to find a way to tell me gently that he couldn't let me so I wouldn't go crazy. "You never stop surprising me, Arlo. I will teach you whatever you want to know on two conditions." He waited for my nod and pulled a ragged piece of paper out of his pocket. "First, you see the counselor that Laurel has set up for you to see, and you let us help you. It's not your fault that you can't control yourself, but that doesn't mean we can keep letting it happen." He offered me the paper.

I took it, unfolded it, and found myself looking at a cartoon of myself, holding a sign above my head.

Can you hear me in the back?

"Why did you keep this?" I hated what it represented. I could feel the same feelings I felt when I drew it as if they oozed out of the ink.

"Jack was right. You have an important perspective that the people of Eidolon need to hear. No one else can tell your story but you. Those are my conditions. You talk to the counselor and learn from them, and you tell your story to the Resistance. When you are comfortable, you can tell all of Eidolon."

"You want me to help with the Resistance?"

"You're one of us. You showed us all that when you advocated for yourself and didn't let the Senator and your Commander take away the rights you took."

I didn't hear much after he said I was one of them. I told Gage that we belonged at the embassy and at school. I told him that we would always have that family but hadn't realized that I didn't believe myself. Seb filled that lifelong hole in my world.

The situation wasn't perfect. I had to return to the Tower every day. I had a permanent marking under my skin so they could always find me. Imma was still missing, but I had a name, a voice, and something to say with it. I found where I belonged, fighting against the system that stole me from my family and myself.

My hand rested on the back of my neck. My fingers brushed the lightning fractals clawing their way out of my hairline and the raised area from the tag.

Everything about me was different, changed forever, and I had the marks to prove it.

I nodded. "Deal."

Thunderstruck

Down to Dust
Project Livewire, Book 2
Coming October 2020

Chapter 1

NO ONE WOULD MISS me if I jumped. The scenery flew by the open doors—a streak of heat yellowed green above an unending sky. Father's train moved just fast enough that staring at the ground for a landing point made my stomach churn. A wall of wind pushed back when I leaned out. The speed made me second guess my calculations about the likelihood of a safe landing.

An arm wound around my middle, yanked and spun me into something hard. The subtle blue of a steward's uniform blocked my view. "I know it's a smooth ride, Miss Pressman-Persaud, but stops can be rough. It's not safe to stand near the door." I hated myself for being relieved.

The stewards, like Elias, were the only people on the bustling campaign train who had spoken to me in the twelve hours since we left Tower City. Elias latched the door with a code I wasn't supposed to know, and I buried my face in his chest until my limbs stopped shaking. Each breath felt like it would burst into a sob.

I wiped my face on the shoulder of my blouse and sniffled. "The odds of living through the jump are almost as good as not. If I protected my head and didn't land on any rocks, I might make it." As a hypothetical, the odds seemed decent, but luck hadn't been on my side recently. At least if I died, I would die trying to do the right thing.

Elias' face furrowed with genuine concern. "Do your parents know that you think about jumping out of trains enough to calculate your odds of living?" Most people didn't know what to do with the precious bits of information I'd curated.

Behind him, our small, myopic world flew by. "You could fill all 154 stories of Central Services Tower with the things my parents

208

don't know about me, Elias." He knew better than anyone that my father hadn't acknowledged my presence all day. The train was opulent, beautiful, and fast–everything my father and the others who ran Eidolon from the guarded room in the Justice Center at the heart of the 154 story Central Services Tower demanded, but that didn't make it any less a prison. Her work, their work, always came before me.

Elias took me by the hand. I gave the door one last look and cursed my cowardice. We would be at our first campaign stop soon, but I couldn't sneeze without the whole territory seeing it on camera when my parents campaigned. Living through the fall was more probable than sneaking away during his presentation.

The doors to my wardrobe stood open. A young woman, a few years older than me, but dressed like a woman older than my mother, snapped the hangers aside one by one. "Good. You're here." She wore lipstick one shade of berry outside of what my mother would call tasteful, and it had slid down onto her bleached teeth. She dug through my belongings as if they were her own. "I'm Lyra." She tossed a mint green jacket and knee-length skirt at me. "We'll be stopping soon, and your father sent me to make sure you know what he expects of you."

I took the suit even though I hated it. It made me look dead. Flashes of Arlo's pale skin, his bruised, swollen eyes filled my mind. I didn't want to think about that. I had to focus on the task at hand. "I was starting to wonder if Father knew I was here. That suit is too small; it's for a child, and the color looks awful on me."

My jewelry dangled from her fingers. "He knows. He's not happy about it, but he knows." She set aside a brooch and earrings. "Dead is better than what you are, which is tarnishing your parents' reputations by associating yourself with a criminal. That suit looks like what a good little girl wears when she is on the road with her daddy. Every time we stop, you need to look the part of a good little girl with her daddy. He will leave you alone–we will leave you alone–so long as you behave yourself during the campaign stops. Do what you're told, wear what you're told, say nothing, and smile when you see a camera. Suit up, we stop in five minutes and are live in thirty." She slammed the closet shut behind her and left me alone.

I picked the ugly suit up and shoved it back into the closet. The simulcast would come on any minute; I needed to be away from my cabin so I couldn't hear it say Arlo died from his injuries.

Elias cleared his throat. He'd stayed so quiet and out of the way; I'd forgotten he was there. "How did you get the door open?"

"My mother restricted my terminal access to information about the campaign, the train, and the daily simulcast. She doesn't want me knowing anything that hasn't been filtered through Central Services approval. I memorized the procedural manuals." I was always good at remembering things, so good that mother sent me away so she could make sure that if I told anyone what I found, there would be no proof of what I claimed. My mother didn't like when people threatened her image, and Arlo's freedom threatened her whole world.

"Where is it you want to get so bad that you'd risk the jump?"

My finger fell on the wide ring of Tower City, but I pulled it away. The home I wanted to get to, the person who made it special, wouldn't be there. "I don't know. Somewhere where I'm not one of the only ones who sees what is wrong here."

I'd been given so many patronizing smiles like the one that stretched across his face in my life.

Poor little Imma, too naïve to know how the world works.

Like most of Eidolon, he couldn't see that things were not as they seemed. He saw what they told him to see. "The borders are closed to keep us safe from the marauders in the badlands. There's nothing out there, Imma. The nearest civilization in hundreds of miles away through nothing but high plains and dust storms. You'd die of exposure from the sun and the lack of water long before you reached anything."

Elias was old enough to have gone through conscription and come back. They'd altered him but didn't know it. My parents made sure that no one who served their mandatory military term on the borders remembered what they did.

I needed to know. Arlo showed me everything I didn't see

before. Before I met him, I believed what they taught me in school, that the Central Services System that divided Eidolon into Residents and Citizens made things fairer for those who needed it. Nothing they did made things fair or better for the people who needed it, and Arlo paid the price for exposing the lie. I needed to see for myself that what I found when looking for Arlo's past in my mother's files was true. "Elias?"

"Yes, Miss?"

"Why did you want to leave?" It was cruel of me. I hated myself for testing the hypothesis on the only person who had shown me kindness since I left Arlo's side.

He puzzled through the question but smiled. "I grew up in the Tower. All I wanted was a place where I had a chance to be more."

I could have turned back, but I wouldn't. I needed to know. I needed to see for myself. "Why did you stop looking for a way out?"

He leaned against the wall and crossed his arms over his chest. "When I was a little younger than you, I spent hours in the Tower Education System computer lab, obsessed with finding out what was beyond the borders." His eyes went blank, and his skin flushed. That simple look back was all it took to fail that simple little bundle of wires Services installed in him. His veins stood out on his skin as if they were too full to fit. A single drop of blood trickled from his nose, and he dropped to his knees on my cabin floor and rested his forehead and the carpet.

There was nothing I could do. If I called for help, they would arrest him. Services depended on the vast majority of their populace being implanted and compliant. One wrong move and, like Arlo, he'd find himself locked up in the Tower for life.

Arlo was different. He'd been through so much more and had so many of those little routing circuits put into his head. It wasn't fair. He wasn't a soldier. He didn't deserve what Mother and Father did to him. Elias didn't deserve it either. He pulled himself up, his chest heaved. The heat in his skull fizzled, and he scrambled to his feet, eyes wide, nose bleeding. "How? Why?"

"You agreed to it when you completed your time in service."

"But why did you undo it?"

To see if I could.

"Because I wanted to believe that you listened and you believed me, but you couldn't do either without your whole mind. Now you have it. You were leaving, said you had things to check." His fevered skin was almost too hot to touch, but I cupped his cheek. "You're bleeding. Go wash your face and let me get dressed."

Elias swiped a hand under his nose and stared at the smear of red. His eyes danced between it and me, but he did as he was told. His faculties were too scrambled to argue.

By the time Lyra returned, I'd put on a simple black dress and the jewelry Lyra picked for me to look like I tried. My shoes pinched my toes and cut into my heels, but I knew better than to put something else on. My mother expected me to "wear my power in how I presented myself." She'd dressed me like a smaller version of herself since I hit puberty. I missed the comfortable clothes I'd worn at the NonVerbal Linguistics Embassy as an intern. I'd felt comfortable in my own skin for the first time in my life. Lyra came in without knocking and looked over my appearance with pursed lips. "At least you look presentable."

That smear of magenta still bled down her teeth. I wanted to do to her what I did to Elias and then wipe the stuff off her, but she was Civil Service Corps. They trusted her with Eidolon's secrets and had no implant setting limits on her. "You have lipstick on your teeth." I tried to push past her, but her manicured nails dug into my upper arm and dragged me back. "Take your hands off of me."

"Your father wants it impressed on you that if you choose not to cooperate on this trip, he will not hesitate to send you for behavioral therapy or conscription instead of on to civil service corps. You live a charmed life, Imelda, and it's yours to throw away."

"His threats would mean a lot more from his own mouth."

A bigger hand covered hers. "Miss Pressman-Persaud asked you to let her go," Elias said. His skin had returned to its normal color, and he'd wiped away all traces of blood. He smiled—the same kind of phony smile I'd be giving to Father's voters and his cameras when we stopped, but I could see the light in his eyes. I wouldn't have noticed if I didn't know he'd changed in the few moments since I'd last seen him. "She's just a kid getting her rocks off. Don't let her get to you."

Lyra whipped around and appraised Elias. "You want to babysit her until we stop? Be my guest. I have real work to do." She flounced out and took the last of my patience with her.

I sat on my bed, full to the brim with anger I wasn't allowed to express. I punched and clawed at my pillow, but it wasn't enough. The pressure of all the expectations, the lies, the secrets, and the uncertainty was too big. I pulled the pillow to my face and screamed until I was dizzy. Everything felt so hopeless. "You can go, Elias. I promise not to jump. Not tonight, at least."

His head bowed, and he stalled. "Someone said you knew the boy from the Resistance video. The boy who surrendered."

The boy who surrendered. The boy whose parents surrendered him into the hands of the monsters who raised me. Closed-circuit security cams in Tower City caught the troops sent by my mother—though she told me I was being ridiculous when I accused her—attacking him after he followed their directions. He lied on the sidewalk with his hands on the back of his head. He begged for an interpreter when they demanded his name. He surrendered, and they beat him into a coma. I more than knew Arlo Cooper. I knew his heart. He knew mine.

Hot tears flooded my eyes, flowed freely down my face. "It's all my fault. He is where he is because of me. He wanted to keep his head down until he was old enough to make a life for himself, and I pushed him to see what he was missing, what they took from him. I needed the distraction of him, and I nearly got him killed. If I had left him alone, he would have run away from them. He would have hidden. They never would have known where he was if I had left him alone!" Despair hit me. "No one will listen to me. I'm just a dumb kid, like you said. 'Getting my rocks off.'" My chest heaved, and I didn't try to contain the sobs.

His hand rested on my shoulder. "I listened, just so you know. I believe you. Can I bring you anything?"

"Something to stop the train."

Elias sat at the computer terminal; his fingers swirled over the rim of a water glass. "I grew up a Resident. It wasn't great, but we had it better than most on the 115th floor. My class took a field trip to the Public Garden one time. We weren't supposed to, but I picked a flower, and my mom put it in a water glass on her bedside table since the Warden's didn't normally look in the bedrooms when they did checks. She came back from work to find our apartment full of smoke and safety officers. The sun through the window hit the glass and set a dishtowel on fire. Ten floors were evacuated because of a scorched towel." He set the glass down. The afternoon sun streaming in through the windows went focused into a perfect circle of light on the floor. "What happened to my apartment?"

I wiped my face and sat up. Maybe I'd gotten ahead of myself thinking his implant burning out would be helpful. "The shape of the vase focused the light and heat. Every dumb kid knows how that works."

He took the pillow from me and pulled me to my feet. "Yeah, but not every dumb kid has the fire protocol for this train memorized or has access to the maps of the route. Not every dumb kid knows that a stranger she just met has something in his head, keeping him from remembering. If a kid like that were thinking straight, she'd be able to figure her way off this thing. A kid like that could change the world as we know it."

A kid like that—a kid like me—had been pushed aside her whole life. A kid like me had never been good enough. He left me to pull myself together, but his words echoed in my head throughout father's speech.